The Register

Studies in Austrian Literature, Culture, and Thought

Translation Series

Norbert Gstrein

THE REGISTER

Translated and with an Afterword

by

Lowell A. Bangerter

ARIADNE PRESS

Ariadne Press would like to express its appreciation to the Austrian Cultural Institute, New York and the Bundesministerium für Wissenschaft, Forschung und Kunst, Vienna for assistance in publishing this book.

Translated from the German *Das Register*.
©1982 Suhrkamp Verlag, Frankfurt am Main

Library of Congress Cataloging-in-Publication Data

Gstrein, Norbert, 1961-
  [Register. English]
  The register / Norbert Gstrein : translated and with an afterword by Lowell A. Bangerter.
      p.   cm. -- (Studies in Austrian literature, culture, and thought. Translation series)
  ISBN 1-57241-012-4
  I. Bangerter, Lowell A., 1941-   . II. Title. III. Series.
  PT2667.S77R4413   1995
  833'.914--dc20
                                                     95-1619
                                                        CIP

Cover design:
Art Director: George McGinnis
Designer, Illustrator: Anna M. Gaitan

Copyright ©1995
by Ariadne Press
270 Goins Court
Riverside, CA 92507

All rights reserved.
No part of this publication may be reproduced or transmitted in any form or by any means without formal permission.
Printed in the United States of America.
ISBN 1-57241-012-4

We would have been able to develop so many of our inner talents to an astonishing degree, if we had not been born and raised in Tyrol.

> Thomas Bernhard, *Amras*

...and every Austrian wishes he could be an American for just one minute and can't resist feeling right with the world.

> Richard Ford, *The Sportswriter*

PROLOGUE

Now, yes, now it's starting with a twitch, a vague trembling, a flickering of the air—or at least that's how it seems to him as he awakens. In the darkness, in the blackness individual images suddenly flare up. They are gone again already, and before they take up more time as entire sequences with only brief blackouts, blinks of the eyes, he can hear the sound swelling. It is a clattering and pounding, loud, too loud in the compartment—while outside, the triangle of lights plunges silently into a snow storm from perspectives that constantly change in the fog, in the premature night.

Momentarily lost again in his abstruse thoughts, Moritz knows that he has escaped from the old expectations: he had succeeded in ridding himself of the recurring dream of an acquaintance, a traveling acquaintance, as he put it, and when he uttered the words they seemed like a phrase used by other people, a phrase for people from a good family—if there was such a thing. In any case, the tingle of excitement was absent. Was it a question of age? In view of the very slight changes—in himself or in general—that was the question. It had already been posed long ago, and he even related it to what happened around him. Thus the wish for inaction had always been suspect. Even the suggestion that he could retire, could have retired, caused him to flare up at the phrase *eternal rest*, and he was forcibly reminded of his tenth birthday, when he had silently looked at the birthday cake, with its candles, and had not concealed his alarm at the fact that the number suddenly had two digits. As if spellbound, he had begun to observe, to imitate the twenty-year-olds, in their clothing, their language, or the way they acted. He had followed them into their cafés, into their dance halls. There he had motionlessly watched the dancers, often for hours. He had watched how they moved, how all their movements dissolved in the light, in its flickering, into individual images of standstill. Then the suddenly undeniable feeling of belonging had sometimes almost seemed like something obscene, a thought that he quickly, often far too quickly, disposed of. And if anything remained, it was envy of those bodies that so intensely belonged to themselves, so readily obeyed, or rather were far beyond any obedience. Whenever he even tried to envision them naked, his own nakedness always seemed ridiculous again, and he saw himself after a bath or the way he would be after a bath, stretched out on the bedroom floor, using a pair of tweezers to remove the bristly hairs around his nipples and across his sternum. And the extracted hairs were like spider legs—an occult symbol —on his violently heaving belly.

In the darkness outside, several small railway stations slide by like toys. Their meager light falls on ghostly, deserted scenery, and the nearer they come, the more it seems as if the power-line poles are all that is alive, wind-blown, frozen in bizarre forms beneath snow and ice. Later, a low, brightly lighted building appears at the edge of the valley floor. It is already visible in the distance, as large as a soccer field, with a name on its roof in enormous characters. The same few letters are repeated many times on the tarpaulins of the trucks that are parked in rows in front of the building. Visible in the light behind it is the adjacent densely wooded mountain slope. Villages pass by unrecognized, inaccessibly far away. Each is like the others. Then the tracks run alongside the highway again, next to the fog-covered river. In its mist the clearing of a transformer station comes into view. There is a building with barely recognizable blurred outlines, and the lighting along an adjacent lane, two rows of wind-blown street lamps, seems to zigzag into the forest. At the edge of the woods is a barbed-wire fence with a sign: military training area—and he remembers: Once, during a field exercise, he had advanced with his company, storming a railway embankment in the light of a falling flare. With his assault rifle in his right hand and a grenade in his left, he had fired shots from the hip, stumbling right into the middle of the clatter of blank cartridges. And finally, when he had lain pressed against the slope in the cold, following the trains with his eyes and sometimes screaming amid the noise as they rattled past, the pale bluish cloud of sparks and the flickering on the roof of a locomotive had seemed to come from a real battle in the flashing, changing brightness of the night.

On the slope beyond the river he can see the illuminated lane of a ski lift, a clearing, as wide as several streets, with a building outlined by fluorescent lights at the end of it. And a little later, after it has been dark for a while, the silhouette of the mountains appears for the first time, set off sharply against the lighter sky.

Then Moritz must have nodded off again. While dozing, he sees himself the way he has so often seen himself before, on the approach to a ski jump. And he doesn't wake up before the jump. At the same time, a jumble of barely visible images appears to him. They are on the verge of being unrecognizable: a chaos of highly piled concrete blocks with smoke rising from them, devastated land, waste land, westward.

He is startled when a woman enters his compartment, sits down across from him, and looks at him as she bends over her knitting. She crosses her legs and places them next to him on a newspaper that is spread across the seat, and between her knee-high boots and the hem of her skirt he can see a strip of her black stockings. From time to time she nervously pushes a nonexistent strand of hair away from her forehead, brushing it back with extended fingers, far back into the nape of her neck. Her lips are narrow, severely drawn lines in the otherwise soft face. They twist violently in a tortured grimacing in rhythm with her hands. No, she doesn't look as if she would say anything unless asked. Her gaze is too vague, as though it were not adjusted to the right distance. When she looks up with a start, her almost colorless eyes are bewildered—and at one point he doesn't think he sees anything in them, and another time, as foolish as it is, he thinks he sees a promise.

Their mutual silence perishes in the noise of the journey. Now, at the mouth of a ravine, it comes in from outside, loudly filling the compartment, reverberating from one rock wall to the other, doubled, quadrupled, octupled. As if they are at the same elevation, in many places the river—or probably better said, the brook, with its narrow course—and the railroad tracks seem pressed between the bank of the stream and the rock wall. At the end of the ravine a rock quarry with milky white stone stretches for a distance into the slope, visible in the light of a construction shed. In front of it two enormous trucks with wheels almost as tall as a man stand face to face like prehistoric animals, bulls in a struggle that will decide everything.

On the flat land adjoining the ravine the train stops on an open stretch for a while and finally moves on at walking speed. It maintains the same velocity until finally, growing undiscernibly slower, it comes to a stop next to a station building with a large, oversized sign that bears the name of the town.

It's twelve o'clock on the railway station clock—noon or midnight, wrong either way—when Moritz jumps down to the platform with his legs outstretched, right into the middle of a motionlessly rigid, irreal world. In the background the train starts up again. No, it doesn't start up after all. It's an optical illusion. At the same time, another passenger gets off, so awkwardly that he falls off the running board, sprains his ankle, and stands there motionless for a while. And when he slowly walks away, he bends his hip before each step. It is less provocative than ridiculous. On the other side of the tracks, a uniformed man steps out of a shed and looks along the stretch of rails for a while, into the fog that is growing lighter, into the snowfall that is hardly visible any longer. Then he withdraws again. A dog appears out of the darkness at the end of the station building, dragging a leash behind it. It doesn't bark, but before trotting back, it stretches its muzzle high into the air as if set in motion from outside. At a trot, the conductor hurries along the train, slams the open car doors shut, and climbs on at the last moment. In the noise of arrival, Moritz walks toward the exit, toward the platform underpass, without turning his gaze away from the red, reddishly blurred glow of the disappearing taillights. And when he turns around one last time, suddenly—that's how he sees it—suddenly Vinzenz is standing there, right in front of him, and he doesn't know what to do or say. He simply regards Vinzenz like an apparition and sees, sees again, again defenselessly, how alike they are.

*

On the plain at the mouth of the ravine Vinzenz is awakened by the conductor. On one side he looks out of the stopped train into his own mirror image; on the other he looks out across the passageway through a gap in the curtain, and at regular intervals the glow, the play of light and shadow from entire convoys of passing automobiles streams in from outside. But there is no sound. The sudden stillness, the sudden standstill in his ears is so penetrating, and with the absence of all sound there also seems to be a break in the continuity of things. Without hesitation he lights one, *one*, as he puts it—he doesn't call it a cigarette—and inhales the smoke in hasty, violent puffs. His cheeks sag, his mouth narrows, and when he exhales the smoke with one eye closed and the other halfway open, the cigarette clings to his lips and hangs down loosely. And without taking it out of his mouth once, not one single time, he smokes it down, throws the butt into the air, and watches as it smashes to pieces and scatters sparks on the ground.

So far, so good; he had wanted to sleep through the trip—and had slept. But from time to time he had stared into the light, into the twilight, and when it grew dark, into space. In the changing scenes, in the window frame that remained the same, his perception seemed limited to recognition. The sentences that occurred to him all seemed to have the same, almost nostalgic beginning: *always, still*. He was alone in his compartment most of the time, but once, briefly, on the way from one station to the next, a group of children came in, and later, a few stations further on, it was an old woman, clothed in black. She was agelessly, sexlessly senile. Without saying anything, she entered, spread herself out across from him, and began to scrutinize him, so that he sank behind a newspaper as a precaution against endless stories about sick people, children, and grandchildren. And finally, when she said something, he pretended not to understand anything—and he remembered: Once during his school days, when he was hitchhiking, a driver had addressed him as a foreigner, with some sort of infinitive, one-word, and two-word sentences. And for some reason he had accepted them without correction, defenselessly, as if he had no language of his own, and had answered with the same stammering; and that had been the first time. A second time, years later, abroad—"where he really was a foreigner"—a man made a mistake with him during idle conversation, and when he silently rebuffed him, he was astonished at his own violence.

If he wanted to, while dozing he could see his grandmother in the old woman. She had recently died. He remembered how she had sat in the living room and knitted stockings and socks from woolen remnants, how she had shifted her position with the moving sun, or, on days when the weather was bad, how she had remained where she was, from time to time devouring one of the cookies that she bought by the bag. And if somebody asked her: "What is it, Grandma, are you eating something sweet?" she immediately stopped chewing or simply screwed up her empty, toothless mouth. Embroidery, darning, and knitting were her tasks. In recent years she had no longer done anything else. And when she said anything, it didn't fit the situation. She told legends of heroes and saints, prophecies, and whatever else there was. Or sometimes she pushed an armchair in front of the television set in the evening and watched all kinds of things from a distance of a few centimeters. She was hard of hearing and near-sighted, and she watched everything, whatever happened to be on, preferably speeches by the pope or some clergymen or dignitaries, and if it wasn't quiet, she could curse and scream and wish the worst things upon everyone: war, world war, or the end of the world. Was that why he was always on his guard with old people?

At first Vinzenz appears to be undecided. After arriving, he remains seated in his compartment for a while and abandons himself completely to the desire to travel on, out across all borders. And again he is sustained by the childish idea that he can't really be anywhere, anywhere at all, if nobody knows about it. Nonetheless, there he is. That much is certain when he looks in the mirror and sees his sleep-ravaged face, his disheveled hair: *like an audacious lothario, or rather one who has been caught in the rain*, he thinks absentmindedly—but proudly as well—while he stands there half bowed. And when he straightens up, he tries to laugh.

It's twelve o'clock on the railway station clock—noon or midnight, wrong either way. In the façade of the depot building the illuminated letters of an advertisement flash on and then disappear again in an unsteady, unreadable background glow. Next to that: two illuminated windows, and above them, like in an oil painting, the half circle of a golden yellow moon. The light on the platform is dim. And in it he recognizes a man as he gets off, and immediately he thinks: *It's Moritz.* And while he walks behind him toward the exit, getting nearer step by step, he simply looks at him and sees, sees again—and again defenselessly—how alike they are—or at least that is what people say about them when they don't know what else to say.

*

We hadn't seen each other for who knows how long, probably since Father's funeral as chance would have it, if you believe in chance; but it was probably more likely that we had avoided each other. There were reasons enough. We didn't want to be reminded face to face of who we were, especially recently, when it had seemed less and less real and hardly worth mentioning anymore. *Of the same flesh and blood* was a concept that we could use to hang ourselves, and in the same category were words like *pregnancy* or *stable warmth*–and what they seemed to designate was gloomy and dull. And when *original sin* was then added to the others, everything became a chaos heavy with mystery; and we reacted with disgust, with destructive and self-destructive wishes that we never quite confessed. In many situations we regarded Kreszenz, our sister, as the only connecting link, and when we took positions against each other –which occurred again and again–it was like one of the constellations of our childhood, where one of us had always lined up with her against the other, at least until she remained behind, grazed, battered, pulverized between us.

Why had we really avoided each other? To be truthful–reasons, reasons–to be truthful, everything was idle talk. And just because there was something that we didn't want to talk about, it became an event when we did talk about it, about Magda–and our love stories, the confusion of our love stories.

In the taxi, *transportation to and from the railway station,* we sit silently together in the back seat and avoid looking at each other. Our gazes are directed straight ahead at the wetly glistening street that is covered with snow in many places. There is nothing to say—as always—and we pretend to pay attention. We are especially careful not even to touch each other. The forest passes by in the darkness on the left and the right, impenetrable. And there are no buildings until we reach the edge of town, where it becomes lighter, clearer. Then there are gas stations, a row of farm houses standing next to each other with parallel gables, the stockyard, the low building of the central market, and, a bit further on, the soccer field, as if frozen in the floodlights, with its high, seemingly blurred wire-net fences. Players run around between them, but their running seems static, as if they are standing still, and the next moment, when we look again, they have changed their positions, in an unfathomable game, like little tin soldiers that we can move any way we please. Next to the soccer field is an automobile dealership with several cars that are for sale standing outside, and a mountain of old, broken-down wrecks that are pressed together. There are high piles of stock, cylinders of dull black tires of different sizes in the background. In the light of the headlights, on the edge of the road, a wooden fence equipped with reflectors rattles past, extended for a bit by a guide rail, a misshapen, twisted thing with a ragged cadaver lying hidden at the end of it, no longer recognizable, a red-black heap. And it seems weird that as we travel for a while across open, undeveloped land, even at a distance each approaching automobile seems to be steering toward its goal, a collision.

From time to time the driver's eyes, which are far apart, appear in the rearview mirror as two slits, pinched together in the light from the oncoming traffic. The alternation of light and shadow plays vividly on the back of his bald head. Drops of perspiration have collected in the folds of his neck. They glitter and become invisible again. Hat wearer, hat or cap wearer–does he call himself a chauffeur? He smokes one cigarette after another, lighting the new one on the butt of the old one before he extinguishes it, in a mixture of longing and revulsion. And what is exciting is the fact that he also talks the way he smokes. From the dregs of one story he always draws forth another–and we become witnesses of some arguments, fist fights; we're confronted with weddings, amorous escapades, and other intimacies, and don't know why. On the local radio station, passages of a story are quoted: "We've learned to use a few words to rid ourselves of vital questions, a concept, a remnant from a long-forgotten religion class, and we don't associate with people who intend to surrender to them. The only result is meaningless, general twaddle anyway."

We're on our way to Magda's wedding–we don't say it–and what we withhold from each other are memories: memories of shared summer days in the city swimming pool, of our aimlessly urgent wandering around, of motor scooter trips that the two of us, the three of us made on Saturday afternoons, on forest and meadow roads far out into the surrounding countryside; memories of the enchanted, wildly overgrown monastery garden where we crept in to steal fruit; memories of the empty wing of the monastery, a building that was several stories high, where we had gained entry and sometimes sat in a narrow cell at night, breathing in the dusty air, the dismal secret of a monk's loneliness, of a terrifyingly senseless world; memories, too, of our first kiss, of Magda's soft, large mouth, her warm, wet tongue, how we had said, "I like you," both of us in the same way, and had shoved our hands beneath her dress, seeking support against the bells of the monastery clock. Once, on a whim, on an Easter Sunday, we–the two of us and Magda–had set off a whole dozen fire crackers in front of the monastery gate, along with who knows how many whistling rockets and a cannon cracker. And while we retreated, the monks rushed up with their wooden shoes banging and clattering. They stopped in front of our hastily erected sign, our sentence framed in a spray of stars: "The Lord is here." In our common diary we wrote: "How good it was when she closed her eyes." It was that or something similar. When she opened them as if surprised, it always seemed as if they opened up, figuratively speaking, and we thought we heard a clicking, a clinking, before every movement of her eyelids. Or we heard Magda say they were gray-blue in the snow and blue-green by the sea–if somebody was insolent or old-fashioned enough to ask. She became furious when somebody called her red top, or fox, or Absalom, or began to sing or to murmur something about her hair. In Magda's diary there were secrets, stories about lost or unrequited love. And if it was reciprocated–that occurred as well–the letters hopped and danced, ran bent, dubiously slanted, toward the edge of the page, as if they wanted to go beyond it, leap into the room, impetuously into happiness. Then a few lines later there was sorrow again, tears and plenty of end-of-the-world frame of mind. And it was an index of her half and three-fourths lovers with technically precise descriptions of all completed kisses, tongue kisses, lung kisses, lasting kisses, all neckings, pettings, *sic*, with entire lists, blissful cascades of words and phrases, like *out of my mind* or even *in seventh heaven*, estimations about measurements and size relationships, conjectures about a great past, a glorious future–and completely unnecessary stick figures of men, stick figures of women, and hearts. We laughed about the phrase *propriety bow-wow*. One thing is certain: Once, when she served as a model for a painter years ago, we went along. And from our high seat, a compartment in the framework of a garret, we watched the artist take measurements–artist, that's what he called himself. We saw how he sometimes stepped in front of the easel, moved Magda, turned her, then how he stepped back, as if in front of a perfect picture, a portrait, and finally began, with real brush strokes.

In the vicinity of the brewery we see the traffic jam from a distance. And from the taxi, as it moves more slowly, we see how the snow has been caught in the bushes all around, and how it lies on the hedges in a thin layer that is perforated in many places. In the glow of the headlights, an abandoned automobile appears on the edge of the road. A few meters further on there is a second one, and finally–art and reality–a rusted bicycle, or rather, what is left of it. We have passed the post office, with its enormous parking lot, gone past the regional academy, the boarding school, a building with a roughly polished façade, high, barred windows, and an immense wall around the garden, past the dairy with its gateways and ramps, past the *Post Hotel*, the *Stern Hotel*, the swimming pool, the concrete block of the secondary school, and, before we know it, we're past the middle-class houses in the center of town, past village fountains that stand next to each other with fountain saints watching over them, squat figures with golden yellow halos. And the driver tells us: "In just one week, they not only vandalized the recently erected cross in front of the churchyard several times, covering and smearing it with dirt, but the fountain saints also got their share, with swastika banners and officers' caps crammed down over their halos." Meanwhile the taxi is moving more rapidly again. It turns into the street with our parents' house at the end of it, past chest-high fences, past orchards–and the domestic bliss upon bliss behind them–with small, pretty cottages. In the summer you can see people sitting on benches in front of the entrances, as if placed there for a photograph, a postcard idyll, often three generations in harmony, in harmonious stillness, while construction noises always come from somewhere, in the evenings, and all day on weekends. Storage spaces have been cut into the vertically rising cliff at the end of the road, only protected in front by wooden partitions. And in front of them lies a pile of metal, hardly visible for the rust against the rust-colored stone. And there it is: our house, as we still call it, even if it does belong to our sister. In front of the adjacent pasture–it looks low and broad–there is a two-story building without a balcony. Scooped together, raked together in front of it lies a dirty, half-decayed pile of leaves. A snowman stands there. Only when we draw nearer do we recognize it as a woman with heavy, pendulous breasts, with red buttons for nipples and the head of a straw broom as a straw-blond coiffure. At her feet there is a wooden box, probably used as a platform. The handle of a shovel juts from the split upper surface, and not far off to the side a little hole has been dug in the ground. "As children, and even less later on, we were hardly ever able to call our sister *Sister,* or even use the word in a fixed idiom like *a sister's fate,* let alone say her name. Or if we did say it, we always had to add something to it, in derision."

Our sister had had her children at short, almost the

shortest possible intervals. In only one single instance, between the next-to-the-last child and the last one, had there been a period of time, and it was said that she had had an abortion. It had been a long time now since we had been clear about it, and with every visit we had to ask again, "What's your name? And yours?" just to be sure when the little ones were lined up in front of us, one smaller than the next, with the smallest one, the son and heir, at the end of the line. Then our sister stood proud and weary next to them, a woman who seemed indistinct, oldish. And we always became embarrassed again. We often didn't know what to say anymore when we saw the large, gleaming eyes of the children, and we prudently looked past her. Her happiness seemed incredible when we thought of how she had run around as a child, over sticks and stones–that's the only way to describe it–in shorts, with her hair tied high on her head in a pony tail. And hadn't she had the greatest plans, to go away sometime, out, away from the city, away from her home town, out of the country where a person was nothing or was simply regarded as guilty, right from the start? With an envious look at mother, she could often talk about another, a better life. She could talk about the way she would be. But perhaps it was nothing but talk, a little girl's big dream, when she said she wanted to study, study, study, and if at all possible abroad. There could be no thought of children, she blurted out laughing, breathless with laughter. A traditional marriage in the usual sense was out of the question. Then her eyes always grew expectantly large. With her head high, her hands on her hips, her elbows cocked wide, she stood there defiantly and looked at Mother, sometimes at Father, too, certain of victory. And it wasn't just her gaze that made her believable, it was her slender form.

And her voice underlined what she said, as if everything had to be as bright and as high as it was. The sound of it was still there later, the way it always climbed one note too high and suddenly fell—a fall that did us good and simultaneously caused us pain.

We had indifferently spent the time of our sister's wedding in a wedding party that we were duty bound to join, and we had hardly spoken to anyone during the entire day and the evening of dancing. Drunk, sunk deep into our armchairs, we sat there and watched the dancers, the couples, as they mingled with each other. And in the perfect ambiance that was all around us, in the hall that was decorated with Chinese lanterns and balloons, in the crowd of too festively dressed people who were walking up and down, the thought of our sister's disability maliciously came to us, only for a moment.

To be sure, *disability* is an antiquated word. She had told us herself, and it was the first time that we thought about her sexuality. We were forced to think about it, but even later it was hard for us to imagine that our brother-in-law—he was long gone—could be the father of our nieces, the father of our nephew. Something ridiculous always clung to unrestrained fertility, and we only accepted it when her childbearing had ended. But we continued to use the word *reproduction*.

*

She has her hands clasped between her knees with her shoulders stretched forward. Changing from time to time, she crosses and uncrosses her legs, rocking her upper body back and forth in a rhythm of her own. It is her girlish attitude, her hide-and-seek attitude, that Kreszenz displays as she sits at the kitchen table. And when she jumps up, it is only to pull the bathrobe together over her breasts; but all at once she rises and steps to the window. Outside it is afternoon, twilight; and she watches tensely as an automobile appears at the edge of the forest above the house and disappears, bouncing down the bumpy road, unreal. Its up and down seems easily visible, the pulsation of its outline, its hectic expanding and shrinking, and after a while there is another one, and another, and again and again—nothing else. As the snow begins to fall, she stares absently at the children's dovetailed sleds—"Thank God, they're away from home!"—with their runners curved upward in front, rounded backrests, and straps that run across the small of the back. Sprinkles of the first flakes are visible on them. Suddenly we hear the shouts of playing children. They stream in loudly and then gradually fade away somewhere in the forest. The noise of an approaching snowplow intrudes into the shouting, and with it the image of a vertically rising exhaust, the image of a lid hovering in the exhaust gas. Through the noise of the engine we can sometimes hear the scraping, the scratching of the blade on the asphalt. And she feels it, feels it up and down her spine, and suddenly feels that there is a draft. Her hands are pressed against the cold window pane before her, with her fingers stretched out wide, as if there were flying or swimming membranes between them, like the hastily sketched lines of a drawing. The snow comes down heavier and heavier, and there are real crystals. The bare spots of the asphalt become darker and darker against them, individual islands in the otherwise snow-and-ice-covered surface.

In the living room it is perfectly quiet as Kreszenz sits down on the sofa and begins to polish her fingernails and her toenails. She does it carelessly, and when she is finished, she shakes her arms and legs and stretches them out away from her body. And as always she finally takes her feet in her hands and touches the calluses on their soles. They are like rasps, as she had already said as a child, from going barefoot so much, and it is the word *child* that she can't get out of her mind, *childhood*, with its unavoidable, always constant images: a trembling arrow stuck in the cardboard; the lid, an enameled lid in the screw threads of an inkwell; the sundial on the monastery wall; the position of the sun–they are apparently intact insignia of happiness. She playfully strokes her shins, her knees, her thighs. And suddenly little space remains, little time remains. She senses her fingers, as if they are unreal, and already lying down, she exposes her pale white flesh, gray-blue in the twilight of the room: her belly, glistening with perspiration, her breasts, her nipples–and "Yes! Yes! Yes!" she screams with her hands jammed between her legs, like a stake in the center of her trembling, wriggling body.

In the distance we hear the peals of a bell–the stroke of twelve. A dog begins barking at the top of its lungs, breaks off, and immediately starts again, and only in the sound of an approaching automobile does its whimpering fade away completely, displaced by the bellowing of a man. It was already one of those afternoons–in conversation Kreszenz called them *philosophical*, but to herself she used other words entirely or was simply afraid to call them anything. "I can't complain...," she always began, and tried to interpret the sudden bend, the gloom of her perception, the slowly blackening field of vision with its uncertain edges. Then she ran from room to room, looking for something to hold on to, or she drew a bath and remained in the water for a long time, protected in the warmth. Or she went out, sat in the setting sun, or raced up and down the streets of town, entered stores, and strolled through the aisles. And she always had to touch, handle something, let her hand run across a wire grating in passing, across the rough-grained boards of a wooden fence, across a rough, unplastered wall or the plaster of a wall. And she was not satisfied until she drew back her fingers scratched, ripped open at the tips, bloody. In her worst attacks, she slashed the backs of her hands with a razor blade. And when blood came from the cuts, it was the word *bloodletting*, visible to the eyes, and she saw hordes of people who had had their veins opened, hysterical women, unconscious people, apparently dead people, in her slanted world of images of a past century. Or she saw herself as a child, hidden with other children in a cabin, filthy with dirt and smoke, listening to the low voices–they were thrillers and horror stories–and she heard herself ask in the stillness, in the audible crackling of the fire: "Are you going to kill yourself? Can you imagine doing it sometime?" In all that time she had abused herself again and again, with nails, needles–just the meaning that the term *knitting needle* carried contributed something. Or it was the fragments, the splinters of a carefully broken glass, and over and over again the hooks, blades, and points that protruded in every direction from her Swiss army knife. It didn't take much: in front of the window a group of people strolling past–their soundless walking, their gestures could be enough; or a wrong number on the telephone, the silence that could never be interpreted conclusively. Or a car drove up, a dog began to bark at the top of its lungs, in the distance the bells suddenly pealed–small matters, and nothing was too small.

The ringing of the bells in the Plague Chapel bursts

forth urgently, excitedly in the silence, close nearby, and Kreszenz counts along attentively. *It can't be twelve o'clock already.* She goes into the bathroom, closes the door, and in front of the mirror, forehead to forehead with herself, she says: "Stop crying, you cow!"–while she fills the tub. She looks unflinchingly at herself as she hesitantly climbs in–it's always either too hot or too cold, and she adds a bit of cold or hot water. And she stretches out and says, "Ah, being dead must be this nice, if it's nice." It's a pretentious sentence, and who knows where it comes from, from a radio or television advertisement, from the pen of some self-styled dandy. "They'll come in a few hours, Vinzenz and Moritz. And again, defenseless as always, as usual I'll think how similar, or dissimilar they are. They're exactly alike. And at the same moment I'll think that my thinking is wearing out in recognition, in repetition, in a dull *aha!*"

*

Red in the face from running back and forth, Kreszenz stands in the middle of the room and talks, talks, and talks: "And *woman*, what a word; for a long time I couldn't speak it without embarrassment, or only in the sense of *old woman, married woman*, and when I was finally able to, it had long since become a household word. Then, in accord with my instinct to defend myself, I forgot the tediously learned usage as quickly as possible, but I considered the most insidious associations to be innocuous. I could say *female*, *girl wonder*, against the grain of general talk."

Then suddenly she says, "Cheers! To the bride!"

And we say, "Yes! Yes! To Magda!" And we clink glasses with her.

We see dried flowers in the corner of the room that is reserved for God–and that there still is a corner of the room reserved for God. But otherwise the living room seems like the waiting room in a railway station. Its atmosphere is like the laboratory atmosphere of a stairwell, with barred windows, yellowish white, mirror-smooth walls, probably washable, and a stone tile floor. A paper target is taped to the door, with holes from darts–they are also all around it in the wood–and its center looks like a peephole. If you don't know anything, you expect to find widows and widowers and elderly couples behind it, with a smell of decay and cologne. A fire extinguisher has been mounted beneath the crucifix, and in front of it personal and household effects stand ready to be moved: cardboard boxes piled on top of each other in skewed heaps, large, tightly filled plastic bags, mutually supporting each other. At first glance it is an ungainly, lifeless pattern that slumps together of its own accord. The necks of the bags are tied closed with multiply knotted strings. The ends of the strings are distributed across the crumpled, glistening surfaces, giving the sacks the peculiar appearance of exaggeratedly large gifts: cat-in-the-bag sacks, surprise packages. On top of them, layer after layer of jackets and skirts lie piled on top of each other beneath skins of transparent plastic. There are pants and shirts with their creases and pleats pressed, starched. And close by there are shoes in all heel sizes and colors, pair after pair, carelessly placed inside each other or with shoe trees whose construction–oxidized metal bows with wooden blocks at the toes and heels–immediately extorts a comparison: like torture equipment that nobody has ever seen before. Next to them, framed pictures lean against the wall with their front sides turned away. There are planks, the glistening lacquered boards of a disassembled shelf, a few bent brass strips, and curtain rods with remnants of curtains. Two open suitcases lie in the middle of the room, and spread out on top of them is a woman's suit with the sleeves of a blouse visible beneath it. An ironing board stands there, with burn holes and spots. Its cloth cover is colored as if urine had dried on it again and again in new layers and shapes. In a proud row on the table in front of us stand several wine bottles, plates with canapés, cubes of cheese, and cookies, pieces of cake on a silver tray, and entire regiments of glasses. For variety, cigarettes, cigars, and matches lie ready in a wooden box, and in the middle burns a candle that has just been lit–and so on and so forth. Is it nothing but the model for a still life picture? Is it only the background when we talk–or rather refuse to talk–and when we sink into constantly changing memories?

THE REGISTER
PART I

1

"Nice of you to come." Kreszenz is sitting down, looking expectantly across the table at us. Her tone is too friendly; her gaze is vacant, turned inward, and it seems like she would rather retract what she said. She moves bottles back and forth in front of her and arranges them differently. Or she brushes away crumbs with her fingers, from every possible, every impossible place; or she forces herself to be calm. That's how it seems when she interlocks her hands and places them in her lap, squeezed together so that they're bloodlessly white and blood red at the points of pressure. And when she looks around there is a nervous twitch around her mouth. "I thought that you would avoid Magda, after everything that has happened."

We look at her and know what she wants to hear. It's always the same, a confession of guilt or at least an admission of our involvements. "Why?" we ask. As always we act as if we don't know what she's talking about. "Why should we?"

We can only hope that Kreszenz still doesn't dare to ask the right questions, that she will be satisfied with the old childhood stories, or will not be not satisfied. She behaves, surrenders in resignation. We watch as she takes her glass and drinks it dry without putting it down. Her swallowing noises and swallowing motions seem exaggerated, as provocative as possible, and while we look at each other she pours herself another drink and takes another sip that she swishes back and forth in her mouth–a drunkard's whim. And no, she doesn't spit it out. She wipes her mouth with her napkin and puts it back on the table folded together in a triangle, and when she coughs, really hawks, again and again, we are anxious, or at least pretend to be. Then she says, "Magda...,"–we don't understand the rest of it–and continues, "We went out together from time to time." And she seems to be aware of her impact.

We move away from each other, as a precaution: "Should we take that as a threat?" But now we're picking up our glasses and saying, "Cheers!" And as we bend forward to clink glasses, we can't help but laugh. And Kreszenz joins in, or better said, at the same moment she laughs at the top of her lungs, throws back her head, and remains that way for a while, suddenly frivolous it seems, light-hearted–and she remembers: "She's out of place. She's been away too long or not long enough. That was my impression whenever I saw her from a distance, when I couldn't help seeing her on one of the shopping streets, or in the *Stadtcafé* where we went after shopping, and even when we didn't go there and did something else. She went there and seemed to be seeking the company of her old acquaintances, her girl friends, as if on the one hand she wanted to belong. But on the other hand she seemed to keep her distance from the outset. Just the way she dressed–in black, exclusively black, or in black and white–was enough, or the fact that she smoked cigarettes without filters. There were little things, childish things, and one time it was regarded as silly, the next as refined, when she had them bring a glass of water with her coffee. And even her interrupted education, or the one that she had never really begun, was something in those circles, at least something different..." She breaks off, seems to hesitate for a moment, and finally says, "I don't know why she picked me, of all people, considering the way she ridiculed them when women with baby carriages and shopping bags stalked past her, dressed up or worn out." And she looks at us, and for a moment it is as though her fate were our fault.

"Maybe it was because of us," we force ourselves to look at her. "Maybe it was really because of us." We can't escape the idea that they quizzed each other, and we don't know what this is supposed to be: a tribunal?

"When did you two see Magda last?"

It probably can't be anything else with Kreszenz's stale concepts of morality. We only know that we will tell her nothing, as always. Or we'll be as general as possible, as unrevealing as possible—and memory, memory: Magda's wedding is tomorrow. We slide together when the window behind us trembles from a blow, from a snowball. And when we turn around, we see a slushy spot that is splattered in all directions on the black, shining windowpane. Pushing a trickle of water in front of it, tumbling lazily, it slides down and stops on the window frame at the end of its snail track, formless, melted. Suddenly there are shouts, and as we bend forward and stare into the darkness, we see a group of people with torches throwing snowballs left and right at the houses. One of them runs out in front, another turns a somersault, still another makes a flying leap into a pile of snow. And as they grow fainter and fainter and disappear into the forest on their way to the *Schloßhotel*, Kreszenz says, "*Polterabend,*"* nothing else, and it becomes unpleasantly quiet.

We use the opportunity to look around, and it appears that everything is the way it has always been, aside from the things that are being moved—"Mother's stuff." The same tiled floor is there, the same carpet, the

*Traditional wedding-eve party

same indestructible furniture. And the same pictures are still on the walls. On the wall across from us hangs an etching of the city, with dozens, a real chaos of church steeples, and behind us, when we turn around, we see a coarse Hemingway portrait, a grainy enlargement that can be summed up in one phrase: "Father's quirk." The pictures in the corner are also unchanged; they haven't aged in all these years, or at least not visibly. There's Grandfather, still puffing on his cigarette, and still appreciatively, it seems. And Father with a headband that we never saw him wear. With his head tilted back, he's looking into the distance with squinted eyes, perhaps following an airplane with them, or a phantom. And we're there too, again and again, with vacantly glistening eyes that are hollowed out by the flash, in the obligatory family photographs with inscriptions on the back, Christmas nineteen such-and-such–delayed-action shutter release. We look at each other. We look at Kreszenz. Kreszenz looks at us. And for a moment–sentimental, to be sure–for a moment it is as if we were transported back and were children, children again.

Stage Directions

We would probably begin with the street, with a camera pan along the street in front of our parents' house, past chest-high fences, past orchards–and the domestic bliss upon bliss behind them–with small, pretty cottages, where in summer people sit on benches in front of the entrances, as if positioned for a photograph, a postcard idyll, often three generations in harmony, in harmonious stillness, while construction noises always came from somewhere, in the evenings, and all day on weekends. Storage spaces had been cut into the vertically rising cliff at the end of the road, only protected in front with wooden partitions. And in front of them lay a pile of metal, hardly visible for the rust against the rust-colored stone. As children, winter after winter we climbed up the gently rising slope behind the house. And as long as sand hadn't been strewn, we rode our sleds–lying backward or on our bellies–over a starting trail that became broader and broader, down into the road and its hairpin curves. And when there was no snow on the ground, it was our tricycles. We wildly pumped their pedals, and finally, when we couldn't keep up with the pedals anymore, we sat with our legs stretched out in the air in front of us. Or later the scooters–and we kicked and kicked or stood in a deep crouch on the footboards and clasped the handles of the steering bars high above our heads. There was hardly any traffic, and the few neighbors drove upward right along the edge, at a walking pace, and they got used to honking, so that we could hear them from a distance and break off our ride in time. And there was another gravel road with potholes and puddles that often remained for days after storms, and if it hadn't rained for a long time, the automobiles trailed clouds of dust. Later, on the asphalt, the snow only remained for a short time, and we had to hurry if we wanted to sled, and when we stomped on the brakes of our bicycles, there was a smeared rubber skid mark instead of the meters-long brake marks in the gravel.

Would we really begin with that? Or with slides, with a series of slides, as none-too-elegant as possible, in black and white and with an exaggerated clicking sound when one slide changes to the next, faster and faster, so that you get dizzy from watching and finally *don't see anything anymore, or only what you already know? Or as garish as possible? In the vicinity of the Plague Chapel that was visible for a long distance on a hill behind our house, year after year, on Sacred Heart Sunday, we set fire to an often house-high pile of fruit boxes, firewood, and branches that had been dragged in from somewhere. And later it was automobile tires, or if we were lucky, even enormous truck and tractor tires that burned for hours, sometimes even until the next morning. They were doused with gasoline, cans of gasoline, and once–if we remember correctly–once we pushed a burning tire down the slope and watched it begin to roll, roll, roll, and finally break through a garden fence, and bounce onto the road, where it wobbled a few meters further and remained lying there burning, blazing, quickly surrounded by a horde of wildly gesticulating onlookers. Is that garish enough?*

    As children we didn't like to be photographed, and actually there were hardly any pictures. In order to produce anything at all for our album, our photo album, we would probably have to mix fantasy pictures among the few real ones, chimeras of some kind, images that don't deviate, or at least not all too far, from the norm. And we would either differentiate them from each other by their degree of vividness, or leave them undifferentiated. And either way, we'd look through them over and over. "In the bright sunlight, turned toward each other, they stand in the garden in front of the house on their first skis, on their wooden skis with cable bindings and laced boots, sometime in the late winter. All around them, bare spots can been seen everywhere in the snow. And while Vinzenz has boastfully erected one ski and rammed the end of it into the ground, Moritz seems to be on the verge of crying, or at least he looks that way with his thick knit cap tied together under his chin."..."Vinzenz leans in front of a tapestry of photographs. He is wearing a hat with a feather in the hatband. His gaze goes right through you. Moritz, on the other hand, makes a roguish impression, with bangs, freckles on his nose, and wrinkles, laugh wrinkles in the corners of his eyes."..."In his thigh," quickly turning the pages, "in his thigh there is an arrow with a broken shaft, and a trickle of blood runs shakily down it."..."We strike and push at each other with ski poles, Count Ferdinand, Sire, Count Sigismund."..."And Vinzenz's nose is broken."..."While Moritz wears his first glasses, a pair of health-insurance glasses with temples that are too long. He seems to be looking crosswise, past the spectacle frames on both sides, with hungry or restive eyes."..."They're standing arm in arm, peculiarly contorted, bent over a door handle, and what you can't see: the tip of Moritz's tongue frozen to the metal handle. And now, now, or now he tears it loose and steps back a few paces, and Vinzenz...did he pinch him?" Whatever the case, it was always a matter of tricking each other, and it was a real game, a sport, and the victor, the more clever one, seemed assured of Father's applause from the outset. We were wary, and we struck when we saw the slightest advantage, out of fear of his laughter. And actually, many of the things that we did, we did simply to counteract the suspicion that we were sticking together, that we could stick together. *"We play soccer."..."We play tennis."... "We play."* In reality it was no game, and when Vinzenz lost and Moritz didn't keep quiet and began to enjoy his victory with all kinds of comments, at some point it always became too much for Vinzenz. Then he beat Moritz to a pulp. Or if he escaped or slipped away with the promise to quit, and then continued to make trouble from an apparently safe distance, Vinzenz chased him. And it was really a ritual, with hymn and antiphon and exchanges that grew faster and faster. "Rigid, stiff as a post, we wait in front of Father's car in our Sunday trousers and Sunday sweaters. And we have either come back from somewhere, or worse, we are just leaving."... "In his confirmation suit Moritz, no, Vinzenz, Vinzenz stands erect with a candle in his hand, and," a few pages further, "Moritz too."... "Father, Mother, Vinzenz, Moritz, and Kreszenz." They repeat themselves, obligatory family photos. "With smeared mouths and buckets in our laps, on a slope full of blueberries or mountain cranberries, we sit back to back, or, hardly visible, in the top of a tree." In the fall they picked the cones of the stone pines. And depending on whether or not they had first laid them in the fire, they pealed off the scales with gummy or sooty hands and faces that were smeared with pitch or soot. Then they picked the kernels from the red, red-violet flesh. And they were supposed to bite them open so that the inside remained whole, and when they let it dissolve in their mouths, if anything at all, it was a sacred act. And actually, later, when they had forgotten to celebrate it for the first time, it seemed like an outrage, like a crime, a fraud committed against their childhood.

 We would not be able to avoid showing pictures of a day, a summer day when we were alone with Father in the city for some reason. It was a unique event and didn't need much to be that way—it needed no more than its actuality. Otherwise he avoided being alone with us, and the reason was that he didn't know what to do or say. And what's more, in situations like that he became *aware of it. We knew that we couldn't presume grand things—we would degenerate all too quickly into sentimentalities. Nor could we incessantly ask why: whether he was taking us seriously for the first time, whether he wanted to exonerate himself, and if so, from what, or if he himself had become sentimental and was going into the city with us alone in order to make up for who knows what—explanations, explanations, explanations, one more important than the other, one as insignificant and small as the other. Weren't pictures alone enough? We walked on his left and his right, striving to keep up with him without starting to run, and when he greeted somebody on the street, we also greeted them. Or we looked away when he looked away. We imitated his wordless nodding, and for the first time, probably for the very first time, we thought we were very grown up. We trotted behind him awhile and caught ourselves as we parodied his walk, exaggeratedly erect, with broadly swinging arms. And when we got out of rhythm, we inserted a skip, and on we went. We ran ahead for a stretch, or ahead and back, ahead and back, ahead and back again and again, and looked around for him. In his suit—he only wore it on very special days—he always occupied the center of the picture. And in it he seemed larger than usual, like a real lord, or at least he was addressed again and again as "Sir," as "Professor." And he really was a sight, striding along, without looking left or right, while we whizzed all around him with glistening, really glistening eyes.*

From an indistinguishable series of Christmas Eves that were always the same, the only one that stood out was the one when something went wrong: Father dropped a set of crystal glasses, and we watched him sit there cross-legged, affected, far more than he had to be, clumsily gluing the fragments and splinters together. And it was clear that for him it was a matter of gluing together an unforgettable moment. That was the only way it seemed possible to picture everything again, beginning with who knows what trifles: with the battery-powered tin cars that we impatiently tore from the glistening red and gold wrappings, with Kreszenz's Negro doll, with the imperative painfulness of *Silent Night,* which had been practiced earlier as Father and Mother sang and we stood silently and shamefully in front of the Christmas tree that was said to be lit, or burning, in the splendor of its candles. Unforgettable, the scent of wax and pine needles, mixed with the smell of coconut mounds, vanilla croissants, Linz eyes, and other, nameless cookies. Yes, in the beginning was the memory, and if you had paid well at the time, it seemed willing to reveal its charms, its most opulent flesh. Then it bade you enter, it let you in, into its innermost recesses. But otherwise it turned you away, buttoned up, so that there remained a retching and a stinging somewhere on its surface. And you weren't sure if you had caught something or if it was only wishful thinking again. Time seemed to dissolve in every direction, and the little catastrophes subsequently gave it a structure. Again and again Moritz's fits were cited for orientation purposes: had something been before or afterward? *Fits* —we didn't have another word for it, when, out of rage, out of fury or pure malice, during his bawling he forgot to breathe and collapsed, red, blue, and green in the face. When that happened, we became alarmed, struck him wildly in our fright, and didn't stop hitting him until he gasped for breath and looked at us in disbelief with his squinted eyes or silently began to weep. Or Vinzenz's electrical accident: once, on a school excursion, he had been careless enough to grab hold of an electric fence, a barbed-wire fence. And he didn't get free until the teacher had cut through the strand with a rock, and when he took him by the hand, he immediately gave him a ringing slap, followed by a sound thrashing. And they said—in order to heighten the effect even more—that the pasture behind it was the pasture of the breeding bull, our first or really only real god, a golden calf. It was an enclosure that could only be reached by way of a hanging bridge, and as the bull stood there, bursting with vigor, jet-black, in an attitude that seemed fixed once and for all, or as he walked, with almost springy, unstoppable strides, he was a sight that still had free play in our dreams. Prehistoric in size, he finally expanded beyond all limits when we encountered his name, Nile, in the index of a map and followed the river with our fingers again and again, across thousands of kilometers, from the area of its source to the fan-shaped pattern of the arms at its mouth.

In the pasture on the edge of town they learned to ride, on wildly bucking calves. And in a bet about who could remain longest on the back of a yearling, they pawned Father's wristwatch. And what about the loss of the chronometer—*chronometer* was the word—a silver-cased pocket watch with large, ornate numbers on the enormous mother-of-pearl-colored face, with a heavy, silver chain and a cover that could be opened with a click and closed with a clack? Did it really happen on the unavoidable boat trip to somebody's—Vinzenz's or Moritz's—first communion? And as the sacred heirloom sank in the water, was it an end-of-the-world situation? One way or another, one misfortune followed another, and together they made up their much-invoked, happy childhood. There were kicked-in pieces of glass in the summer, broken legs in the winter. And each time there was a story to go along with it. There were entire rows of slain frogs, clipped to the neighbor lady's clotheslines by their back legs, and the blows that they received then. There was the test of courage: swallowing June bugs, depending on whether they were still alive or already dead. Or you paid a price each time for your cowardice—in the beginning it was a shilling; later the price was five shillings—and watched from a safe distance as the few existing heroes attained immortal fame, and gradually a fortune, with their art.

In the fall when Vinzenz started school, we played at a construction site for entire afternoons. We often climbed around for hours in the damp-smelling rooms, up and down scaffolds, across narrow plank walks, always searching for new discoveries. And that was where it happened, during a fight, or because of carelessness: Moritz—yes, it was Moritz—pushed Vinzenz from the top rung of a ladder and watched as he crashed down with full force onto a half-dried concrete floor.

And when Vinzenz came home from the hospital—good luck mixed with the misfortune—he no longer went to school, and they began school together a year later, and—and nothing. Pupil and teacher stories.

And after that, summer seemed to be the most productive season by far, especially when we were out in the country with new playmates. For the first time there were other girls besides Kreszenz, tall young things with slender limbs. We listened to every word when they used atypically stressed words and discolored vowels. And we began to listen with unfamiliar excitement when they said "Oh yes," "Oh, of course." And in their sly innocence they always got what they were after.

We could tell the story about our almost complete standstill, or even our movement backward, if necessary even in ancient, worn out pictures, arranged differently, if necessary in painful pictures of a rural idyll—even if we say that it isn't worth it, and that you'd need a narrative approach, a memory that doesn't hop from one misfortune to another, that doesn't amass anecdote after anecdote but evenly illuminates the spaces between them. But for some reason, we continued to narrate erratically.

And even later, when they talked about their first love, about long-faded love affairs—they called them that for lack of a different term—they never went beyond one and the same story: Then Vinzenz always expounded on how he had buried his girl friend's bracelet in the sand somewhere by a lake, while playing, how he had hunted and hunted, had finally even thrown her necklace high into the air above the supposed place, and had seen it disappear without a trace. And then when they had plowed and plowed the beach a dozen times, they had attacked each other, exhaustedly and desperately, and for a moment nothing had had any meaning but the moment itself, his, Vinzenz's body and the woman's body. And Moritz's little lament concerned a female classmate whom he had unsuccessfully pursued for years. And when he was whole again, for revenge he still acted for a long time as though he were half blind with love and stupidity. And meanwhile she had become a buxom, chubby woman, married to an insurance agent, a civil servant, and when he met her, she always looked at him from empty cow eyes, let her eyelids flutter lazily, with a steadfastness that made him think how robust, how durable she was. And he wondered how he could have been infatuated with this hulk for even a moment.

In his memory it seemed like a unique farce, with a shy, cockeyed, up-and-coming Casanova and an uncertain-looking three-quarter woman in the main roles. And more than anything else it was a scene on a swimming pool platform, their useless quarreling over a lost tin ring that had slid into a crack between two boards. "Quick, quick, get it," she said moodily. And he replied, "Why, what am I supposed to do with it?" And only when he crept back in the streaming rain and crawled around searching for it in the mud, was everything fine, really fine, even if he did feel miserable.

We hadn't known our grandfathers. As if they had known what might possibly happen to them, what grandfatherly fate, what picture-book era with every imaginable chitchat, with visits to the circus and the zoo, with merry-go-round rides and ice-cream-eating grandchildren, they had already run away years before we were born. The one had gone on what we imagined was a sunny Sunday morning, as he came from an early drink without looking left or right. A man who didn't watch where he was going, he walked—wanted to walk across the main street. Not long before or after that, in spite of all the warnings, the other one kept bustling around a horse, and suddenly, with a single kick, it caved in the front of his skull.

What they knew about their grandfathers—it was little enough—came mostly from Father and Mother, sometimes dutifully on an anniversary or told disjointedly in sudden remembrance. It was always the same stories that they had often heard before. But their grandmothers were tight-lipped; neither the one nor the other had ever said much of her own accord, for whatever reason, or without any reason—who knows why? But right from the start the life story of their paternal grandfather was dominant, in a family tradition that unrestrictedly gave priority to everything that came from that direction. And it went so far that Father spoke of his genetic and pedagogical potential. It was responsible for the few of our traits that he accepted, and every flaw was placed on the heads of Mother and her ancestors. Under his influence, without knowing better and lacking other heroes, they had made his–Father's–father their hero, and it was he whom they meant when they said "Grandpa"–as if there had always only been one, just one.

Father's pride would have been enough by itself, the superiority that he displayed when he talked about his father and said that of all their ancestors he had been the first who was not stupid enough to break his back as a farmer for nothing again and again. On the contrary, he had been clever enough to make a fortune with his cunning, his craftiness, and *have people work for you instead of working yourself* was his magic formula. It was linked in our imagination with the image of a man who lay on the bench by the stove day in and day out, rubbing his hands and watching his business flourish, as if of its own accord. Sometimes it sounded as if he had been the one who taught them to walk on two feet, as if he had surpassed generation after generation of failures and yes-men as if they were nothing more than silent fellows who believed in fate and would hardly have been worth talking about if there had not been some event at one time in their history, a coincidence of historical importance. Repeatedly, in every possible variation, it was said that when fleeing from the Council of Constance, Prince Frederick, Prince Frederick of Tyrol had found a hiding place with their ancestors and had raised them to the rank of nobility for it, peasant nobility, but nobility nonetheless. From then on they had been called *von*, and had been exempt from the military and free of all taxes for who knows how long.

We acknowledged that each time with a nod: not bad. And we were caught up in the most audacious dreams, as knights, as robber barons, Count Ferdinand, Sire, Count Sigismund, burning with eagerness and anger to defend our master's honor, with lance and sword, against all defamatory and malicious tongues, against the emperor, the pope, and God.

But from the beginning we were most impressed by Grandfather's years as a smuggler in the period after World War I, even if we learned little about it, as good as nothing in detail–and even that didn't seem bad.

Their fantasy had been awakened, and in ever more colorful images they projected a wild scenario, with a cattle drive over the nearby border, herds of cattle and flocks of sheep all thrown in together with liquor and weapons deals. And they turned the reality of a basket-laden man sneaking over the fields with a rucksack full of cigarettes upside down. Nevertheless, that activity had already established the foundation of his fortune, and he had added to it in the period that followed, in some sleazy deals with a road construction company. As a result, he was able to erect his hotel immediately, without credit, without a dime, as they said over and over, in an inimitable style, here a bundle, there a few banknotes, a thousand here. And with what was left he was frugal or generous, depending on his mood.

We imagined that he was actually as he seemed to be in photographs: a bit stiff in his dark suit and vest, in the pose of a respected, honorable citizen. An upstart who acted like a parvenu, he had what he called a healthy contempt for everyone who hadn't made it, or worse, hadn't even attempted to make it. And included in the image was a certain amount of social life, with one night a week spent drinking, and with idle conversation that often lasted for hours among men whom he met on the street. And on Sunday mornings he enjoyed an early drink. All in all there were a couple of dozen pictures, standard snapshots; but there was one that made them wonder: Grandfather–who knows where–leaning against a bridge railing between two unidentifiable girls, a tall, lanky man, with rolled-up sleeves, with a cigarette that was noticeably crooked in his mouth, with strands of black hair pressed against his forehead by the wind. And each time they looked at it they saw his roguish laughter behind the dark lenses of the sun glasses, his laugh wrinkles, and the consciously assumed gaze of a cunning seducer.

Was he a ladies' man? Or was he one of the God-pleasing, sexless creatures to which everyone in our family was bent and shaped, if not while still alive, at least after his or her death?

One winter, when he was a ski instructor at the Arlberg–we're only telling what we've heard–they say that Grandfather possibly–and maybe without suspecting anything–had the encounter of his life, even if talking about it did begin as a game. In the beginning they laughingly said that it could have been so. Then it quickly became a certainty. And when the old story was dug up about Hemingway's months in Schruns, Vorarlberg, they saw a magic charm in it–tourism, advertising for tourism. And they dragged even the last village idiot in Schruns in front of the camera, in front of the microphone, and had him reminisce about it, after half a century, in partially unintelligible, partially concocted mumbling.

Then it was on everyone's lips and in everyone's ears for a couple of weeks, and at the time Father was just beginning to be a writer, a real writer. And there was no longer any doubt that Grandfather had gone skiing with him, with Ernest Miller Hemingway, big game hunter, deep sea fisherman, ladies' man, and that they had made the most daring ski runs together. And more than once they had played cards all evening and spent all night drinking for all they were worth. In any case, the time was correct, and it wasn't far from Arlberg to Schruns, and vice-versa, or into the Silvretta area. And at that time there still weren't too many ski and mountain guides, so that a foreigner would unavoidably come across Grandfather, the best and most dependable one— what else? And he was probably the only one far and wide with a few scraps of English, or who was at least arrogant, clever enough to act as if his "Yes" and his "No" and "Thank you" and "Sir" were already enough. We didn't attach much importance to the story, whether it was accurate or a figment of the imagination, and would have easily forgotten it–after all, who was Hemingway?–if it hadn't been for Father and his craziness. He began talking about it repeatedly, and he lovingly, almost tenderly said, "The old war horse," and that he had had to learn something or other from Grandfather. Or he sat at the kitchen table, reading the appropriate passages aloud in a hoarse voice, the Schruns passages from Hemingway's memoirs. Then he would moan, "Hemingway, Hemingway," in a tone that always made us wonder if his admiration was directed toward the text, the man, or only his fame.

Again and again, even if only by chance, the topic of conversation was the war, the first or the second— *world war* was never said. And in the silence that always followed, every word seemed like treason, not because they had anything to hide, that is, no more than others, but—at least it seemed that way—because they were gradually getting their fill of the remorsefulness of the late-born that was hypocritically promoted everywhere. So they remained quiet and didn't even say that they preferred not to talk about it. For, if someone in a circle of lying penitents dared to say: "What does that shitty war have to do with me?" sometimes he was already regarded as a reactivationist or a National Socialist or an anti-Semite. We didn't know what circumstance, what coincidence made the one grandfather—Grandpa—a thoroughly apolitical man, into a so-called opponent of Hitler, and what circumstance, what coincidence drove the other one to name his daughter, who was born at the beginning of the war, Adolphine—a monstrous name. We only knew that the opposition of the one hardly went beyond a few disparaging words uttered while intoxicated, and that the admiration of the other was nothing but a blind *hats off* to the reputed road-construction strategist, to the employment-providing officer. We knew that or thought it—just what did we know? Only that his halfhearted *no* led the one as directly into the war as the other one's blinders did him. Yes, yes, that was what we knew, and anyway, in two wars the two of them together had served who knows how many war years as contemporaries, regardless of their attitudes, or even if they didn't have any.

In the years after World War II, Grandfather began to add on to the hotel, and he expanded it significantly before his death. He leased two shelter huts from the Berlin or Brandenburg section of the Alpine Society, and it was said again and again with a mixture of pride and incredulous head-shaking, that he had sold glacier melt water brewed into a thin tea at the most exorbitant prices to some semibarbarians who came along. At times he was totally unresponsive. It would happen one day and then again a few days later, they said. And with that they designated the rhythm of his regularly occurring ill humor, and finally the ill humor itself.

A pigheaded man, a cunning, contrary man, he was actually one of the so-called tourism pioneers in the good old days that Father invoked again and again, the days before the proud Tyrolean people degenerated into a horde of bootlickers and toadies, and the holy country into a rental brothel. And all his life he is supposed to have met foreigners and guests like a force of nature, with completely or halfway tautological sayings: "If it works, it works, if it doesn't work, it doesn't work," or: "Do what you want, because you'll do what you want anyway." In his way he was a forerunner of all the later ski-lift and hotel emperors. And did it really come from him, the saying that we should let the Germans into the country, clean them out thoroughly, and kick them out again stark naked? It was important that what he did, he did against the ill will and the resistance of the world, or at least that's what they said from time to time. Nothing was dumped in his lap, in his cradle, and we heard again and again about all kinds of acts of sabotage during the time when he was building and expanding, about bands of thugs from the neighborhood who tore his newly opened nightclub apart before he was even aware of it —and so on, and so on. And it was friends, always only friends, who else? Sometimes Father seemed to get wrapped up in that very fact. It fit his self-image well to be the son of a persecuted man. And we had to be careful, even later on, not to see ourselves as the persecuted grandchildren when we remembered the loneliness, the one-man loneliness of our hero, along with Grandmother's assertion, after thirty years of widowhood, that if given the choice she would not have married him again under any circumstances–even if he was a good, upright man.

What else is there to tell?–In a library in San Francisco, during a year of study in the U.S.A., Moritz ran across the photograph of an Indian chief. It was an Apache on the cover of a book, Geronimo, Vittorio, or Cochise. And he remained sitting in front of it for who knows how long, daydreaming, confused by the similarity. It was as if he had reached a destination, at last, as if he were there at last. And as he walked outside with the picture in his waistband, it was a late afternoon with a warm wind from the ocean, with the soft play of light and shadow in the west and whole swarms of very young students in the streets. They were still children. Very often he had told them the most unbelievable things, just to hear how they said "Oh, no! Oh, no!" in amazement, or "What?" And for the first time he saw Grandfather closely related to the American dream.

Expulsion from Paradise or *Light in Deep Darkness*–
Father must have felt both ways when they paid the way for him–the second-born son–to leave the village and his youth and begin life in the city as a teacher–that's how he put it, in his familiar, only all too familiar literary tone–with a niggardly inheritance, the gratuity portion, a bit of charity that was nevertheless still good enough to buy a house on the edge of town. But if you looked carefully, only the loss remained in his eyes that glistened with tears, in the suddenly interrupted movements when he began to talk. He was a sentimental fool, and

the relief at having escaped was artificial or part of a tailor-made world, of a survival strategy to change the perception of it, if reality itself couldn't be changed. Or it was only embedded in insults directed toward backwoods people, toward village and mountain dolts who had remained behind, in attacks of love-hate, or in his cursing, and it was completely arbitrary. In all that time, you see, he had never made himself at home, and what's more, he hadn't even tried. It was his belief–learned and never laid aside again–that the place of his childhood was Mecca. And just a few kilometers outside it was foreign country. It began in a drawing of borders that had hardened over centuries, with a different language, a different way of thinking, and other forms of insanity. So much resistance was directed just then toward the city, a so-called district capital, even if it was still such a godforsaken place, a sleepy pile of houses that had never been kissed awake, with a few thousand narrow-minded people and bureaucrats.

Even if it was against his own conviction, Father defended the village and the villagers in conversations, if a scandal, a hint of a scandal had become known and the neighbors were wagging their tongues because of some small thing. Their carping brought him to that point again every time, and when he said something, it was in the language of the village, and he never deviated from it, from its clarity and severity. That elevated it above all the fuss and the speechifying, all the timidly servile hemming and hawing with "My God," and "Do you think so?" and every possible excuse that fearfully sought after a skimpy respectability. It usually didn't take much, when one of them came out of a valley on his pretentious day–as superficial as a handshake, to put it derisively–with a whole supply of suitable gestures and sayings, and painted the town in a beer hall. It was quite enough if he stood a round or two of drinks with a hand gesture that was as careless as possible and yelled for liquor at the top of his lungs, but by the bottle. And the whole crowd of philistines was in the greatest uproar for a week or more, in a mixture of envy and openly displayed disgust. But Father saw a sign of a different, an anarchistic world in it, when he had them tell him about every scene in detail. In the retelling it became who knows what, an event, and he often wavered for days between great, grandiose ideas and a peculiar carewornness, as a domesticated, degenerated descendant, as a failure.

It was not the first, the construction and pioneer generation, it was their sons and grandsons who invaded the city with their inherited money or money that they had swindled together, or even with only the suggestion of money. You saw them shopping in the central market. You saw them in the stockyard. They came to district meetings of some local society or other, and on many Sundays they appeared in hordes at the soccer field. Or they actually played the family game of a Sunday walk in the inner city, bringing their wives from dingy kitchens especially for the occasion, decked out and crammed into fur coats or designer clothes and accompanied by a more or less wild confusion of children. What was so great about that? In our eyes, no matter what, they seemed like uncouth oafs, and we didn't think much of their boastful stories. We were simply amazed at their success in directing their empires—hotels, ski lifts, and all kinds of trivial affairs—as if it were a small matter.

And what was peculiar, or not, was the fact that when we got to hear something, it was always, first and foremost, stories about automobiles. Their thinking seemed to revolve around them—always in a circle—around the joys and adversities of mechanical locomotion. And they were not just cars, they were limousines, luxury limousines. From week to week there were new reports about who had bought which model again...with the price, performance, and top speed, or about who had had something stuck or welded on. The so-called connoisseurs were obsessed with detail. And finally even the most unbelievable rumors about the first Rolls Royce hardly aroused astonishment any longer, not even when they heard that its owner was repeatedly seen with it at the garbage dump, with a grotesquely rusted garbage trailer, or that inside and outside of the valley he approached all of the filling stations and car washes with special wishes, and that he treated the car like a dog or some other pet, with a whole list of terms of endearment and all kinds of foolishness. That made the story of Alban and Attila downright innocuous—Alban and Attila were the mayor's sons. It was nothing but a prologue that promised much or everything, when it was said that when they first started school or a little later they already had their first, fully operational electric cars, and that they had raced them in the corridors of their father's hotel palace during the preseason and the postseason.

There were the most peculiar customs. The driver's license examination seemed to be the final initiation rite before the real entry into life, into possible death, and the wildest tall tales entwined themselves around it. Tricks were played, the riot act was read. There was anecdote after anecdote, and that alone made clear what it meant when you failed the examination, what a humiliation, what compelling evidence of complete failure it was. And the index of the roads seemed like an excerpt from a secret self-help book. It had precise data about all kinds of accidents that had happened at some time or other, whom it had snuffed out at some time and place, what it was called, with speed limits, curve for curve —eighty, a hundred, a hundred and ten—conjectures about the corruptibility, incorruptibility of who knows whom, predictions about radar traps, and so on, and so forth. We also always got to hear how expensive something was, for example—why not?—for example a hotel, or piece by piece the construction of its shell alone, its furniture, just its... And sometimes it went like an inventory, point for point, from the largest things to the smallest, porcelain and silver utensils, and number was added to number, and that it was thousands, millions went without saying. Or if it wasn't numbers, it was concepts: they said *heliskiing* or *helicopter skiing, surfing, sunbathing,* or *deep-sea diving, wild boar* or *bear hunt,* and the associated countries could never be distant or exotic enough. They casually said *rags* when they talked about clothes, and then dropped the names of cities like Paris, Rome, or Milan besides. They called a car a *unit* or an *automobile,* and usually the words alone had enough glitter, independent of what lay behind them.

    Always—again and again when he had visitors from the village, Father was like a changed man. Once or twice a year our uncle—Father's brother—unexpectedly stood in the doorway. Or he met an acquaintance on the street and brought him home without any hesitation at all—if it was an acquaintance and not a stranger, the friend of a friend or who knows what. Then he dropped everything and excitedly ran to the cellar for the best bottle of wine. He had Mother scurry quickly to a store and serve only the choicest delicacies, little salmon rolls with thick, oily layers of mock salmon, entire nests of boiled egg halves that were often still warm with smears of black caviar, Milan sausage on Vinsch Valley bread, and all kinds of little things that were reserved for feasts and celebrations. *Two-man spread* was his phrase, and he often sat the entire night with a man who seemed to be everything: childhood friend, father confessor, drinking buddy, and lover. And if you looked into his eyes the next day, they were swollen, red from crying in a mixture of senseless boozing and an inevitable, miserable sentimentality. We avoided him on days like that, or even the night before, and even Mother limited her presence to what was absolutely necessary and was more nervous than she ever was otherwise. And sometimes she seemed to be ashamed of him, of his courtesy and his all too voluble shame.

We only got to the point of kissing hands on the rare occasions when our aunt came along. Or perhaps if the entire family appeared, with male and female cousins in lederhosen or sailor suits. Then we had to show off. We were forced to put up with all kinds of compliments— "How big!" "How bright!"—even if their smiles and laughter and false gladness only meant that we were needy wretches. And for revenge we named them after long-range bombers and battleships from a children's card game, and we shot them down unfeelingly again and again.

Conversely, when Father drove to the village, it was also an event, with a splendid beginning, with his expectation and exuberant joy. Only the ending sometimes missed the mark, and he came back a day or two later like a man who had been flogged. In our uncle's hotel they greeted him as if he had only been across the street for a moment, with a mixture of casual matter-of-factness and unmistakable equanimity that they put on for the reception of a guest, any guest at all. And they put only the very best in front of him, without understanding his euphoria, his childish excitement about small things. And they listened to him for a while and then left him alone under some pretext, entangled in the confusion of his all too vivid memories, his fantasies. In the restaurants, when he went out, he was greeted with much ado. Wherever he went, they began talking with him immediately, and it only took the right group sitting together, and it was already the beginning of the end: with a card game where they wagered life and limb, with a drinking tour, a drinking tour from Pontius to Pilate, as the saying went, and with all kinds of gibes and mischief-making. And the key phrase was: *with absolutely no quarter*. The most audacious, impertinent ones called him *Teacher*, at first in fun, but as the evening continued, the mockery in their voices kept increasing. Their outbursts of laughter were aimed solely at him, and sometimes he almost seemed to be asking for it when he took everything seriously and in the next moment didn't see the seriousness of his situation. They played with him, and it was a comedy when they approached him like supplicants, as if they were not very bright, and asked for his blessing, so to speak, his opinion about who knows what—it could be anything at all. And while they tried to stifle their laughter, it started, and he talked, talked on and on, in an attack of ridiculous self-infatuation.

In their eyes it was probably an unnecessary act, at least at first, a resounding flop, when his first contributions appeared little by little in the local newspapers—a handful of Advent poems, a Christmas story, an almost embarrassing children's story—when he actually began to write and saw a stroke of genius in everything that he took in hand. We called him a woman playing a man's role, a bursting rifle barrel. Wasn't he their mouthpiece? Nevertheless, after an initial fright they wanted hymns from him, hate tirades, and above all, free pages of advertising. They wanted him to carry their petty vanities and quarrels out into the world: ski instructors and philanderers, child-labor users and illicit employers, or whatever else they were–shady characters of all kinds. It generally went well for a while, but little by little they continued to reinforce each other more and more. And finally, sometime around dawn, when one of them was drunk enough–too drunk, as they said–and suddenly went all out, they attacked him, reproaching him for his civil service salary, shilling for shilling, a ridiculously small sum and at the same time a fortune. He was paid twelve, fourteen times a year, and performance: zero, an impertinence. And it was not too foolish for them to say that with their taxes they sustained a horde of parasites, an entire regiment of beggars like him.

We didn't know who it was. Was it the pale-skinned, freckled girl who attended our class for a few weeks in elementary school, or was it a child from nursery school or from our neighborhood? We only knew that it was something very special: our first red-headed girl, face to face.

Usually they gave a plump girl with widely protruding pigtails the brush-off. A Pippi Longstocking type, in their memories she wore a square-cut, garishly colorful dress.

And besides that there was, above all, a picture of her with us, while our fathers attended a lecture by Otto von Habsburg. We raved about a magnificent court, a splendid reception, without leaving out a single fairy tale. And later it was all the more shocking when His Majesty, an ordinary figure, dry and powerless, the scion of a great family, did us the honor for the first time on television. Even his—even her name—Felicitas—seemed to be a promise, and we reversed all of the ever-so-bad characteristics—in the vernacular they went hand in hand with hair color—to their polar opposites and made a fairy out of the witch. Outrageous sayings, hundreds of years old, or older: she must have blasphemed, or she must be in league with the devil or some kind of demons—all kinds of abracadabra. And even Father's witty remark was senseless enough, namely, that redheads were the spawn of mediocre novelists, the mainstay of their inspiration or at least their sales. And when he said it, he was visibly convinced of it and even more sure of himself.

And Magda? We had become acquainted with her—that much was certain—before we entered secondary school. There were all kinds of games—heaven and hell, cops and robbers, who's afraid of the black man?—and she was there. Or she was often there when we threw a ball against the doors of the bus garage on the post office square all afternoon, until somewhere in the vicinity someone came out on a balcony wildly yelling and gesticulating. There were children's festivals in the city hall, amusement parks with swingboats and bumper cars. But more than anything else it was the unavoidable television evenings.

Right at that time, in his apartment above the bakery our baker made his television set available to others one or two nights a week. It was the first and for who knows how long the only one far and wide, and whole swarms of children, sometimes adults too, pressed around the chairs, sat on the floor, and watched everything that came on. They sat there like savages, as quiet as mice, watched and watched, and at first repeatedly got into arguments about the mysterious inner life of the apparatus, or listened to the baker's abstruse explanations. He already felt good if he could turn and press the knobs again and again. It was probably there that we saw an adult cry for the first time. He was a large, bloated man with blurred facial features, a thick, sad moustache, and the gaze of a common seal. Remarkably, he didn't miss an evening, and over and over, halfway hiding it, he took a sip from a bottle and seemed not to hear our whispering and giggling. It was the report of the death of a Grand Prix pilot, and he laid his head on the table. He was shaking, and he gulped with a peculiarly violent hiccup. We hardly dared to stir or even to look at him or anything, and were happy to see his forced smile, his laughter at himself, and when he said, "Good, good, it's all right," we embraced him.

Squabbler–that was the word we heard them use when we overheard them talking about Magda for the first time. And as we soon saw, her tirelessly repeated sayings really did seem to irritate everyone far and wide–some old familiar stupid, childish things like: *Timmy tells time til the train at ten,* or, *He who becomes nothing becomes a bartender, and he who can do nothing works for the post office and the railroad,* or, *Long, tall Johnny, short, fat girl.*

"And you? What do you want to be someday?" she had casually asked in a moment of sudden silence. We were sitting next to each other on the bars of a fence, and those were her first words. And for some reason we knew that she would take even the most impossible wish seriously and, as far as possible, even help to make it come true. So what, what? Winnetou and Old Shatterhand, for fun–or not just for fun. And if that seemed too far-fetched, there were always the usual choices, caterpillar tractor or crane driver, helicopter pilot, or more daring: circumnavigator of the earth, world embracer, astronaut.

We ran races together from the beginning, ski races. Sunday after Sunday, in all the villages, even in the most godforsaken hole in the district, in all the valleys of the country, qualifying competitions or championships were always taking place. And we often crept to the agreed-upon meeting place while it was still dark or in the semidarkness and cold of a winter morning, with our skis and poles shouldered. And then we were transported without ceremony in the team bus. And while we sucked at tasteless pieces of dextrose, we went through all of our good-luck rituals, prayers, and pleas for intercession again. Or we surrendered ourselves completely to fate, with pants that were wet with excitement. Proud to belong, we viewed all those who didn't belong as failures. We were a half professional, or what they called a semiprofessionally functioning group, with a coach appointed by the city, a former A, B, or C-Team skier who had somehow been prevented from making a final breakthrough. We had to listen to the story of his failure again and again, in all possible versions, depending on mood and momentary usefulness, so that it rang false in our ears from the outset.

But it wasn't their story, not at first. Their story began with his conviction of his mission, when he overzealously took control of them in the summer, already torturing them with endurance runs, push-ups, and jackknives. And once a week, like a crazy man, with a stopwatch in his hand, he drove them up and down the gravel heap at the edge of town.

The word *flexibility* said it all—man and material had to be flexible. "Stiff as a board" was his worst verdict. He waxed and ironed and filed and ground on the skis; he tossed and screamed us together, and if nothing else worked, he even struck us. He was omnipresent with his shrill voice: *Mamma's boys, stay-at-homes*, if something went wrong. Or he could be completely beside himself and say: "You're winners, you're world champions, understand?" And that was all. Out of fear, if nothing else, we would have wanted to win more than anything else, or to satisfy him in some other way.

When he stood at the starting point before a race and began to implore the tensely formed-up team; when he looked into the eyes of one after another, they knew that it was a matter of life and death. And sometimes it seemed to be more his concern than theirs. They repeated the race's sequence of gates by heart. It consisted of so-called open gates, slips, bores, verticals, and hairpins. And when he screamed "Ski!" they yelled back "Hail!" one after another.

And over and over, in spite of the laughter all around, at the top of his voice he asked the question: "How do we ski?" And we had to say: "At breakneck speed and with music!" and repeat it on his command, in chorus, in a single battle cry up and down the slope.

As a rule, Vinzenz won his division going away, and collected one trophy after another. And everywhere he went, he stood embarrassed on the victor's pedestal, shook hands with some dignitaries, and patiently, later graciously, listened to their speeches, or to what they had to whisper in his ear about pride and honor. And he didn't enjoy his victory until he held the seconds, tenths, and hundredths in front of everyone, bragging pompously to his brother and sister even days later. For nights at a time, he didn't let them sleep. They were confidants, silent partners in his fame and good fortune and money.

Moritz, on the other hand, only won once, and a fog race at that—a dubious triumph. And otherwise he hardly exceeded honorable mentions, always the same ones, so that he superstitiously surrendered himself to cabalistic trifles with lucky and unlucky numbers.

And it was just as superstitious when Magda sprinkled holy water on her skis. Otherwise there wasn't much to say about her, at least in that regard, only that she seemed to get lost again and again in the forest of poles on a slalom course. And sometimes in the middle of a run she turned and while doing so said, "I don't want to go on," or, "Does anybody know how, does anyone know where we go from here?"

And suddenly—as never before—Father was proud of us, at least it seemed that way. And if he somehow showed it in his obligingness and his often exaggerated support or in the way he began to cut out the sports articles from the newspapers—from the district paper, from the *Blickpunkt*, and from the daily newspaper—then he couldn't help himself. In a countermove he had to offend us. He had to say, "Well and good, but that's all nothing at all compared to Grandfather's art, yes, art." And then even he had been an ace in his time. Sometimes when he finished there was nothing left, and if he noticed it at all, then later he tried to apologize again and again with new pieces of equipment, with shin guards, jet stays, and always with skis again and again: *Kästle* or *Kneissl* skis, *Kneissl SS–Snow Storm, Storm Stride,* or *Super Star*. Was that before or after the time when we began to think about why we badgered Magda, why we teased her, only to badger her, to tease her all the more without response? And if nothing else occurred to us, it was always because of her hair: copper-red, rust-red, fox-red.

2

"We always went to the same café, usually early in the evening, when it wasn't full yet. A few customers sat alone at the tables, especially men, men of all ages. And when we entered, their eyes seemed to be directed at Magda, torn back and forth, enraptured. And she knew it, she must have known it, decked out the way she was."

"Isn't that a bit exaggerated?" We don't let it show that we flinch when Kreszenz pauses, all the more when something really flashes in her eyes, something like triumph. And to elucidate, we take our glasses and clink them together once more. And we know that she can't do anything but refill our glasses swallow for swallow. That's how far she is from having ceased to behave like the little people. Just as compulsively, from time to time she says, "Eat! Eat! Please take something. There's plenty here!" And she points with a munificent hand gesture at the snacks that are spread out on the table. What lies behind it is nothing but Father's frugality, not to mention his stinginess. And we, we dig in. We eat everything indiscriminately, canapés, cubes of cheese, and cookies, without stopping. And we don't forget to say "Mmmmmm!" again and again, or "Good!" We sit there erect, as erect as possible, at the mercy of our origins, masters in the exercise of old habits, old obedience.

There is a sensuous look on Kreszenz's face: "From our usual seat, a sofa across from the door, a genuine lookout post, we watched them come,"–she forgets to say who–"watched how they looked around, sat down, and immediately disappeared behind oversized newspapers. And finally—we made bets about that—finally there was always one among them who wound up at our table" period, or rather, period, period, period. She's always interrupting herself, it seems, so that we inevitably think that there is more to it. Or at least she gives that impression, and probably on purpose. It's as if she tries to give her words something—who knows what—besides their meaning, something monstrous. Is she conscious of her theatrics? "We more or less resided there. There's no other way to put it."

As she says it, we suddenly hear the doorbell. We have failed to hear the sound of an approaching truck that has stopped in front of the house. Then, "Just a moment! Just a moment!" and she's already jumping up. "I'll be right back." And while she hurries to the door, none of her murmuring is intelligible.

We remain silent. We hear Kreszenz talking. And even though we are alone for only a few seconds—fortunately—it suddenly becomes cramped without her. We can't slide far enough away from each other at all, but are thrown back. And it is just as if Father were at the door and were going to enter at any moment and utter one of his sayings or say something else: "Should I read stories to you?"..."Well and good, well and good, but who's going to pay?"..."Everything or nothing, doesn't that mean everything?"..."We won't give in." And suddenly—at least it seems that way—some of his melancholy is tangible in the room, and we look at each other meaningfully, much too meaningfully. "Peculiar, isn't it, after all these years?" We hear—"Pssst!"—we hear footsteps in the hall—silence, nothing. Kreszenz has already returned, and behind her in the doorway stand two men, so broad in their work clothes that they hardly have room next to each other. They nod to us, and we–– "Should we help?"––we watch her supervise them as they carry away box after box, plastic sack after plastic sack, and gradually the rest of the things that are being moved. And with shoes, pairs of shoes in her hands, she minces along next to them and talks, talks, and talks. Finally only the suitcases are left, and while they carry them out, she quickly pours liquor into glasses and hurries after them. We hear her ringing, high laughter, nothing else, interrupted by the laughter of the men, closer to a wheezing, a real fit of coughing. The sound of the departing truck penetrates from outside, and when she comes in again, it's still written on her face. She says, "So...," interrupts herself and then continues, "that will help everyone," and we know or don't know––we don't want to know at all––what she means. "Just don't bother us with stuff about the old folks home."

Silence. We wait––and suddenly: "What's that?" We say it simultaneously and listen. Kreszenz stiffens: Shots, there are shots in the neighboring woods, first isolated, carried here by the wind, from all, seemingly all directions. Then there are more and more, salvos. And we hear the faint, muffled hammering of a machine gun, with immediately occurring images of cones of fire hacking into the sand, dirt spraying up, and figures diving for cover or evading with something like dance steps. Or they are images of a parabolic arc into a slope, sprinkled, exactly punctuated with tracer ammunition. And we give vent to our relief: "Austrian Army," and we stop listening as the noise loses itself in the alternately barely silent, no longer quite audible rumble of a helicopter.

For a moment it is unpleasantly, unnaturally quiet in the living room again. Not even the stillness itself seems to be real anymore, and it is all the more unreal when Kreszenz says, "Sometimes we didn't leave until after midnight, and Magda often allowed herself to be persuaded to go on alone with a man, with some man or other, to a dance hall or who knows where. And the next day, or when we saw each other again, there were stories. Stories there were, I tell you...." And again what she says moves along with much more meaning than it really has, underscored by an extremely weighty silence. As always, when she isn't sure of herself, she has casually, carelessly begun to poke around unceremoniously in her teeth with a toothpick. And she distorts her entire face, roguishly it seems, into grimaces that are always different. It doesn't matter whether we look at her or away, and from time to time she pulls it out, sniffs at it, and stares, apparently thoughtfully, at the zigzag of bitten, broken places. And suddenly—we very wisely avoid her gaze but don't let her out of our sight—and suddenly she rouses herself and says, "What else do you want to hear?"

*

It was probably when we entered the secondary school—it must have been then that he started saying it, or even before, and we just didn't become aware of it. It almost seemed to be built into his thinking, into his so-called system, that he was disturbed by their existence from the very beginning. He said that there was always only room for exactly one generation at a time. The others were too young or too old and had to wait and see what was left for them—a truth that he described as elementary. And no wonder it sounded cheap, banal. Maybe he was driven by the fear that his time was already past and theirs was just beginning, and he lapsed into a glorification of the past and gave them no future. Perhaps it also had something to do with the fact that overnight, so to speak, he moved into a bedroom by himself and from then on avoided Mother or looked past her with squinted eyes. Or was that only our imagination, an interpretation prepared after the fact? From then on, over and over he simply rejected what had previously been his unimpeachable educational principles, particularly the admonition: "Pull yourselves together, go all out." Now he indifferently said, "What for? You won't accomplish anything anyway." When it concerned them, everything bad was suddenly called *typical*, and good things were met with the observation that they would burn their fingers yet after all, on the practical truth of life.

And it didn't take much—he only had to have seen a politician on television who didn't suit him; he simply had to have encountered the right person—worst of all, the chancellor, or the finance minister, the pig-head, as he called him, the state pig, or his purse keeper. And in his favorite term of abuse he could reduce us to a single concept: *socialists, complete socialists,* and *failures.*

We quit running to him with all our discoveries, all of our ever-so-small successes, out of fear that he would wipe out everything, or even worse, cut it down. And we became accustomed to being—or to being like—born underachievers. But now and then we got our money's worth, at least for a time, in an attack of megalomania and exaggeration, in one sweeping stroke. There was nothing between forced self-underestimation and a wobbly extravagance. And he, of all people—Father, of all people—was our example. He was denounced in the entire school for his submissiveness, for his rash agreement to everything that the director proclaimed. And to compensate for it, they said, his authority in his classes was consistent and complete. And we, when we heard something like that—words like *servile, slave of authority*, or who knows what—we didn't even try to defend him. We were ashamed or weren't even ashamed, depending on the situation. And finally we no longer recoiled from the last step: to repudiate him.

That was when he began to read his serious stories aloud at home, for every possible reason, reasons that he even invented if necessary. Or he didn't need one. And all that meant was that there was nothing that wasn't good enough for him. It came totally unexpectedly. After supper we were still sitting at the kitchen table or together in the living room, and suddenly, smiling, laughing, with a vocal fanfare, as if it were a magic trick, he pulled out a manuscript and said, "You'll permit me"—he couldn't possibly have said anything more stupid. And then he began. We were at his mercy, only gradually able to judge when it would seize him. And based on that assessment we avoided gatherings, especially ones of the entire family, or even only the slightest suggestion of inactivity. And we were surprised again and again, when he suddenly interrupted a film on television, or it was some other unexpected move—and he read. Or Mother wanted it, in a kind of obedience that hurried on ahead in the hope that she would get him that way for some purpose, or that he would at least be in a kind mood for a while. Usually he read with a deep, constantly monotone voice. And when it sometimes seemed to fail, he depended upon his slowness, introduced pauses at the most impossible places, and actually almost came to a halt, touched by himself, by his stories, and more and more by emotion itself. And at the end he sat there motionless for a while, with his head bowed, finally looked up, apparently reluctantly, and asked, "Well?" or simply looked questioningly at us. We knew we had to be careful. Silence, a commentary, some reaction, or if there wasn't any—everything was wrong. Right from the start, he dismissed praise, even the slightest attempt at it, with a gesture of his hand. Or he said, "You don't seriously mean that." At the same time we very wisely withheld criticism, even if he sometimes ever so urgently requested it and didn't leave us in peace with his pleading and begging. And if Mother brought herself to put him in a predicament, he seemed to have simply been waiting for it, and he attacked her. Or he was suddenly silent, who knows how irritated. One way or the other, in the end it always seemed disillusioning, and for a while he walked around as if he were hung over. Or he withdrew completely, and we sat there with the same taste in our mouths, the same tastelessness that we had on all of the Sundays when the radio was on in the living room and Mother stood at the ironing board and sang or whistled along with the hits of the request program.

We were surprised when Father presented the bill to us for the first time—*Register* was his word—in an account book covered with black cardboard that had swollen to twice its original thickness, with enclosed and glued-in cash slips, receipts, and vouchers.

And unbelievable but true: all the expenditures were entered in detail, what they had used and had, since their birth, beginning with the diapers and the baby food, year after year the food money and an amount for clothing, Christmas and birthday presents, and school supplies. Vinzenz's hospital stay was noted, eye glass after eye glass that Moritz had broken at one time or another, whatever it was, what they had lost or broken, Father's wristwatch, the chronometer, scooters, tricycles, and bicycles, ski equipment without end.

And when it was added together—Vinzenz, you this much, Moritz, you so much—it amounted to a substantial sum, one that would continue to grow in the course of time, to a frightening six-digit figure, to millions and millions. Were we really worth that much?

In any case, now and then he wanted to know how and when—"How and when will I get it all back?" And there was no doubt about his seriousness when they tried to reassure him with their sometimes childishly small, sometimes wonderful, grandiose dreams of what they would earn someday as who knows what, as business tycoons or managers. But nonetheless, he consistently kept them short of money, without a dime of pocket money for a long time. Or he only gave it to them reluctantly, and they were denounced far and wide as skinflints, misers, when they had nothing. And in spite of that they didn't divulge the reason. On the contrary, in order to avoid something even worse, in order to avoid even more ridicule, they said they had cash, enough cash. And when they had debts and couldn't pay them, they were sometimes beaten to a pulp.

All in all, Father promised us that we wouldn't receive anything, anything at all free of charge. But by the same token, neither did we have to take anything, zero to zero. And really, he didn't do anything to us. He did virtually nothing at all. He didn't beat us with a wet lash while we were tied to a post, didn't shoot us to the moon or to the place where the pepper grows. He didn't slap us one, two, one, two, back and forth, marching in cadence, didn't swallow us unchewed. He didn't let us die a wretched death, didn't grind us into sausage, didn't gas us to death–threats, all of it only threats. So that we occasionally became frivolous and began to stage an almost macabre play, with the roles always distributed differently: "Son, I'll bend you." And after a pause: "Please, please, Father, break me instead."

During attacks of bad mood–he called it *world-loathing* and *self-loathing*–Father withdrew more and more to his books, into the book room that had been expressly set up in the attic, his holy of holies, into what he sometimes called the only possible conversation, into reading–even if he probably didn't read, not much, but simply sat around doing nothing, as dozens of books seemed to prove. They were on the table, on the shelves, piled on the floor, uncut, sealed, or packed in wrapping paper. Often we saw nothing of him for an entire Saturday or Sunday. Or if we saw him somewhere in the house, he gave us to understand that it was better not to see him, and walked silently past us in his dressing gown, in slippers, unshaven. We said derisively, "Pssst, Father has locked himself in. Father is in survival training." And the regularly occurring excursions were cancelled. Crowds of people, masses were most likely to attract him on such days, and those must have been the first and probably also the only occasions when he mingled with people in the city, totally of his own accord, with the city people that he otherwise despised so much. He was seen as an onlooker at tent festivals. He was seen in the shopping bustle of the inner city. He always seemed to know in advance where something was going on, a commotion, a tumult, and he went there. He was seen everywhere, welcome as well as unwelcome and uninvited at weddings and funerals. One autumn he went to the soccer field weekend after weekend. He stood or sat erect in the proletarian audience that he had reviled repeatedly, amid hordes of cursing, shouting lumberjacks and backwoodsmen. And even if he held back, he became excited. It gave him a thrill. Hot or cold shivers ran up and down his spine in the sudden din when *it* began: a spectacle, a unique farce—when it came to violence, fist fights on the playing field or in the stands, or when the referee was no longer sure of his life and had to leave the field under police protection, soaked from head to toe with beer, being booed and screamed at. In all that time, Father seemed to be concerned about things that he otherwise condemned from the outset. Much that he did, he did for the first time, but what was bad was that he became presumptuous. And when he drew comparisons, entire chains of comparisons between our behavior, our progress and that of some relatives, or when he let himself be carried away with speculations that we were different, or no different, depending on circumstance, mood, or utility, it could never be done without gossip. There were stories, rumors, especially about uncles and aunts. Terms like *slowpoke, chatterbox*, or *lothario* were used, and we mixed up everything, deliriums, and permanent deliriums, divorces, mental illnesses, committal to the insane asylum: "In the courtyard a constant ritual of kissing and grabbing, and finally, with frightened, jerky movements, the poor devil fled into the house, into the lap of a meanwhile thirty-year-old virgin."..."In the eternal struggle against constipation, against her gas pains, her stomach pains, her sullenness, and the desiccated landscapes of her wrinkled face, your aunt had command of an entire arsenal, a squadron of laxatives"—and so on and so forth. We listened and didn't understand, not really, why he could waste his time with such trifling matters. What did any of it matter to us–the muddle of fate?

In the summer after our first year in the secondary school, arguments between Father and Mother were common, and their course, step by step, hardly differed from one time to the next. As a starting point, a trivial thing could never be too small. A wrong word, a tone of voice, and from a meaningless squabble a full-blown fight developed in seconds. We lay in the next room and listened: monosyllables, blow after blow. Sometimes it was words from a past that we had thought was forgotten: *Monster, Murderer, Arsonist.* And no, if we blocked our ears it didn't continue; it was only a buzzing, a whirring, a humming–silence–blackness in our skulls, a thousand-cycle tone.

Stage Directions

We would have to use violence and so-called violence scenes as sparingly as possible. Unbelievable, but true, all too quickly they seemed implausible, exaggerated, and their effect collapsed. At one moment still repulsive, in the next they were already something to laugh at, or at least they were no longer any reason for alarm. When Father struck us, he struck us properly, with a switch, with the carpet beater, or whatever it was. There was no nonsense, and if anything at all, that seemed to be his way of taking us seriously. The harder he struck, the more he believed that we were being treated like real men, and that he was only doing something good to us. And he didn't abandon the idea that we would be grateful to him someday. It didn't take much–and it often wasn't clear to us what the problem was—for us to be punished. And he always punished us immediately, and as severely as possible, that is to say, severe punishment was the only kind that existed. And the only difference was whether he struck unconsciously, without looking where—more than once we had bloody noses or bruises all over our bodies—or cold-bloodedly. He had us line up in the evening before going to bed, and smack, we got it in the face. And they were not cuffs or boxes on the ear—what harmless, ridiculous words— they were slaps in the face, as rough as the words, or hits in the teeth. He was that mean. Sometimes at first he only pretended to strike and watched to see if we twitched, and whatever we did, even if we stood still, without twitching, it always seemed to be the wrong thing. And either it was finished with a single blow, or he had us count up one, two, three and back down, and it was only over when we reached zero—zero, as if nothing had happened.

Then he looked at them calmly, said, "So, now you can go," and turned apparently absent-mindedly to his newspaper or a book. One summer they had clashed with their male and female cousins in the village, over some trivial thing or other, or in an argument about whether Grandfather was more their grandfather or their cousins' grandfather. And they had immediately been involved in a wild brawl, and when they stopped, with torn shirts and pants, there was no question of whether they were guilty or not guilty.

We were in for it, and with the intention of setting a warning example—as he said again and again—Father locked us in the refrigeration plant of our uncle's hotel, sat down in front of it, and watched to see that nobody let us out early. And we, out of fear of touching somewhere, stood as motionless as possible in the darkness, in the stink of meat and decay, in the stink of decaying meat where the room seemed to shrink more and more. And we swore to each other that someday we would pay him back for everything, with interest and interest on the interest.

We were no longer children.

In collisions with Father they had taken it lying down for far too long and had only really begun to defend themselves little by little. At first they had hesitated and only imitated. But then they had gradually taken on the behavior of adults without experiencing the leap in development that was repeatedly invoked: "Wait until I get big!"–"Yes, when you get big, what then?" In reality they had remained small: in their dealings, in the forms of their association with him, in the way they continued to cower before his authority, in the way they evaded him, in the way they beat around the bush when they were posturing, or in their seemingly selfless consideration for his drivel and whims, for his intricate, complicated obstinacy. He seemed to have them in hand with his illness and hypochondria alone, with the threat of becoming ill if something didn't go the way he wanted, or even when he was just inclined to frighten them, to harass them. That meant: watch out, avoid contradiction or anything at all that made him suffer–or at least he skillfully pretended to suffer. And sometimes their perception seemed to be excessively sharp because of an almost innate guilty conscience, and they even saw the end of the world in the slightest aberration. Again and again they held back, and when they finally couldn't do anything but say something when he went too far, it was not what they would have liked to say. Rather, it was a hodgepodge of accusations of negligence, a jumble of swallowed morsels that were undigested, suddenly spit out. And if there was a goal, their outburst missed it completely, went far beyond it, or it struck everything indiscriminately. And in the countermove, when they had regained their composure, they were inclined to view every blockhead, every imbecile as a master of his discipline, a master of the art of living. He was an authority, if he identified himself with age, title, boasting, or money—they called it *eloquence, superiority*—or if he just knew how to use the right phrases, if he was continually dismayed, concerned, spoke in proper statements like a politician, like a flock of politicians. Or later, years later, there was another comparison: like an artist, a so-called artist or intellectual from the East. And they felt like they were small and stupid, paltry, a piece of dirt, and another piece, Vinzenz, Moritz, products of a much, much too often cited Austrian soul or soullessness.

The stories of their first love affairs were quickly told. If they told them themselves, they confused everything or never got beyond one and the same story. But they left much of it blurred or completely concealed because their roles were less than honorable: that of the frustrated charmer, that of the ice-cold hothead. Everything seemed to have shrunk together into a few images. And what was typical—if anything at all—was how they stood waiting, waiting again and again, somewhere in the rain, often enough in vain, or in freezing temperatures in a winter night, or the way they strutted to a rendezvous—or date, in its innocence—in old-fashioned Sunday pants, bold-plaid trousers, yes, trousers, a model of ridiculousness. How could they have told about that or about how awkward, how clumsy they were when it came to placing, performing a kiss cleanly, unhesitatingly, stiff as a board, as if in front of a jury, or when they prattled utter nonsense and simultaneously looked as if they were out of their minds, confused, or completely insane?

We saw a game in everything—*sport* was a different word—or at least we acted that way: It was always a matter of which of us spoke to a girl first, or even better, was spoken to. We made bets about our success, talked about twelve, fourteen, or sixteen-point bucks, and about shooting them. And we assured each other of our unserious intentions. There was nothing worse than being suspected of being in love, effeminate, whiny. And for lack of the slightest adventure, we showed off, lost ourselves in daydreams, sayings, "Convex is the breast, ah, is the hump of the witch, concave her..."—but there was no rhyme. And we didn't say *girl*, we didn't say *woman*. We said *female entity* when it was unpleasant to say something else. And we put together a prototype of every garish chimera, with the legs of a black African long-distance runner, with the pelvis of a ballet dancer, sometimes with a handful of breast, sometimes brimming with opulence, with the shoulders of a female swimmer, with the face of a starlet or a star. And even if we didn't agree with each other, there was never a doubt about the highlight: Magda's hair. We made a visual estimate from time to time, and we were not certain if parts of our bodies—our sex organs—were not too small, too large, or actually incorrectly developed, or if the growth of our beards came too late, or what identified a person as a man: chest hair or none. But gradually—in some magazines, in street and gutter conversations—we saw what was in vogue and what the standard was, and we breathed a sigh of relief when we knew that we were not all too far from an average value—within a precisely defined margin of error. Yes, it wasn't much, and most of it, if not actually all, was only in our imaginations anyway. And there was confusion there, with an entire cabinet of girls that we knew, and we depicted to each other in the most strident tones, how we would jump over our shadows with a single leap—quick as a wink into happiness.

In the neighborhood there was a young lady—we said *young lady* just to be cynical right from the start—who came past our house every afternoon at the same time. And we rushed from one window to another to catch one glimpse and yet another. We called her *butterball* in a recurring phrase: "Imagine that you pound, you powder the butterball." And while we unabashedly stared into the triangle of white, swelling skin in the neckline of her dress, or watched the insides of her thighs rub together with every stride, as they gave weight, stability to her gait, we were as quiet as mice. In her movements there was something arbitrary, and we said that they weren't carried out, they happened. Her head came first, followed by her neck and breast, and when it seemed that she had to be off balance, a leg swung forward, extended its swing in a goose step a bit beyond the point where her foot would come down. And when her foot touched down, her shoulders shot back, and it began, it started again from the beginning, while even the swinging and striking of her arms gave a reason for assumptions. We had never really seen her face, and we didn't notice the reddish-blue discoloration until sometime later. It was a stigma, a birthmark. Whatever it was, we didn't see it, or we only saw her beauty all the more, and imagined again and again abducting her, seducing her, using a lot of liquor to make her submissive—yes, a faux pas. There was no other way, not even in our most reckless fantasies.

Repeatedly—another faux pas—in one continuing grotesque story, we posed as masters of the house in front of our cleaning woman, when she came to clean once a week on Father's school afternoon. And Mother usually wasn't at home either. We watched her shamelessly as she worked, and actually kept a sharp eye on her, as we had been assigned to do: "Watch her, please. Watch and see that she doesn't steal, that she doesn't swipe anything, that she doesn't forget to wipe and wash a corner, or that she doesn't sit in the outhouse with a cigarette in her mouth." And little by little we made her into an object of our constant observation—and certainly not with unselfish motives. We decided to set out some bait for her, as irresistible as possible, and if she entered the trap, it would be her own fault and she would have no other choice but to be submissive to us. For that purpose we robbed our shared piggy bank, exchanged coins and paper money for a brand-new thousand-shilling note that wasn't tattered or crumpled yet, and laid it out in its full dimensions, length times breadth, on the living room carpet. Hidden in the closet, trembling with excitement, we could hardly wait. And when it got to that point, when she came, pulling a vacuum cleaner behind her and talking to herself, we were forced to watch as she stopped in front of the banknote, wavering, at least apparently, picked it up, carefully, affectedly, between her middle and index fingers, and held it searchingly to the light. And no, no, and no again! She laid it on the table, shrugged her shoulders, and disappeared without further ado.

In school—again, another faux pas—when we were in the secondary school, a rumor went around for years about a female teacher. It was said that she was rather promiscuous from time to time, at class parties, throwing herself at some silly fellow, a greenhorn, a choice baby face, always of one and the same type: dear child, dear child. And she supposedly did a slinking dance with him on the dance floor, breath-takingly close together, or even began to neck right out in public. And we idiots believed it, passed it on unbelievably embellished with words that were much too big: *obsessive* and *nymphomaniac*. And we calculated out, counted up, when it would be our turn, disappointed, again and again, when she did nothing.

How unreal it was. The women in our immediate vicinity seemed all the more real. And we made them pay, or at least tried to, with sensitivity in the truest sense, when we–supposedly out of fear–slept in the same bed with Kreszenz, or pretended to tickle her while playing –tickle-tickle–and strayed with our hands time after time. And one time Mother lay on the living-room couch, sleeping, snoring, and we stared intently at her dress–it was out of place–at her half-uncovered lap, a crater–we knew that much.

On an arterial road at the edge of town we saw a whore for the first time. She was a young, a very young woman who walked back and forth between one roadside tree and another, in a kind of blurred casualness. Or while leaning against a tree, she stopped to light a cigarette or to stare into the darkness, waiting. And impudently, boldly we tried to follow the cars of the customers when they drove away with her, further and further away from town.

And finally, a few weeks after their first discovery, while walking in the woods they even discovered the *scene of the crime*, a place at the foot of the gravel heap.

From then on they occupied their observation post night after night, hidden in a bush. They saw how at intervals of often only a few minutes again and again a car appeared, approached slowly, and stopped with its lights turned off. And sometimes, in the light from a passing car, in a sudden flash of light they saw a man bent over the passenger seat, rocking up and down. And as if it were lifeless, turned toward them was a doll's head laid far back, with staring, open doll's eyes.

And that's how we also became witnesses of an incident, a difference of opinion between her and one of the guys. We saw her jump out of a car, give the car door a smashing kick, and begin to curse and scream in the light of the headlights. She outdid herself, exaggerated like an actress. And after that one sentence remained in our memories: "I'm not going to let you hammer your way through me for a few pennies, you idiot!" It was guaranteed to make everyone laugh when we repeated it when and wherever we could.

For some reason we also told Magda about our notions and failed attempts, but the stories were always smoothed over, with the most serious improprieties eliminated.

What did they expect from that?

We were in a dilemma, and from the beginning even our language seemed to stand in the way of a solution.

Pride always resonated in their stories too, but it seemed to be a well-balanced pride, and they remained zealously mindful not to go a step too far. Or if necessary they stood up for the exact opposite, with an impertinently displayed youthfulness. Sometimes, when they had a good start, or when they intended to create confusion, it seemed as if they wanted to boast, to indulge in lies, and only as the story progressed to its bungled climax was there no longer any doubt that they were only recounting another misfortune. They probably knew what others would think, when they admitted coquettishly enough that they were failures. They knew how little credibility their words had—at least people contradicted resolutely—even if they refused to accept it and repeatedly said, "Hypocrisy, Catholic crap," or in Father's words: "It's socialistic imbecility to make a winner out of a loser, just because he admits that he's a loser."

We avoided Father more and more.

They knew his schedule, and if at all possible, they got out of his way early when he was still at a distance in the corridors of the schoolhouse. Or they squeezed into a corner, if he unexpectedly came toward them.

If his classes ended at the same time that ours did, we hid ourselves well and watched, as he walked across the schoolyard, stiff as a board, with his head held high in an official posture—a caricature of his usual slovenliness. We waited for him to drive away and walked home or took the bus. Sometimes we escaped one of the hallowed, communal midday meals that way. And what was peculiar was that worse and worse and even worse excuses seemed to suffice: minor, even the most trivial catastrophes of all kinds. But when we stopped excusing ourselves at all—we said that we were old enough to do as we pleased—that was too much for him, and we had to make an effort again, or better said, not make an effort. It was enough if we said anything at all, if we blamed each other, or whatever, as long as we at least adhered to a superficial appearance of obedience.

Did Father succeed in remaining true to his own

ideal concept of a world of individuals left to their own devices? Whatever the case, by this time he was also at the soccer field on workdays, sharply, properly focused on the youth team games, with Moritz in the forward line and Vinzenz at the goal. In the winter he drove back and forth through the country, into the farthest corners, to see Vinzenz win bigger and bigger ski races. And Father also won, and there seemed to be nothing left of his fear of being surpassed, outdone. Suddenly, when he spoke of their future, instead of a verdict, more and more often they heard the question, "What will become of you?" Or he was even certain of victory: "You'll really amount to something." And he took them seriously in their inclination to be aimlessly active, when he said, "Every step is a step further and a possible step toward success," or "Being in motion means getting the jump on your fate." And he probably also had the effrontery to say, "He who rests, rusts."

His most important, his real concern never came until the very end, when he could no longer be held back. Then he recited platitudes, banalities without end, and at a foreseeable climax he arrived at Grandfather, at a supposedly natural correlation between money and genius. At least that was the formula that we reduced it to when he wanted to know what was successful and in the next moment briskly—or hesitantly, with all kinds of corrections—gave the answer himself: nepotism, fatalism—especially after he became a writer, a real writer.

Among his colleagues in the school there was only one with whom he had private contact. But even with him meetings occurred only very rarely, and usually for a good reason. They got together to drive to a seminar, a continuing education event, or a graduation ball, or to go to a café after school. And once or twice they played tennis in the schoolyard. And one day a shy, ordinary man was at our house for dinner–just once and never again, either because they preferred not to overdo it, or because Father suffered in the role of the host, or for some other reason. In any case, nothing connected Father to other teachers, to the lives of other teachers. He seemed to avoid them more and more, and he finally cut them off completely, limiting his conversations to only the most necessary things, even in school. Or he tried to humiliate them, as he did once on an excursion, when he bought rounds of drinks and finally invited everyone to dinner. And in the night and on the following morning, when he came home and we saw him drunk for the first time, he could hardly be pacified because the rabble accepted his invitation as a matter of course, so much a matter of course that it hurt. In his cynicism he went to the point of beginning to collect money from them. It made no difference whether it was for the victims of an earthquake or those affected by a famine. And when groschen after groschen had been counted out, he made a speech in the conference room and rebuked them for being a group of well-nourished stinkers in a state institution, who were obviously too short-sighted, too stupid, or simply too stingy to give more. Then he scornfully distributed, strewed handful after handful of coins, and who knows, perhaps he gathered them up again himself, to make them pay for their miserliness. In his contempt, he couldn't go far enough. And we supported him. We weren't the children of a teacher, we were the grandchildren of a hotel owner. And when it mattered, we called our teachers–just as he did–painted post-office workers or railroad men, or said that it was ridiculous to give the title Professor to a good-for-nothing. And in school we were virtually looking for conflicts. We weren't satisfied with some childishness or other, with the usual pranks. An "unsatisfactory" in behavior was our declared goal. As a precaution, we devoted ourselves to a higher art of impertinence by going to class well prepared in order to expose the knowledge of all teachers and senior teachers for what it was. On principle, we wanted answers to questions that were unanswered or unanswerable. And we pretended to know more. Or if we really did know more and were completely successful in exposing somebody, that was enough incentive for us, at least sometimes.

Moritz pushed the game to the extreme or far beyond it. Intending to checkmate a mathematics teacher, an old, completely senile gentleman, in a few moves, he spent weeks, months deeply engrossed in a specialized area of mathematics—linear algebra, analytic geometry. He got more and more deeply involved in it, went on and on, and began to go into raptures about it. He talked about the beauty of the logical conclusion, about the beauty of numbers, and completely forgot to talk about his purpose; or he remained silent, and it was the silence of a wise man. He could sit for days in front of some problems that he had devised for himself. He could study for days, and there was a rumor that in his so-called—it was actually called that repeatedly—thirst for knowledge, he stole every one of the few mathematics books in the book store, a jumble of popular science material or books that pretended to be scientific—as he differentiated them arrogantly enough—in addition to one or perhaps two strictly scientific works. And on days like that, when he had stolen one, he went for a walk or locked himself in his room, and if we met him somewhere late in the evening, or not until night, he was exhausted. It seemed to be a purely physical state of exhaustion, recognizable in his external appearance–in his wildly disheveled hair, in the glow of his eyes. *Worn-out* was probably the term, or *peculiar*. While around his mouth and in his lips there was continual movement, and he succeeded in drawing an observer completely under his spell.

What he actually did? We spoke of his fantasies, and what remained, besides unintelligible explanations, were piles of paper. There were sheets covered with writing that we saw clipped together, piled on top of each other, or strewn all over the floor in his room. And whether we knew it or not, they were filled with Arabic numbers, with Latin and Greek letters–thick alphas, betas, and gammas written with a flourish–with the symbols of arithmetic operations, lines, points, and brackets, and an integral that resembled a disguised treble clef in its exaggerated execution and its curlicues. There were geometric figures whose names, when pronounced, seemed almost erotic: rhombus, parallelogram, trapezoid, and deltoid. There were circles, drawn with a compass around a puncture, a tiny hole in the paper. There were ellipses, hyperbolas, limbs of hyperbolas, their metaphorical, repeatedly vain approaches to asymptotes, and one, two, three sheets with parabolas and a proverbial longing for their ends. It was too little for him to solve problems again that had been solved by generations of pupils and students, and he didn't spend his time apathetically, stubbornly calculating out columns of examples. That was a waste of time, nothing but a waste of time. When he talked about his vocation, when he was overcome, in moments of unshakable self-confidence and awareness of his mission, he seemed to believe that a great discovery lay immediately ahead of him. And there were times when he constantly carried a volume containing unsolved and unsolvable mathematical problems around with him, with the notion that he would solve at least one of them. Time and time again he tried the four-color problem and the great problem of Pierre Fermat. He tried his skill at the trisection of angles, and to crown it all at the quadrature of the circle. And what came of it were approximation constructions–iteration processes without scientific value. The paper was already black with them after a few steps, in a confusion of curves and lines. Or there was cabalism, lucky and favorite numbers, 4, 7, and 17, all prime factors of a numerical series, or the squared numbers minus 1–and so on and so forth. He also indulged in unfulfilled prophecies of his advancement, and in such moments, nothing, really nothing, was too much for him.

Meanwhile, a kink seemed to have occurred in Vinzenz's development, upward or downward, who knows? Often he had a day off from school, sometimes even longer, to go to a training course or to a race. But every jump from one level into a higher one always involved more and more time, and from the beginning everything served him as an excuse. He had a whole list of excuses, and if he no longer knew which one to use, it didn't seem to matter if he was unexcused. Or he had Father sign something afterward, or he signed it himself. In the upper grades–late enough–he was enrolled in the secondary school for skiers. And from then on he no longer had to depend on that sort of tactic. On the contrary: in the late autumn and in the winter he was seldom in school. There really had to be continual bad weather, or no snow far and wide, or a gap in the race schedule for some reason–or who knows what. Otherwise he was on his skis, as he liked to say, for four or five months. And the rest of the time he prepared to make up for everything that he had missed, at least in the beginning. And when he gave up on it, he tried to escape from exam after exam with race results that were as impressive as possible and with all kinds of tricks–and nothing more.

We had–or did we have our own life, reason enough to be happy, content, to look confidently toward the future? Anyway, there were possibilities enough, and first in Father's, but more and more in our own minds as well, it grew into a certainty that everything lay open before us. We simply had to clarify what we wanted.

In Father's predictions there was no doubt about their subsequent course. Importantly and proudly he told everyone who wanted to know, or whether they wanted to know or not–relatives, acquaintances, and sometimes even other people–what they would become. And when he talked about their prospects, their prospects for the future, he always went into rapture: "Moritz will study mathematics because he is calculating,"–a poor play on words–"and Vinzenz, yes, Vinzenz..."–and if he paused at all, then only to heighten the effect and to murmur blissfully, "He already earns money in his sleep, prize money, Gentlemen, whether you believe it or not, prize money and victory bonuses." Otherwise there was nothing to say, at least not in front of others. And later, when he kept calling us on the carpet, it was an ever constant hodgepodge of aphorisms and peasant lore, of superstition and old, familiar warnings–especially about friends and females, "Frrr-ffff." That was his canon, his code, as it had been the code of his father and his father's father, and probably a whole line of mule-headed men before them.

*

One summer, when they were at home alone for a few weeks, in the garden they discovered a cat crouching motionless in the uncut grass, and when she was seen the next day and the day after in the same position, in the same place, they had to entice her.

We placed ourselves at the front door with a bowl full of milk—and how should I put it: we tried to imitate the hissing sound that we had heard so often—a smacking sound—or even to meow, and we waited. We saw how she raised her head, how she stretched and came closer step by step, with front paws that reached far out over the grass, with back paws drawn after her, turned out to the sides. And when she stopped at a safe distance, she was ready to jump. And she did jump, yes she did. If one of us moved, she leaped away in great bounds, and who knows when she came back again—we didn't wait anymore. But after a while the bowl that we had placed there was always licked clean.

From one occasion to the next the distance grew smaller. She didn't jerk back at the smallest movement, and they finally succeeded in touching her, with the tips of their fingers, and little by little with their whole hand. She now popped up at shorter and shorter intervals—or put differently, she appeared. In the mornings she sat on the kitchen window sill. She stood in front of the house door sometime in the afternoon, or lay, when it was sunny, on the roof of the shed. And she strolled around in the garden in the evening, sometimes late at night, enigmatically slowly, decelerated. We gave her something to eat—and before or afterward there was a constant ritual. We took her by the front legs, lifted her at arm's length in front of us, and tried, at eye-level, to subdue, to break her staring gaze with its different, very differently centered focus. We made faces, yelled, or spit saliva in her face, spraying it with our breath. We shook her, swung her, or simulated a free fall with a sudden downward movement. We talked. We began to talk to her, to speak nonsense; and we mutually outdid each other in the invention of newer and newer sounds, newer and newer noises, or in chorus, in bird calls in two-part harmony. And there was no longer any doubt about it. She had found a new home with us.

When did we see that she was pregnant? Or did we see it at all, and if so, in what—in her unusual behavior, in her swollen belly, in a change in her nipples? We had seen how a tomcat from the neighborhood mounted her, tried to mount her, while biting firmly into her neck. We had seen how she escaped again and again, with a lightning-quick turn, a blow of her paw, how she screamed, made a long, screaming bound, and came to rest at some distance away in the grass as if she were dead. And finally, after a while, she pushed herself closer, closer and closer, toward him, with peculiarly twitching movements, completely unprotected, apparently ready for submission. And everything began again: *rape, attempted rape*, and *mating behavior*. Signs, there were signs enough. But we probably didn't notice until it got to that point: a kitten, a kitten, my God, a kitten. We were startled when she stood in front of the house door with it in her mouth one morning, motionless and, as it seemed, waiting. And we were surprised, even more surprised, when she walked past us into the house, walked back and forth in the house, in the hallway, and finally in the living room. And when she lay down, we were—we were fathers, or at least it seemed that way to us in the first moment. And we immediately began playing the roles of nurses. We threw the old cat on her back, held her paws far apart, and lay the kitten on her still swollen belly. We saw how it moved across her belly with its mouth, in rapid movements. Then it finally stopped at a nipple and began to suck, kicking with its front paws—our term was *milk kick*. We listened when it purred, an apparently hasty purr. And when the old cat began, in her rhythm, in her own tone, we stared at each other and only turned away, caught, when we realized that we had stared at each other, and with such exaggerated pathos. Sometimes we took it, the kitten, in our hands, opened its mouth to the extent that we could, with thumb and index finger, and let large drops of our saliva drip into its throat. And it drank, it swallowed with quick, slobbering licks, and we, we were . . . or were we happy?

Anyway, we didn't think twice about it when a pile of vomit lay on the living-room floor. We shoved and pulled the old cat through her own mess, with her head in front, and we only stopped when she was completely smeared. Or rather, we put her, a trembling, kicking bundle, into the toilet bowl, closed the lid, and flushed it a couple of times, quick as a flash. And from then on it went around. In the following days, totally arbitrarily, time after time we dumped a bucket of water on her when she lay stretched out in the garden. We threw her in a high arc, sometimes from a rise, a stack of lumber, or a gravel heap, onto the tin roof of the house. She wasn't able to hold herself there. She immediately began to slide, to run, and finally fell stumbling or bounded down. We tried to shove a straw or a piece if wire into her anus and didn't let her alone until we could no longer bear her screaming. We grabbed her by the back legs and whirled with her in a circle with our arms outstretched. We tarred and feathered her, with candle wax and shreds of paper melted into it. And when she cleaned herself in all kinds of contortions, she looked like she had been plucked. When she escaped—which happened repeatedly—we took it out on the kitten. We shoved its head into a glass full of water. We pulled and tugged at its legs, jerked it up by them, or threw, whirled it far into the air, and outdid each other with newer and newer altitude records. And when it came tumbling down, its eyes were sometimes bloodshot, and flaying with its paws, it sought for a hold. We made it scream, and we only stopped when it had finished screaming. And we hung it in a curtain, let it hang, clinging by its claws, and after a time it slid down, centimeter after centimeter, lost its hold, held itself, lost it again, held itself—or didn't hold itself, was no longer able to hold itself.

Finally, one afternoon they discovered a canister of gasoline in the garage, poured it all over the kitten, set it afire, and watched calmly as it went up in flames. It took one step, still another step, screaming, and stood still, silenced, and collapsed. And while it was still burning, they were already catching the old cat, riding their bicycles, running with her back and forth through the town, and letting her go at the edge of town, at the base of the gravel pile. And nothing remained, or only a blurred consciousness of their guilt.

3

"With a few students, probably students, Moritz lolls around in front of the university. And with his arm stretched out wide, he points to a sign next to the entrance, certain of victory, it seems. And what's there isn't legible, only a glittering and sparkling in the sunlight that strikes the side of the building."..."He assumes the attitude of a hunter over a slain animal, a predator—Vinzenz—with one foot resting on the bumper of a limousine that glistens with chrome. One hand is propped on his hip, the other raised high, balled to a fist, or rather clasped around a rifle that isn't there. And in the corner of his mouth he has a cigarette. He is in the process of puffing it, and it seems as if its glow is the only fixed point, the only point of color in the black and white."..."Unrecognizable at first glance, very tiny, in a bizarre landscape with falling shadows...—Moritz, it is Moritz, dwarfed by house-high, apartment-house-high parallelepipeds, pillars, and capitals of ice, meaninglessly isolated or standing in groups, almost like ruins whose geometrical severity is penetrated again and again by a confusion of undescribable forms."..."Vinzenz on skis—how should I say: with his legs spread wide apart, bent, with vaulted shoulders and arms raised protectively in front of his head. It's the picture of a steer with its horns lowered for the attack that comes to him or doesn't come. He's precisely centered between the gates of a slalom course decorated with red and blue pennants."... "A hall with bombastic plaster-of-Paris decorations on the walls and crystal chandeliers hanging from the ceiling—in the middle of it Moritz, no, Vinzenz, sits bent over a little table, apparently writing, and in a spiral around him stands a line of people whose faces can't be distinguished from each other," and turning more pages, "A man—or is it a woman—a man stands across from him, face to face." And further—"Magda, yes, Magda—a gigantic half-length portrait, as though surrounded by a halo, with her illuminated, glistening hair."

We look attentively, page after page, without knowing why Kreszenz dug out the photo album, without wanting to know why, lulled by the wine. We drink one glass after another, and to be sure, we don't think anything of it, as they say. And we watch as she turns the pages from time to time and again smooths out the crease that has already been smoothed out, not without looking at us first. Sometimes she wipes the whole palm of her hand across the paper, and it's as if she were trying to frighten away the ghosts of a past time. At the same time, it appears that her gaze invitingly or even challengingly says exactly the opposite. Or she bends forward and tries to blow it—whatever it is—she tries to blow it away. And it seems as if she expects a commentary from us when she pauses for a long time or points exaggeratedly at something, something that is usually obvious anyway: "Father's sayings were always a scream."..."As children you were always together"—or when she says, "Remember, remember," or otherwise invites us to do our duty. We don't do it, or only hesitantly. And suddenly it seems clear that she is looking for a real conversation; once and for all she wants to hear from us what she already knows anyway. "Why don't you say anything?"

We move apart again. We seem to limit ourselves more and more to moving apart when in doubt, instead of saying something. And it has an effect—and it's the effect that it's supposed to have—as if we were moving away from our own mirror images or even from ourselves, without anything more than what is obvious lying behind it—not symbolism or anything else. And our horror is only pretended. Or at least it's a different horror than Kreszenz imagines. "Perhaps there's nothing behind it, nothing at all, or only a fantasy."

Either way—"You can't always kid yourselves"—we should have known that we can no longer come to Kreszenz with appeasements, with confessions of our limited ability to remember, our speechlessness—even the word alone...—or with some other nonsense. And when she speaks, all of the playful friendliness is gone from her voice. Suddenly her entire appearance seems changed, unconditional, all at once more definite. And it is as if she has only been waiting for a key word, or rather, for its absence, to strike. Suddenly creases seem to have become visible in her face. Behind her glasses—all at once I notice that she is wearing glasses—behind them, with contracted pupils, her eyes seem to spray sparks. And in her suit—who knows why she put it on—gray, light gray, with dark gray seams—she is suddenly older and actually like a businesswoman, like the caricature of a businesswoman: timeless, ageless, with glowing streaks of glistening lacquer that still looks wet on her overly long fingernails. "Magda..." That's her customary timid beginning. It is uncustomary in its directness as she continues: "You have—I'll say it plainly—you have Magda on your conscience." And as she says it, it's as if with *you* she means not only us, but us men, and with *Magda* she means Magda and herself.

As we listen, from outside, probably from the woods, we hear a sound, a creaking, cracking, snapping that is unclassifiable. Then we turn ostentatiously toward the window, but there is nothing, no more sounds. And as it grows quiet–even quieter, it seems–the silence is the absence of the sum of all possible sounds–of all possible distractions: rustling in the forest, the noise of automobiles, the footsteps of passers-by. And when Kreszenz begins again: "In town...," and says who knows what, we don't listen. We only pick up some fragments when they are repugnant or absurd enough, "filth," or "awful mess," "wild marriage." And we're only startled when she says, "Moritz, talk."

*

In the autumn before the second winter games that were held in the city, in the so-called state capital, an excessive self-confidence, an aroused, wildly salient local patriotism raged in the whole country, even far more than usual. It was there in tavern conversations and in politicians' speeches that could not be distinguished from them, or only with difficulty. It was on radio and television, synchronized or apparently synchronized with all the newspapers. "Men and women of Tyrol," the words were fawning and fraternizing, and after an appropriate pause–at least it could be imagined that way: "the eyes of the world are focused upon us." And written, spoken, or even only suggested, the sentence seemed proof enough to everyone that the city was a center, a natural world center. Its name, indiscriminately mentioned with the melodious names of all kinds of metropolises–no matter how much it didn't belong–was again and again and again a reason to be proud: Alp city, sport city, and sport capital. And if it was the upper end of a scale, there were enough discouraging examples at the lower end, in some border, and trashy, and Ruhr districts. And it was clear that in every corner of the world they knew who and what it was. They knew what was concealed behind it, what glitter and sparkle, what glow.

What was really concealed behind it? In the streets of the city there seemed to be only one breed of people. They were crafty in more ways than one–and only at second glance was a jumble of different eras, styles, and fashions visible. Among business people, secretaries, and students, recognizable in their appearance as city people, again and again you encountered people from the country, even in the inner city. The younger ones didn't differ from their city contemporaries, or only when they wanted to appear exaggeratedly elegant or urbane. But with older people you could tell immediately, by their gaze–the way they could look at apparently obvious things–or by their still clearly rural clothing, especially on the weekends, on Sundays, when they staged their play with a cast that consisted only of extras, in their Sunday suits and their Sunday costumes among closed stores in deserted shopping streets. Or sometimes one of them even made an appearance with his tractor, in the sparse Sunday traffic, and rode in, so to speak, on his high seat, among streetcars, buses, and tourist carriages. Or you met groups of fully equipped skiers, with skis and poles, in the middle of town, or mountain climbers with back packs, and you were on the point of going crazy in the foehn, in a landscape that closed in, oppressed from every side. Again and again divisions of seemingly ancient figures paraded. They were figures from the past, from the people's theater, and with their brass bands and riflemen's guilds they gave the streets their loden-stiff, fan-draped appearance, their very own air. And suddenly passers-by seemed less real, as if they didn't belong, and they lost more and more of their authenticity, their existing or nonexistent glow. And everything was the same; but things were only regarded as authentic, placed in a decent light, or viewed as brand-name products, if the notation *Tyrolese, Tyrolean* was added to them, entirely in the sense of the old, ancient, inveterate saying: "He who is a Tyrolean is a human being, he who is not is not."And it was that very thing that still gave weight to decisions. Or to put it another way: there was incest in the narrower, in the narrowest sense, and incest in all institutions. Even the university that was called *time-honored* stood in a questionable light with its staff of resident officers and a few professors from outside of whom it was scornfully said that they wouldn't have gotten any position otherwise, or that they had come to ski, or because Italy wasn't far away. And even if fraternities didn't necessarily have a say, their sash-and-saber-sheathed appearance remained a normal scene in front of the dusty busts of Nobel-prize winners from the prewar era–famous people or some who were not. But just what significance did they have compared to the world renown of some loquacious, garrulously doting mountain climbers? Discoverers, inventors–all of them were nothing by comparison. Oswald von Wolkenstein. At least it was always the same names, always the same people, when they talked about the country's great ones. And our, yes, our provincial governor was always included–there wasn't a native pope or antipope yet. And people were convinced that they set the tone in everything that counted. And it was not so bad to limp along behind otherwise, especially in the arts, in the so-called fine arts. Nevertheless, a few times a year there were performances of old music in one of the churches, and hordes of eager, overexcitedly enthusiastic women stalked, pranced in high heels to the performances and exuded their artistic taste, in muffled *ohs* and *ahs*, in applause that broke out, restrainedly broke out and broke off again and again. From time to time in the halls of the city, there were evenings of folk music before sell-out audiences, and people forgot themselves, seemed to forget themselves in unrestrained whistles, in shouts of "Bravo!" and a slowly swelling applause that finally swept everything else away. There were readings by local poets before relatives and acquaintances and a handful of stalwart comrades-in-arms. And afterward there was always a laboriously conducted discussion. There were exhibitions of the works of mediocre painters, vernissages, with words of apparent approval that seemed to be expressed without purpose, and background noise that could unambiguously be interpreted as *yes* or *no*. And there was a theater, a so-called provincial theater, hallowed with the geographical addition *Tyrolean*, and a few stages that were literally, a few that were figuratively in the cellar, where they devoted themselves to second and third-class folk pieces—and so on and so forth.

If it hadn't been for the cinemas, but what do I mean cinemas: they were movie theaters—gigantic auditorium and screen, and there was a curtain that opened noisily—in movie houses that weren't packed. And we still continued to go there later when everything was different. We went to see a film—even though it was probably a bad one that had been shelved—alone or with a few of the lost, forgotten ones, instead of going to one of the new box-like cinemas with their 8:15 films, or instead of joining the etiquette-conscious audience of a program cinema, at a so-called cinematic event.

Near the railroad station there was a low, gray house

with windows that glowed red at night and a view of a jumble of parallel tracks that criss-crossed in front of the platforms. It had an old, uniformed man as doorman—he seemed more like a porter, more like a chauffeur. And when you entered, he touched the brim of his peaked hat with his hand, or said something or other, when you were already standing in the anteroom in front of a dour, anorexic woman. And when she rang the bell, there was a swarm of made-up, fancied-up girls with a smile that repeated itself in all their faces, with a sometimes hidden, sometimes clearly displayed scorn and an unsuppressed or only barely suppressed contrariness. And yes, when you climbed the steps behind one of them, to the rooms on the upper floor, you were momentarily... How should I put it? You were momentarily elsewhere.

*

When Moritz came to the city to study, he was already determined to leave with his science, as he pretentiously put it, as quickly as possible, to go out into the world. At least that standard statement corresponded to his detachment when people came to him with warnings of a black future, with idle and futile calculations about probationary teachers, teaching positions, and who knows what. Just what did that have to do with him? In lectures he usually sat far back, far away from others, and copied from the blackboard like a man possessed. And sooner or later he was denounced as being unresponsive and moody, as having packed his days full of hours in some lecture hall or other, from the crack of dawn until sometime at night, with light falling at constantly different angles as his only measurement of time, or later, with a twilight that lasted for hours, a timelessness that lasted for hours. From home he went to a lecture, from a lecture he went home. And in between, before, and afterward there was work, work, work–even if it was nonsense–and his dream of a successful start, a vertical take-off out of nothingness.

But little by little his already trite enthusiasm for the beauty of the logical conclusion, for the beauty of numbers–his enthusiasm in general disappeared in seemingly empty attempted explanations. Or it was suddenly aimed at the lives of great mathematicians instead of at their work. From one day to the next he began to read a series of biographies that were comparable in tone. And out of chimeras and everything that he read, he began to create a prototype, an ideal and dreadful image that he put together from a thousand fragments. He proceeded indiscriminately, or he based his selection on constantly changing criteria, on different books each time, ones that were usually written by second or third-class people from the discipline, would-be or unappreciated scientists who were sometimes apparently under pressure to compensate for their own failures with exaggerated admiration and newer and newer hymns of praise. And thus arose the picture of a man with a striking face, a face that was called *striking*–an aquiline nose, a narrow mouth that breaks off abruptly at its edges, at its corners, an apparently dented, protruding chin, and eyes drowned in tears in their sockets. And he had probably –at least there was a rumor to that effect–already been a compulsive calculator at the age when he started school. And he had been recognized in his younger years as a very, very extraordinary talent. And with pampering and coddling a life devoted exclusively to science began. But it was to be one in which he really lived for it, with an absolute schedule, with established times for work, meals, rising, and retiring to bed, with or without a wife—in a well-calculated expense-profit computation it didn't seem to matter—and with uninterrupted work, work that could not be interrupted by anything in the world, not even by the end of the world itself, twenty-four hours a day, three hundred sixty-five or sixty-six days a year, year after year after year.

In many circles it was regarded as heroic to die young, with modes of death ordered strictly according to the degree of their honorability. Suicide always seemed to be a plus point, or you died in a duel carried out at dawn, in a long-past century. But on the other hand: a long, long life. And actually anything could be proven, based on the inconceivability of dying, now, at this moment, or from one moment to the next.

In Moritz's perception mathematicians were heroes from the start, with their methodology that was apparently far superior to all other ways of proceeding—their "queen of the sciences"—and their ever-recurring claim to exclusive spiritual or mental health. Whatever it was, they seemed to know how to do it better, or more precisely. Either they could do it better or they left it alone. And from the beginning he did not neglect to measure himself against the greatest. He jealously noted who had already done something at what age. And when his birthday passed once again without anything to show for it, he consoled himself with the idea that perhaps, perhaps during the next year..., even if he knew that it was quickly, all too quickly too late, with very few exceptions. There were only a handful of lights left in who knows which decade of life.

Initially Moritz turned to one professor in particular, a German who, at least at first, in all the rumors, even in the most malicious ones, was above the bad reputation, the disrepute of the entire university. And really, what better reputation could he have than to be a taskmaster, a slave driver, and to want to do away with Austrian slovenliness, Austrian congeniality, Austrianness in general? Even before Moritz saw him, he began to rave about him, and more than once he stepped to his defense against a wild, sworn mob, or expressed himself in his favor. He made it clear to everyone that he, not squeamish in choosing his measures, was there to study, to study, and to study some more. And under those circumstances what did they mean by *irritability, overestimation*, or *Prussianism*—a constantly recurring word —either spoken unequivocally or concealed in resentments? In his memory it was a confusion of images, the way he paused in his lecture, standing erect, exaggeratedly erect in an auditorium, and lapsed into a demented, rolling laughter that swallowed itself. And at such moments—at least it seemed that way—switch points in his thinking were most likely to become visible. Or he gave structure to his thoughts in some interspersed comments, when he wrote *to know* or *to have* or, less self-assured, *until now* in gigantic letters on the board and placed a colon behind it as if to confirm it, with hacks that could even be heard in the corridor, or when he said, "Just a moment, just a moment," repeating it quickly, and it was as if he were stopping himself. Over and over there was always a different word that was directly associated with him, but his favorite word seemed to be the favorite word of all of them, all mathematicians: *trivial*. And a problem that had been called trivial at some time was no longer a problem, was unimportant, uninteresting.

Convinced that he did not approach unimaginatively a world that presented itself as unimaginative, Moritz was always astounded when they ascribed to him an exaggerated sense of reality, an exaggerated inclination toward objectivity. There was no other way. He either had to rave about something or leave it completely alone, and he would have preferred to roar out or to weep silently when somebody, an acquaintance, dismissed an ancient, shared, childhood dream with a few words and was contented with less and less, finally with nothing, with everything. Then he had to be careful not to look into his eyes, or arm himself in advance against their hopelessness, against any semblance of hope for a happiness that was always a few sizes smaller. They were soldiers of fortune, world conquerors, or fairy-tale princes. He stated it in his own words pathetically enough: "We always want the highest and are not even ready for the lowest, damned as a species, as a genus, condemned to mediocrity."

So Moritz placed in him, in the professor, his entire confidence and clung to him, even when doubts arose everywhere about his ability–they thought it might be just a skillful pounding of phrases–and about his personal and political integrity: words, words, words, an unparalleled torrent. And he followed him, actually ran after him, with nothing but the wish to see him from his good sides, not pared down to a few weaknesses. At last, one summer, he even traveled with him. And from then on he accompanied him as an assistant, as a so-called glacier worker, summer after summer on glaciers, especially on the Kesselwand and the Hintereis glaciers, taking measurements–measuring glaciers, which was the professor's specialty and hobby.

*

In the skiers' high school things finally went upward, or downward, for Vinzenz, depending on how you looked at it, whether you preferred skiing or school. And after he flunked the first year "spectacularly," as Father put it, with a whole row of F's, at the start of the second year he didn't even go, and later he had to be talked into going. And somehow he was able to get from late autumn into the winter, and when the racing season was over, from spring into summer. But it still came as a surprise when after the first few weeks of class in his senior year, he suddenly said, "That's enough, I don't want to continue," and turned a deaf ear to every art of persuasion and cajolery from the start.

His foundering had already found expression in countless letters, notes to Father from all kinds of teachers or even the school director, sometimes to Father and Mother simultaneously. And they all indulged in enumerations of pranks, little things, and ended, as the *moral of the story*, with a sentence that could be recognized by its very wording as a conclusion: It was about their son, and the fact that he was impudent, lazy, and a liar. As a rule, Father took it laughing–Father, and with him Mother too–or he even encouraged Vinzenz to go on. And when he was angry, Father always took his side against all the accusations, so much that one word sufficed to describe it: *comradeship*. And that didn't exist, of course, except or not even in war. On a parents' visiting day, he even went so far as to say in front of the gathered faculty: "But, but Gentlemen, who will be so mean, so narrow-minded, when somebody is getting ready to accomplish something great?" And he wasn't at a loss for examples. He cited the careers of numerous famous and world-famous people who had finished school with bad grades or not at all: there were hundreds, thousands, hundreds of thousands. As he perceived it, it seemed clear from the beginning that sooner or later, Vinzenz would go on from Grandfather's former greatness with his skiing—even if it was only a fictitious greatness—or at least continue with the life that was held up as an example in the village. And when he traveled to Vinzenz's races in the winter, as a tireless companion, he stood in front of him, he stood behind him, obvious, undeniable. His creed was success at any, or almost any price. And to emphasize it he could recite all kinds of aphorisms, truisms, platitudes. And if he sometimes began talking about the chancellor in the same breath—one of his standards—or the finance minister, we knew where it was leading. The next moment it was always about money: "Money brings happiness, money brings luxury." That was what he said, with exaggerated shrillness and just as if he were looking into a badly positioned camera. And when he laughed and his laughter first came out as coughing, he was completely beside himself.

In his final school year, Vinzenz won the national championship in the slalom. And if the event alone was not reason enough to tell about it, it gained effect in something else, in an interview that he gave on that occasion. It climaxed with his saying that what he won, whatever it was, he won exclusively for himself and not for some abstract thing like the country, for example. He told how words had been put in his mouth over and over, Austria or some other fantasy. And the next day he made headlines in the tabloids: "Lout," "Traitor to the Country," but in quotation marks. They called him selfish, self-righteous, and a loudmouth. And there was only one newspaper that took his side and applauded the fact that he was the first one who quit playing the hypocrite and said what he thought—what all the others thought as well, without saying it. In school there was an epilogue, and Vinzenz was called before the director and had to take a dressing down and listen to who knows what while standing there. But in class he was received with enormous fanfare. He had to tell it again and again, and when he talked—"Quiet, quiet, please!"—it was completely silent.

With his extravagances—how should we put it: With his extravagances and his megalomania, from then on he seemed to kick over all the traces. And in reality, daily, day after day there were encounters with teachers. And if he didn't bring them on, it was they who suddenly used trifles as an excuse to harass him, and there were entries in the class record and detentions without end.

On a whim, Vinzenz decided to sell his car. Bought when he was seventeen, before or after his seventeenth birthday, with his first prize money, it stood in Father's garage for more than a year, resting on wooden blocks. He only sold it in order to buy a new one, an American model. And when he parked it in the parking lot in front of the school, that alone seemed provocative, or when he told how much he spent just to pay for his gasoline, insurance, and his registration. And at the very latest it was enough when he took a teacher by the arm and said, "I do it all just to provoke you." At the same time he began to buy rounds of drinks—in the appropriate style, in a style that would have been a credit even to Father's saints, his village saints—in the only tavern far and wide, with male and female students and teachers as regular guests. And he always said the same thing, "*À toutes*," or, "Steady, steady!" when a waitress began to wobble, or when it began, "Cheers, cheers, cheers." And he smoked and liked doing it. He staged his smoking as an exaggerated act when he snapped a cigarette out of the pack and tried to catch it with a snap of his lips. And when he succeeded it was a feat, and everyone applauded. Or when he took his lighter and—"Attention!"—performed a trick, or simply made it open with a click and close with a clack a few times. Around him—he was always at the center of attention—around him there was always a whole swarm of girls with large, innocent eyes—or for lack of another word, eyes that were called *innocent*—and who knows what uncertain longings for a real, really real life.

Stage Directions

Would we have voices from off-stage or even a narrator? Would we talk ourselves? In any case we would have to be careful not to explain too much or lapse into a schoolmaster or senior-teacher tone, into gestures of presumptuous omniscience, or even worse, into an I-know-that-I-know-nothing behavior that is as enlightened, seemingly enlightened as possible, with the associated artificiality and coquettishness in which everything seems just as permissible. The more unconscious the one attitude, the more conscious the other, all the more ridiculous, all the more false, all the more mendacious. We would have to guard against inadmissible connections as much as possible, against those that are clear, apparently perceptive anyhow, and especially against causalities. Or if we were to begin with them—where? And where would we stop? If we said "because," how far would we go back in a cause-and-effect hierarchy? And then, if it was too simple, always too oversimplified, it would not be right anyway. Actually, as far-fetched as it seemed, it could always be claimed about any two events, that one occurred because the other had occurred. Or at least there was no evidence to the contrary. At the same time, all too simply woven stories always seemed suspect, with introduction, body, and conclusion like we had in school, and we usually already had enough when we simply heard about the necessary course of a plot. In such stories, with their birth and their obligatory horrible childhood, the heroes already wore something like an invisible index number—a Cain's mark. Then step by step everything developed from it, with murder or suicide at the end. Should we say psychologize, *and at the same moment:* a monstrous word? *We would have to be careful not to let that happen to us, not to psychologize like some know-it-alls. And even if we talked about traits and characteristics, we would have to talk about them loosely, with* and *and* or *as the most important conjunctions. In our family it was considered to be a virtue to be able to be alone, with appropriate, never doubted images, and if you couldn't do it, you kept that to yourself, out of fear of being considered a woman, a sissy, or who knows what. If we were tied, we were more likely tied to a place than to people, and for that, if at all, we seemed to be homesick. We had learned our lesson and felt that every meeting with others, except our nearest acquaintances, was a confrontation. And we almost always withdrew from the outset or pretended to be reserved. We said little, or nothing at all, in order not to say anything wrong. And what that was, something wrong, seemed to be different from instance to instance. And really, what we said, we said with the intention of pleasing everyone. And if anything at all, that was our truth criterion in role playing that constantly changed. What we really could do was listen, or at least we pretended to do that in skillful poses, always attentive, inattentive, precisely as much or as little as seemed necessary. And it was an art, the nodding of our heads, the shaking of our heads, the way we said yes or no at the right, at precisely the right moment, or the way we bent forward or leaned back. We knew how to ask questions like a father confessor, and even if they were only sham questions, the person across from us always showed a weakness, and we moved it further and further into the center of our perception. And we suspected that nothing remained at the very end, nothing, nothing, nothing, no matter how intelligent or eloquent someone seemed at the outset. We had stopped listening long before that, and anyway, it was not only what a person said that disturbed us, it was how he said it, how self-evident it was. We always felt that it was an obligation to have to decide. And actually, when we said* yes, *we were already dismayed that we had not said* no, *and vice-versa, or even better, nothing. Because in general, when we uttered something, in the next moment we could utter just the opposite, and in the moment after that the opposite again, again, and again.*

As a basic rule we would have to let our scenes wander around for a long time without a goal, without a purpose, apparently disoriented. And only at the very last moment, when they began to go astray, would we urge them into a trot, into a gallop, so that they would storm off in some direction as if bitten by a tarantula and only come to rest after a while, out of breath. And they would go on in an uncertain rhythm, on and on that way, and ultimately, in a fatal sting: blackout.

In general it was a few weeks of work, no more. It was always the same. In the afternoon, in the evening, they—Moritz and the professor—walked out of the village with large packs, with enormous, specially made dossers with measuring equipment tied to them. They carried a steam drill with a steam-drill boiler, ice axes, crampons, and ropes, and on top, piled higher than their heads, their rucksacks with food, valuables, little things, and junk. And when they visited all kinds of taverns before their departure, they drank liquor, homemade brandy, and tried to enter into conversations with natives. It was a real ritual. Or when the Professor—"I refuse to tolerate that eternal *Professor, Professor* nonsense"—who was suddenly a different man, began with his jokes, they were always the same, his so-called trademarks. And ultimately, when they landed in our uncle's hotel, things were usually pretty lively, with accordion or guitar music and singing and shouting that could be heard far and wide. It was all the quieter when they finally left, side by side at first, on a narrow gravel path that changed to a still narrower, ungraveled path with a center strip of grass, with meadows, pastures, and only occasional trees on both sides. And finally they walked in single file on a path between black mountain slopes that seemed to stand vertically in the twilight—repeatedly—divided into perfectly straight strips by foaming, white brooks. And if they talked at all, it was always one and the same thing: Moritz recounted his gossip, village stories, and scandals, while the professor daydreamed about the good old days, about the historic moments, the high points of glacier measurement, with much more money and many more possibilities, with helicopters and enough personnel and a whole crowd of willing porters. And when he began raving, after every sentence he said, "What?" usually said it again, even more insistently, and finally Moritz, well... And that way, in a short-winded back and forth—"What?" "What about it?" "What?" "What?"—during the night they reached the shelter that they had been heading for, usually more dead than alive.

Their working day began with a breakfast in the darkness, and when they stepped out of the cabin, the sun hadn't come up yet. It was getting ready to rise in what was perhaps, and perhaps not, the coldest moment of the entire day. They could count on beautiful weather, and if it rained or snowed, there was always a back and forth—"We're leaving." "We're not leaving."—and again and again one of them stepped outside, looked, tasted, and smelled, and finally, one way or the other, they started out. Sometimes they were instantaneously wet, soaked, sometimes sunburned, with swollen, cracked lips and blistering facial skin that was peeling in flecks and shreds. And while Moritz ran from one measurement point to the next with a reflector, over gravel heaps, moraines, or across the snowless ends of glaciers with very visible fissures, the professor sighted in on him from a fixed point.

In one longitudinal and several transverse profiles, measuring gauges were staked out at precise intervals over the Kesselwand and the Hintereis glaciers. They consisted of iron and aluminum tubes bored into the snow or into the ice. From their motion, from the differences in their positions from year to year, the flow velocity, the surface flow velocity of the glacier was established. And summer after summer the transverse profile gauges were placed back in their profile, at their position from the previous summer, while the gauges of the longitudinal profile were permitted to wander toward the end of the glacier without being transferred back.

And again: Moritz ran from one to the other, secured by sight, as it was called, or with a helper on a rope. And in very tricky situations he stopped, or crept onward on all fours. And once, in an operation when something could have happened without warning, he took off his shoes and felt his way across the steep ice in his wool socks, in danger at every step of the way—at least it was more than just imaginable. Or there were other times: when he hesitantly walked across a seemingly fragile snow bridge, with nothing on either side, a gigantic black hole; or when he began to poke around in a smooth stretch of snow, and round, round, and all around, his ice axe broke through; or when he stood beneath a break, and from inside the ice came a noise as from an approaching, suddenly derailed locomotive; or above him a piece of ice broke loose and burst in a pile of crystals, fragments, and splinters. And night after night—a web of dreams, nightmares—night after night he saw himself standing in front of a moulin, a hole bored in a spiral by melt water, sometimes hundreds of meters deep, sometimes reaching clear to the ground, unfathomably deep, a few hand widths in diameter, large, large enough. Or he stood in front of a brook that twisted its way into the ice in narrow bends with smooth walls that glistened in the sunlight. And when it vanished with "S" after "S" into the interior of the ice, he was startled, defenseless, completely defenseless, washed away, or even washed up, battered and abraded, spit out in the cave at the end of the glacier.

One summer a pack horse had fallen into a fissure and had been shot in its death throes by a hurriedly summoned constable. And again and again there were people—mountain climbers, mountain enthusiasts, people obsessed with mountains—who disappeared into a glacier without a trace and came out somewhere years, sometimes decades, centuries later, when the snow melted, undecayed or in every imaginable, precisely discernible state of decay.

As children, when an accident had occurred in the mountains, we had always excitedly watched the mountain rescue team depart, man after man, single file. Or we had watched their lights disappear in the darkness. And once, in the middle of the day, we became aware of a faint sound, and when it was still some distance away, we saw the tiny dot in the sky that grew larger and larger. It was a helicopter approaching with its tail raised. And on a rope, blowing in the wind, there was a shrouded bundle with the head of a corpse jutting out of the covering, rocking up and down, with a corpse's arms and a corpse's legs dangling lifeless. And finally a twisted corpse's body was released, fell, and apparently landed softly in the noise that scattered, tore everything apart.

Glacier advances or retreats—apparently depending on which it was, the professor opened up or shrank back into himself. Yes, he took it personally. And if it was too much for him, if there was no other way, he didn't hesitate to give false measurement results. When he talked, the story of the glacier was also always the story of his own mental condition: ice ages, interglacial periods, nourishing and depleting areas, deep bores in the ice with drilling depths of a few hundred meters. And finally, he always began talking about the already legendary outbreak of an ice lake that had been dammed up by a glacier, and about the devastations that it had caused in the entire valley. Or he talked about the landing of two stratosphere fliers in the snow on the

Kesselwand, the Hintereisferner, or some other glacier. Usually he could no longer be stopped, and when he noticed it, he said laughingly, "Say enough!" But a moment later he would say, "Nothing is enough. I'll say enough. Enough." And he was in his element if he had listeners in the shelter in the evening and could tell everything again and again and again while he was slightly drunk. And he wasn't quiet again until they were alone, in their room, and were drinking a last bottle of wine or were lying with their eyes open, one above the other in their bunks. And sometimes, when he was dead drunk, pseudoquestions, significant questions slipped out of him, about what the future would bring, the meaning of everything, and especially, why?

One day they had actually flown, and as the howling of the helicopter became louder and louder, faster and faster, and it seemed to be on the verge of exploding, in the pounding and jerking of the machine Moritz felt as if he would take off ahead of it and leave his body behind while flying in the air above, outside himself. He felt like he was in flight again, in free fall, when they brushed closely—apparently within millimeters—across a ridge and an abyss opened behind it in the next moment, or when they—feat, feat—simulated a diving attack for fun, or circled in the tightest possible radius, or flew in who knows what patterns in a sky that could hardly be distinguished from the snow. From time to time—odd jobs and work on the side—they also measured ski-lift routes in glacial ski areas, with their masts that wandered out of the track in the ice and stood in zigzag lines after a while. And there was always the danger that they would be bent or that the lift rope would jump off the rollers. Or there were other construction projects, mountain restaurants that had hastily been placed in moraines and after a few weeks were already sagging on their enormous foundations, standing askew over fissures that had suddenly opened. And yes, the professor was a consultant, officially accredited, and often they were invited to different hotels, belonging to different lift companies, for skiing vacations with all the trimmings, with especially assigned ski instructors and so-called female companions. And of course they didn't pay a penny. All in all it was O.K.–*O.K.* was Moritz's term–and sometimes when he stepped out of the shelter above the Kesselwand glacier at night, or out of the measurement station on the rocky ridge in the Hintereis glacier, and in front of him, in a moonlit landscape, there was a starry sky reflected in the glitter of a snow field–how should I put it?–it was all explainable. It was an astronomer's ABC, so to speak, derived with a minimum of air pollution, a minimum of artificial light as minimal interference factors. It was as if he saw how the earth turned around the sun, around its own axis. Or at least his knowledge helped him to interpret the confusion that way and not otherwise, not as the play of nature. On the contrary, he interpreted it as a mathematical play of symbols and numbers, as an artistic spectacle.

*

In the weeks after his departure from school, Vinzenz sat around at home and actually did nothing but train. And when he offered to help Mother, to wash the dishes for her, or to go shopping, or to wash Father's car in addition to his own, he always did it reluctantly, in a fit of guilty conscience that was quickly forgotten again. And in a vague tone that was as benevolent as possible, they said that he was good for nothing anyway—useless. So that finally, or even from the very beginning, he was relieved of all duties. Thus one day was like the next: He got up at sometime in the morning, and when he appeared he was already in his sports clothes—sweat pants, sweatshirt, gym shoes—ready to go, as he put it. Before the midday meal he usually went into the weight room that had been set up purposely in the basement. There he tortured, hardened, mistreated his body on all kinds of apparatus: steel constructions, simple, or with arms, legs, and tentacles, like gigantic, clumsy insects, frozen in their clumsiness. When he was tired, he withdrew with the newspapers into his room, or sometimes, on nice days, into the garden. And he could be seen sitting in the swing for hours, usually motionless. In the afternoon, wearing the same sweaty clothing, he made a long-distance run with various interludes of dexterity and strength training. Or he sprinted up and down the fitness course or the gravel heap on the edge of town. Or he clattered back and forth through the woods with his motocross bike, or over difficult terrain with abrupt rises and drops, with insane, daredevil stream crossings. Or he rode his bicycle, his mountain bike, on hiking paths around the town or in the mountains, with glacier climbs and descents, moderately difficult climbing passages, and real mountain climbs. And it was clear that it was not limited to weeks, of course not. It became months and finally even years in which he sat around at home, acting as if he were getting ready to do something while he was coddled and even supported in his idleness, his so-called idleness.

Winter after winter during the racing season, Father let nothing get near his son, at such moments his only son. He ordered everyone to leave him in peace, not to disturb him in his concentration. And a procedure was established, with the ideal that a person should evaporate into the air if in doubt.

When Vinzenz came back from a race, a reception was always staged in every detail, and depending on whether he had done well or poorly, it was a real festival or nothing. And either way, that meant that he was not accessible at all. During all that time, whether present or not, he seemed omnipresent. And when he sent postcards from training courses in the summer and the fall, or telephoned evening after evening—it didn't matter if he had been away from home for who knows how long, or for only a few days in the nearest spa or winter sport resort—it seemed like exaggerated homesickness. And at some times during the year it was the same when he sent vacation greetings from places that were always different and as exotic as possible, and then always got back ahead of them.

Usually on race days the radio was on at home. Or rather, one was on in the living room and one in the kitchen, uninterruptedly. And when there were sports reports, somebody said "Pssst!" so that we wouldn't miss anything. And sometimes, in the hiss of a station that was readjusted again and again, something actually came, *something*, as we always said. In the winter when Vinzenz ran in the World Cup for the first time, Father didn't forget to proclaim—proudly and certain of victory —that from now on he would also be on television—he didn't think it was too foolish to say TV. And one day we sat gathered in the living room for a live broadcast. And while he was still turning and twisting all the knobs, playing with the harsh picture and sound contrasts, it had already started. Skier followed skier, always accompanied by his same commentary, only so and so or so many before Vinzenz—only five, four, three, two, one more. And then suddenly the broadcast was over, and he cursed and screamed, determined or not to make a fool of himself. It was a messed-up premiere. But even later, it was a long time until he got his money's worth: When it got to the appropriate point and Vinzenz was standing at the starting line, suddenly in the picture, or he was in an expected, unexpected segment, or in a camera pan shot, Father left in wild excitement, sometimes with his teeth chattering, trembling, or he sat grotesquely contorted in his armchair, with eyes that were closed or nervously twitching, with his hands over his ears, and he had lost his ability to see and hear. That meant, the less he heard, the less he saw, the more he talked, talked, and talked. And there was always noise when he indulged in tirades of cursing, in his constant monologues about the advantages and disadvantages of different starting numbers, about weather and visibility conditions, the quality of the snow and the ski course, or when he talked about a bunch of ignorant dilettantes with Vinzenz as the only expert, as an exception. He didn't accept contradiction, or only if he contradicted himself in his exaggerations, and we did well to moderate our own demands in the hope that Vinzenz would win. And in a catastrophic situation–that was the phrase–in a catastrophic situation there were all shades of gray, dark gray, and jet black tones, depending on whether he had been eliminated in the first or the second round, with a good or bad intermediate time, or whether he was in front of or behind so-called exotic skiers in the competition results, and by how many seconds, tenths, and hundredths of seconds. And it was worst of all if he was on the way to a victory and fell just before reaching the finish line. At such moments Father withdrew without a word, and we suspected that it was an attack of his illness when he didn't appear for breakfast the next day, or when he didn't show his face at all for longer periods, sometimes for days.

That was the scenario to which Vinzenz continued to return again and again, always with new medals and trophies and some gifts and prizes–cheap trinkets and junk. And sometimes he had hardly returned and he was already bringing out his souvenirs. Mounds of dirty laundry welled forth from his open suitcases, and it was up to Mother to wash and iron everything. And he said, "Thank you," or not even that, or "Leave it, just leave it, leave it," when the things had been washed and ironed without great ado, of course. And there was no other possibility. Right or wrong, he seemed to see in her and his sister only models of misfortune, captured in overly weighty idioms: *The fate of the sister; Mother's martyrdom.* That stood in irrevocable contrast to Father's nonsense. One day, in a moment of overflowing enthusiasm, he began to distribute victory signs throughout the house, in every room. And he covered one wall after another with posters and placards–Vinzenz in competition, with staring, glaring eyes, with his teeth clamped together, or they were exposed in a laugh, in some victory pose or farce or other. And when he–Vinzenz– began to restrain him, there was always conflict again, with whole lists of reciprocal accusations. But it was never bad, really bad, until the end when he went so far as to call him a poor wretch, or mockingly, a teacher, a teacher type, or when he recited samples of his writing from memory, with all kinds of quotes that were as distorted as possible.

To escape from them–outside the racing season–Vinzenz consistently went out and made the rounds of his usual bars. And he was well-known, notorious, in the truest sense, with his meanwhile regular radio and television appearances. And again and again there was something in the newspapers, in regional and supraregional papers. When they recognized him and spoke to him or even simply began to whisper, he enjoyed it, at least in the beginning. There was a tickling sensation on his skin. It was perceptible in his back and in his neck, when he received a glance as he walked by. And at first he was startled, and in the next moment he became all the more exaggeratedly absorbed, more and more in love with himself. Again and again he sat in a group for hours, with friends, with acquaintances, or even with people that he didn't know at all, strangers. And he let them applaud him. And as an overnight hero, at least in certain circles, even the babbling of drunks, their same old nonsense, their singsong, was important to him. And he accepted everything without any fuss—embraces, pats on the back, and who knows what—in the knowledge that it wouldn't last. In reality there were too many apostles of meekness, artists at submission, and worshipping slaves—and he was careful, even if they were only supernumeraries. But for as long as he could, he let them entertain him, let them pay the tab for him again and again. At first he seemed to do it reluctantly, but by and by it had become a matter of course, a matter of honor, that someone always beat him to it with his money. Or in some bars everything, everything was suddenly on the house. And there were times when it was also customary that the stores didn't let him pay, or only with a discount, or generally in kind, with skis, signed, unsigned, with ski boots, ski poles, and all kinds of things.

Cars, driving cars, and everything connected with them was a special, inexhaustible topic. And Vinzenz could talk, talk, and talk. And even worse, he could momentarily transform some whim into action, and even in that he seemed to be on a par with Father's characters, his village characters, in total contrast to his original scorn. At an age when others impressed themselves and their girl friends with motor scooters or had nothing to impress with, he was already the proud owner of an automobile. And on some weekends in Father's garage there were real tours around his pride and joy—which was propped up on wooden blocks. And there were crowds of excited male friends and sometimes equally excited, sometimes disinterestedly sulking female friends. And he answered questions about price, performance, and top speed, and repeatedly had to be careful not to become arrogant. That was the beginning. And then there was buying and selling. When he developed a taste for it, he changed his cars as if it were nothing. From one day to the next he succeeded in acquiring them, selling them again, sometimes even at a profit. Yes, sometimes he had several at once, and when they stood in the driveway leading to the house or in a row on the shoulder of the road, it really was impressive: special models with all kinds of extras, special equipment, special paint, front and rear spoilers, hardwood steering wheels, bucket seats, tinted glass. Some were equipped with wide tires, slicks, with entire banks of headlights and dual exhausts with an outrageous tone. And if he was in the mood, he added the last touches himself, with rally stripes, entry numbers, and especially his very special earmark of as many zeros as possible or a series of repeating numbers. In town they watched him make a fool of himself more and more. With benevolence or with benevolent head shaking, they mocked him and told suitable stories at every appropriate and inappropriate opportunity, adorned, distorted over time, without knowing what was real when he let even the most daring conjectures fade in contrast with constantly new and different escapades.

It went so far that he was willing to be denied everything else–soundness of mind, integrity, and intelligence–just as long as he could retain his ability to drive. Anyway, when he drove, he drove too fast and didn't let anyone pass him, or, if he had been passed, he passed the car in return with daredevil maneuvers. There was no reason not to drive for a change, and it seemed to be fun for him–a matter of honor, a pardonable offense–to drive a car that wasn't quite safe, had faulty brakes or a wildly wobbling steering system, or to drive when he was dead drunk. And there was no real motive, just a quirk, when he always decided at only the very last moment to fill his gasoline tank, or when he cruised past one filling station after another in a virtual series of experiments and got stuck again and again in no man's land without a drop of gasoline. In a short time he had succeeded in breaking all kinds of course records, in the surrounding valleys, in the valley, outside the valley in daylight and especially in breakneck nighttime drives. And when he was at home in the winter, on some weekends there was no parking lot in town–at least it seemed that way–where he didn't carry out spin tests on snow and ice, with half and full spins, figure sixes and figure eights in the smallest space possible. And the high point, the epitome, was a drive at full throttle on a glass-slick one-way street where the legal traffic direction changed on the hour. He drove between snow walls that were meters high, remnants of avalanches, in a sliding, wildly hopping car that was always jumping out of the tracks and being boxed back in again by the barriers. It was an ancient, dented, bent VW. And when he read for the first time, that among young people in the eastern part of the country it was a game, a sport, to get drunk at some party and while intoxicated try their luck, their bad luck, as wrong-way drivers–arena, the south or the west expressway–sometimes flying blind, with lights turned off at night and at top speed, did he really approve of that?

During that whole period he was involved in collisions time and time again. Sometimes he was at fault, sometimes he was not. Real collisions, not counting trivial things such as dented fenders and paint scratches. Usually it was a rear-end collision, where he shot toward a car in front of him without braking, or inattentively crept along behind someone. And it seemed to be only a question of time until something really happened, when reports of triumph and bad news went hand in hand at home. He made headlines in the newspapers, in the *Blickpunkt*, in the district paper, and in the daily paper– "Stuntman," "Luck in Misfortune," with a row of exclamation points–when he suffered an hallucination, with out later being able to say why, and shot past a bridge and struck the other bank of the stream, in a gravel heap. The car was a total loss, and he was completely uninjured. Or there was the time he collided with a stag, a colossal stag. Or in the same year–it was always reported immediately–he got off the road once more–and nothing: blackout. He crashed into a young forest plantation and was somehow able to get out of the wrecked car–or he had been thrown out and to safety– before it went up in flames like an explosion, in a real forest fire. And when he regained consciousness in the hospital, with a brain concussion and broken bones, he really seemed to be proud of himself.

Toy, status symbol, or proof of his strength, his masculinity. But above all, the car was the only place where he found peace. He retreated to it when he wanted to think or didn't want to be bothered by anything anymore. Or in general, it was where he endured everything. Motion was the only possible condition when it seemed as if no single moment could become too firmly established, too real in a sudden standstill, as if rather, without effort, one moment passed smoothly, without a hitch, into another, dissolving even before it began to spread in its horror. So many things had been said, so much nonsense about the dream that time would stand still or at least pass in such a way that a person perceived nothing of it. Sometimes it was enough for him just to start out unseen, to drive away—away, away, away—especially in the twilight, in the lightless light of a winter afternoon, when hundreds of kilometers lay before him. And if he wanted to, in the darkness he usually rapidly went into a trance, as if he had already been traveling for who knows how long and would continue to do so for all eternity—unreachable.

And he indulged in daydreams. He dreamed that something could happen again, as in his childhood, something completely unexpected—even when nothing happened: at night, when one expressway rest stop was more irreal than the next, seemingly dead, with a handful of visitors, victims of catastrophe—at least it seemed that way—in the unaccustomed light, traveling on a mission that was mysterious, uncertain, even to them. And when he stopped, he was one of them. And he was only himself again in the noise of the engine, when he shifted from first into second, into third, fourth, and fifth gear, opened the throttle, and shot into a nebulous cone of light—with the broken line painted in the middle of the road on one side, the line along the edge of the road on the other—faster and faster, in the bass tones, in the rhythm of real music.

He was always one of the youngest—one of the youngest on all kinds of teams, one of the youngest on the national team. Everything seemed to accrue to him, and he was undefeatable, immortal, when who knows what was in the newspapers. They compared him with Greek and Roman heroes, or there was no comparison, when he won one race after another—either won or was eliminated. He virtually had an habitual place in winner's photographs and on winner's pedestals. And sooner or later, *If you can you can, if you can't you can't* had also become his motto. When he stood at the starting line—it was always the same—the order went into his bones, into marrow and bone, and he felt his body part for part, in virtual jolts of electricity, in a condition where he felt ready to burst. And between one second and the next there always seemed to be one more, and finally, now, now, or now, he could no longer be held back and sprang with a bound from the starting gate. And it seemed—it seemed most—as if he had submerged into a viscous liquid, and he now perceived everything around him only in a blur, delayed, or not at all. What happened was not clear, and either it seemed as though at first he always had to push one moment into the next, as if he had time, enough time, an infinite amount of time, if only he wanted it, or everything slid past him, as if he were not involved. And depending on which it was, during the run he already knew: fast or not fast enough. It was there in his consciousness second by second. But when he was eliminated, a decisive fraction of a second was always gone from his memory, and it was useless to wonder why.

With the team, winter after winter Vinzenz made the rounds of a repetitious series of unavoidable ski resorts in every possible country, and, exciting or not, in the end it was always only courses. It was snow, snow, and weather conditions. It was entry numbers—victory or defeat—and nothing else. As a rule, the entourage arrived on the day before the race, with coaches, managers, and a crowd of stalwart journalists who were continually hurrying ahead or along behind. And sometimes swarms of fans came along, representatives of a shady, dubious jet set, hangers-on, playboys—called that by themselves and others—and their female counterparts. And last but not least—as they always said in enumerating the honored guests—there were politicians with their politicians' wives or mistresses: actors, supporting actors, and extras in an irritating circus. Or was it a nightmare? And when it moved on, on its way to the next station, nothing remained behind, only a few incorrigible natives who still hadn't had enough and were already raving about the next year, when everything would be different and everything the same. It was a constant coming and going, and sometimes it seemed like an insane merry-go-round ride with vaguely perceptible dummies that seemed eccentric as they flew by—on their seats that swung far out into the horizontal plane, amid the clanking, the rattling of the rod linkage—fearful that everything was coming to a standstill in a different reality.

If Vinzenz still took it seriously at first, he quickly succeeded in placing himself at the right distance from it. Just what did he do that was great? In light of his self-doubt and his doubts concerning the cause, *important* and *unimportant* assumed corresponding values from the beginning. In everything that he did, he could see a futility—in everything, as he was relieved of more and more by team managers and coaches. And there was much too much expense, just in the preparation alone, with training weeks in forgotten, godforsaken holes in glacial ski areas. And if they went skiing day after day, fine, but afterward they never knew what to do. They went for a walk, or they were in the gambling hall, if there was one in the vicinity, or they tried their luck in card games for more and more money. And if you were fed up with everything, you went to bed early, alone, alone at last, without an attendant—*attendant* was the word—who had strict ideas about what was proper and what was not, about clothing, haircuts, and manners. The attendants were sometimes preachers, sometimes executioners, and in their presence you momentarily sank back to the status of a school boy, especially when they repeatedly addressed their favorite topics, drinking and cigarettes, only to say nix to drinking and cigarettes. Or they talked about matters, well, matters of sex, and one time they would talk about the strictest, the very strictest abstinence, another time about the exact opposite. And its purpose, in their words, was self-confidence and liveliness.

In close races a few tenths or hundredths of a second made the difference between victory and defeat—a breath, a clap of the hands—zero point, or zero point zero something. But expressed in prizes, in prize money, it was numbers—it was numbers, unbelievable. Vinzenz's attitude became more and more cynical, and finally honors, medals, and trophies no longer meant anything, anything at all to him. And even when he took and accepted everything, it was as if it had nothing to do with him. Or when he sat in a so-called party hall during a celebration, with other chosen people, among sometimes dozens of dignitaries, he let them applaud him, grab him, touch him, and call him a hero in their speeches, a representative, an ambassador, or an emissary of the country. And no, it didn't hurt. "Model Austrian," "Darling of the nation," "Athlete of the year"–he had risen higher and higher in public favor, even though he secretly did not correspond to their ideas of a character type. But he was also careful not to sacrifice anything at all. What counted–what counted was money. And on the one hand, from the very beginning it had always seemed like hush money anyway. During all that time–on the other hand– during all that time there was nothing more beautiful than skiing, with the sound of the airstream and the skis on the snow. And when Vinzenz stopped, he was in a world that alternately tipped, alternately wobbled to the right or the left. Then suddenly everything was in order again, and he immediately wanted to ski onward, ever onward. Then a scornful look would come over his face –at least it seemed that way–one that was directed at himself.

*

In its initial exuberance, his expression was that of a child. Or better: it was what is referred to as the expression of a child–with a new reality that has not yet been erased by speaking, by its speechlessness. When they, Moritz and Magda, saw each other again after a time, they were always immediately on the go. It was time to experience something that was something, with nothing added. Usually they started off late in the evening, made the rounds of one bar after another, and drank for fun until their heads were dizzy. And when they were tipsy and unavoidably began to make silly jokes, it always peaked in the same playing of roles: talking man to man or woman to woman. They sweepingly clinked their glasses, doing it again and again, if that crystal-clear clinking didn't occur. There was only a single sound that was right, and when it occurred, they made a wish, and they knew what they had to wish for: I and you, you and I. And they wished for it, or from the very beginning they wished for something that would remain unfulfilled, and were just as content. There were scenes, scenes like in a movie—without dialogue, quickly strung together, with atmospheric music, or broken down into individual pictures, sometimes in black and white. And in the movie theater it always seemed as if they wanted to employ some quickly deciphered codes to avoid talking, to avoid telling stories that couldn't be told or had been told too often. On many evenings during the first glacier summer, Moritz had ridden around in the center of the city with Magda on the handlebars or the baggage rack of his bicycle. They had ridden in large loops from one side of the street to the other, on untraveled pedestrian paths, or in a zigzag between cars that were caught in a traffic jam and honking their horns in concert. He had walked beside her when they were going uphill, with his bicycle between them, with his hand on her hand on his hand on hers on the saddle, and with large strides that he conformed to her playfully large strides. And spectacular or not, it was an event. Or when they were out and about at night, somnolent, with tousled hair and eyes that glistened in the light, in the glow of the street lamps, walking barefoot in shorts and short-sleeved shirts, they climbed over the wooden fence of the swimming pool on a whim, went swimming in the black, initially ice-cold water, and finally sat shivering, wrapped in large bath towels on the edge of the pool, more and more confident. And that, too, was already enough.

In the movie theaters far and wide there was usually no film that they had not seen, even though many of them had been torn to shreds wholesale or had found approval either in the appropriate tone in some tabloid or in unctuous words in the church display cases that were distributed throughout the city and could not be overlooked. On the weekends, when the programs changed, they went from one movie theater to another, where they saw so-called classics that had already been shown who knows how many times, quickly assembled retrospectives, or new second-class or third-class films. And during the week they went across country, into the theaters of the district capital with their Kung Fu, sex, and regionally oriented films. Usually they attended several showings in one day, and it seemed as if they expected to find in their world the same games and inconsistencies that they saw in the movies, or in going from one film to another. Otherwise they were not content. *Good* and *bad* seemed equally good or bad, when they simply shifted again and again—*events from a reality called reality that was interchangeable with all kinds of realities.* And once—corny, so what?—once late in the fall they had gone to a movie and had come out of it into the first snow of the year. It was as if it were their very first one, with white or greenish-white lawns, white park benches, and cars moving at a walk on the streets with white hoods on their tops. They had trampled hand in hand across flower beds with half-broken flowers. They had run far away from each other back and forth across country, in a playfully staged snowball fight. They had entered a large lawn in order to pace out a pattern, an ornament, with tiny steps. But woe be to them if they saw a sign, wanted to see one, an omen. In roundabout ways they had arrived in an old section of town that was deserted as if for the first time, with tracks in the snow that fled each other radially in all directions. They had stopped and approached each other step by step, to wipe the snow and melted water from each other's faces over and over again, with apparently casual hand movements, and—and nothing. "We understand."

When they went for a walk, they went to the railroad station where they could sit down on a bench in the main hall, among people who were waiting. They were often young people with enormous rucksacks or vagrants with plastic bags and wine bottles. And they engaged in verbal exchanges for hours, focusing on one and the same, ever so meaningless point. Their conversations were interrupted again and again, then whiningly continued. And from time to time their whining changed to a practiced mooching—"Monsieur!" or "Madame!"—and to one or the other: assurances of humble gratitude or a barely intelligible torrent of curses, quotations from the Bible, and aphorisms that they repeatedly thought up for themselves, about their real or at least effectively presented belief in fate. Sometimes it was enough just to cast a glance at the large announcement board with its trains, departure and destination stations, arrival and departure times, its blinking lights, and its letters that rattled as they turned. And from time to time a word appeared for a second, a fraction of a second, in the confusion of their turning. Or they looked for a station, any station, for some reason, or without a reason. And they raved: in so many hours they could be there, in so many hours in who knows what places, in all kinds of cities. So that one night, without wanting to know where it was going, without tickets, they got on a train with wide-open doors that was waiting and ready to depart. And it happened, as they said later with a wink, in an almost biblical solemnity—without saying what. Or if they said anything, they made abstract, mystical comments, affirmed the fact that they had had a wonderful time. In a fragmented darkness that was shredded again and again by light that suddenly came in from outside, they lay in their compartment. It was barred from the inside, with the curtains closed and the compartment window wide open. And amid the smell of sulfur—it was sometimes strong, sometimes not as strong—there was another smell, the smell of summer. It came in clouds, apparently mixed with the noise from the railroad ties that irregularly grew louder and softer. They didn't speak, were careful not to speak, because they knew it would have become a whispering, with failing voices, about everything and nothing. But they touched each other, and beneath their hands they felt their soft, soft and ever softer bodies—"Now! Now! Yes! Now!"—that suddenly grew hard, harder and harder, hard, and finally broke. They felt their bodies give way, respond affectionately beneath their hand movements. And they came to rest with arms and legs stretched far from them, and their faces were distorted, seemingly distorted with pain. Later, kneeling side by side, they stretched their heads into the airstream with their eyes closed and let it blow over them. And when they had enough of that, they played with their hands, held them horizontal one moment, vertical the next, or bent them streamlined, hovering seemingly weightless above a pillow of air, moving up and down in waves.

*

Sometimes there was no free day in Vinzenz's appointment book, especially before and after the racing season—even if he did resist being present everywhere. The public, working with the public was what it was all about, and again and again he let himself be persuaded to do his part. And sometimes it seemed artificial when he acted as if he were shy, coquet. Whether he liked it or not, first of all there were responsibilities toward his sponsors, the ones who equipped him. There were presentations of their newest collections, or a fitness center was opened somewhere, a gymnasium, a so-called sports shop, or there were charity or who knows what kind of events. At least they placed themselves in an appropriate light. And he was present without knowing why, when he had to pose with a beautiful woman in front of a camera. At the right moment he planted kisses that were as wet as possible on her cheeks, or he touched her breasts as if by accident and said, "Oh, oh, pardon me," in a mixture of roguishness and apparent innocence. Or there were autograph sessions. And when he sat at a little table with a stack of autograph cards and gave autographs to a never-ending procession of people without looking up—what was that? Later he repeatedly got drunk. And depending on whether he had to mime the athlete who was true to principle or was sociable for a change, that meant that he secretly poured liquor into his orange juice or went to the toilet and took large swallows from a pocket flask, or that he shyly, seemingly shyly clinked glasses with all sorts of people. And to be sure, there were no excesses, but when he succeeded in keeping his balance, he sometimes seemed immune to everything. And when he left he was happy to be drunk, happy to be alone in an ever so unfriendly hotel room that was almost shabby in its anonymous comfort. And he usually sent away his notorious female companions at the threshold or after an unedifying interlude.

One day—*Efforts to achieve an appropriate team appearance, an attractive external appearance*—a woman with a rhetoric program that was guaranteed not to fail was hastily engaged to give them evening lessons in speaking. "Speaking as speech and language art, the science of speaking and linguistics rolled into one"—the way she said that—with a voice that always seemed hoarse—it sounded like a croak. And there wasn't much in the pains that she took, in her constant repetitions as if mocking herself, and in the other things that she had to say, other than that you were supposed to speak loudly and clearly, with pure vowels—thus "a," not "o" instead of "a"—and with consonants that almost danced out of the language flow. And you were always, always supposed to speak in complete sentences. So there was nothing left for them to do but to repeat mechanically what she said: "Abraham, in the beginning was Abraham," or: "Ih, ih, Nitribitt, igittigitt." And it was important that they always began with "I believe," "I am of the opinion." And instead of "Yes," whenever possible they said, "That is correct," "You are right," "I agree with you."

In the hotel dining room, between tables and chairs that had been pushed together, they learned to dance without female partners. They were instructed in a way that had them turning themselves around each other with embarrassed faces, "One and one and one, two, three," in time to a music that was started over and over again from the beginning.

And manners, they were taught manners, especially

table manners—which utensils when, which glass, with which hand what, and what took place with its counterpart. Or there were trivialities of a different kind: whether the gentleman went before or after the lady, whether he walked above or below her, or not at all—what, well, what? They were made up for all kinds of occasions. They were manicured and pedicured, and when they had shaved, they were placed in suits or pressed or pleated trousers with sports jackets. They wound ties around their necks, so that they looked like prototypes of their kind that were overly well-proportioned. Sometimes they looked like dandies, would-be dandies, sometimes like pimps, and there was always something vulgar about them that couldn't be overlooked. And they always had a certain expression on their faces, dull, vacant, in spite of every effort. And it was one big farce when they went out that way to their interviews. Oh yes, interviews—there wasn't much to say about them, just this much: one was just like the next. What was important was said before or afterward and didn't appear anywhere, or rip, strip, it was cut out. What remained was a skeleton of questions that were always the same, answers that were always the same. And the only thing that seemed surprising in their indistinguishability was how different the results were. One time they came out as model sons-in-law, another time as sex symbols.

In innumerable situations pictures were taken of them, of Vinzenz—he was the star. And from the outset there was no other possibility: all the pictures were excellent. And they talked about "his striking face," "his masculine body," and said that there was something timelessly immortal, just something or other about him. Smiling with confidence of victory, laughing, with sharply embroidered writing–advertisements–on his inevitable head band, he stood, sat, or lay there in effortless poses that seemed practiced because of their very effortlessness. Not one spot on his entire body was free anymore. It was covered with company symbols and emblems. And once, when he was portrayed naked, as good as naked, wearing only underpants and with a pair of skis crossed in front of his lap, we felt compelled to look for tatoos on his body.

*

Moritz seldom came home, especially after Father received his pension, went into retirement as he could say tormentedly–tormentedly or disparagingly–into early retirement like a slacker, a feeble-minded, nothing-but-useless state parasite. That was part of a recurring repertoire. And on his rounds between one meal and the next–always the same, indistinguishable morning, noon, and night–he was omnipresent in the house with his cynicism and his self-pity. And we didn't know what he was concerned about when he came on the scene laughing loudly, too loudly, about contradiction, about agreement, or about something quite, quite different. Sometimes still wearing pajamas in the afternoon, he crept idly around, from the kitchen into the living room, from the living room into the kitchen, shuffling his feet. And he didn't even withdraw to his books anymore, or only to rummage around in a stack of magazines that were hidden under the couch in the library–magazines full of girls with naked breasts, naked vulvas, and naked behinds–and grab at them in their sudden presence. Again and again he talked about a book–a book project–saying that a large portion of it was already there, notes, material, and a title—"A title, I tell you." And the only thing he still needed was a successful beginning, a trumpet call. But did he really begin? He often seemed to be too much even for himself, torn back and forth between magnificent plans for a glorious future—a future as a writer—and his sudden realization that it had all been in vain again, that everything had been spoken into the wind again. And he seemed coquet when he spoke his cliché of a classical loser. Or on the basis of all kinds of acquaintances, on the basis of so-called prominent people, he even tried to prove that there was nothing, nothing at all to be gained, and he indulged in a confusion of quotations: "In view of death, everything is vain," or "*Rein ne va plus.*" And when he thought about Hemingway, and all he said anymore was, "Yes, the old war horse," we sometimes couldn't tell when he meant Hemingway and when he meant himself or another person, someone else. Those were real fits, with an apparently playful beginning that was always the same, and a sentimental ending that was unbearable in its sentimentality.

Generally they were only short visits, and for a while things even went well: a few hours when we sat undaunted at the kitchen table and talked to each other. That's how it was. We talked to each other as if we had only just discovered language. It was conversation that was more an aid, more a safety net when everything had gone wrong. Sometimes it seemed like being in a drawing-room play, like being at a coffee klatch with uncles and aunts, with all the family members, apparently gathered in harmony. And there were innocuous questions and answers that could just as easily refer to nothing as to everything, if there was any doubt. And there was a silence that always began at the right moment. When it collapsed, sometimes it was Moritz's fault, sometimes Father's. One of them always started off at the first cue given by the other, and from then on it went quick as a flash, back and forth in a pattern that was always the same. And it didn't take much. Father's questions: "What are you doing?" "What will become of you?" were often enough by themselves. And when Moritz said, "Well...," or began to rave, using his key word vocabulary—*abroad*, for example, *drop out*—or suddenly attacked, railing at Austria with its Austrian sciences and Austrian universities—when that happened, for some reason Father always seemed to take it personally. Then he became concerned with placing himself in as good a light as possible, or if not himself, with hindsight at least the man that he once could have been—once, in a different world. That way, with his steadfast complaining, his ideas of missed or still viable opportunities, he admitted to himself—and to everyone else besides—that he was defeated. And he had become a loser in a system where there were no losers, at least not in his linguistic usage. And he was no longer able to cope with the confidence of victory that he had preached again and again, with his own delusion that Moritz suddenly embodied in such exemplary fashion. There was always conflict in the end when Father uttered some reproach or other that he had grasped out of thin air. And when Moritz contradicted him, when he said, "I am what I am, and not only that, it's because of you," it was over. And either he left the house as quickly as possible, or Father threw him out: "Get out, just get out, get out!"

When Moritz came to visit again before his departure for the U.S.A.—a few days before—even without conflict there was no doubt about how little it would take: an abnormality in tone, a word. And as they said good-by to each other there was an unbearable mixture of suppressed belligerence and suddenly overflowing sentimentality. It was just as if Moritz were going into a glorious future and leaving Father behind in the past, with his unavoidable fate, his illness, his death—how theatrical, how pathetic. Before he finally left, Father gave him money, of his own accord, and even if it probably wasn't much, the fact alone is worth mentioning.

INTERMEZZO

Again and again I awakened—when I say *next to*, that means *beneath*, that means *on top of*, and *next to*—next to women, next to them. When the first light of morning came through the curtains there was a moment of panic—a moment. I hardly knew anymore how and where. Or the noon, the afternoon sun shone on my face, so that I continued to lie motionless, without breathing. And didn't dare to look, to look at what there was to see, nor to listen to what there was to hear. Or I stared into the darkness with my eyes open wide. Somewhere, muffled, there was breathing, a cough, wheezing, sometimes snoring, or unintelligible words, one, two. And I breathed in the smell, I almost said the smell of our bodies, instead of mine, hers. Or if the window was open: the smell of spring, the smell of summer, autumn, and the odorless winter. I remember rainy days when I was still half asleep and heard the changed noises of the street, hasty steps from the sidewalk, raindrops falling on a roof, the clattering, splashing. And once there was a thunder storm. I awakened and saw how the wing of a window banged against the wall of the building across from me until the panes of glass broke, one after another. And I still remember my euphoria, and how I listened for the tinkle from the courtyard—to hear what there was to hear. I remained true to myself with my uneasiness, with my fear of her first words, her "Well, how do you feel?" Or I told her my dream and wanted to know hers, or to know how I was. I took up a conversation from before, from the day before. I say, *a conversation,* and say—too much has already been said—

something stupid. There was never enough time to argue. And I never failed to begin talking about it. The story came as if of its own accord, from one time to the next, I don't know how. It was the story of my father, and when I began with it, when I talked, there was shameless sadness. And there was the consciousness, the enjoyment. I knew that from a certain point on the woman would be silent, would lay there silent and she would look at me. And once–it was not just once that one of them said, "You loved him very much." And I still remember how I buried my head in the pillow and laughed soundlessly. And only gradually–I forced myself–only gradually did the tears come. Their understanding, their warmth–even the word itself–and their manner. I permitted one after the other to run her fingers mechanically through my hair and creep up to me, closer and closer–the comparison is in bad taste, but nevertheless–like a child. And like a child... No! No! No! I was not like a child. I felt her fingers, her nails–I almost said, her claws–and her breath, which she held–she, she, or she–and noisily let out after a while. I remember moments when I silently gasped for air, because things suddenly closed in on me. Or I turned around and reached blindly to touch her face, her lap, or her breasts with both hands. And when she spoke, I held my ears closed, as if in fun, against her ever constant tone, her voice that was always the same, her steadfast, soporific singsong: hope. It could not have been more hopeless. In my memory, one instance can hardly be distinguished from another. I arose hesitantly, seemingly hesitantly, took her hand or only nodded, and left. I walked softly, playfully, on tiptoe down bright or dark corridors, or ran thundering–I wanted most to scream–down a flight of stairs or a passageway. Or now and then, when I was on the ground floor, I jumped out the window. I still remember: *ecstatic*—it was always the same word—when I stepped out onto the street alone, to go for a walk early in the morning, in the still unused city, with its noiselessness and its familiar and unfamiliar smells. I remember once—it wasn't daylight yet—how I ran into the arms of a beggar who was pushing his things along in front of him in a shopping cart. I was far beyond him when I heard a tinkling sound, and I didn't dare to turn around out of fear—I say, fear—that he could curse me. Or another time, I got into a peculiar procession that was puzzling to me, a group of stooped men who were coming toward me. And it was during the noonday heat when nobody else was on the street, except a few little, old women, clothed gray on gray, with their ill humor—or should I say grumpiness?

I no longer remember how it all began, but it was always the same. It was a small repertoire, and when I thought of the expression—I had been called that once, half in fun, half in ernest—I could laugh again. And while laughing I shook my head: I was an oily charmer. My type—I say that ironically: pardoned in marriage, already pardoned in advance. And actually it always seemed to be one and the same woman with one and the same ideal conception of me. I was supposed to—it was indeterminable, unspoken, of course—I was supposed to be a small, small man, a bit touched in the head, a bit eccentric. Perhaps I wrote poems or had some other hobby that was especially anemic, something like collecting stamps, making music, or something to do with botany. Her wish, her desire to take care of me—it often seemed like a pretext. And the fact no longer remained plain and simple—it was no longer naked—the act of sleeping with me. I remember once—it was in broad daylight–how one of them used the phrase *make love*, and I became frightened. It was a fright that made me pause, and I couldn't do anything but laugh. I began laughing again and again and finally said–I don't know what. I would have liked to have said *fuck* or *screw* and to have seen her unbelieving expression, her overly made-up, suddenly sexless, old-maid face. I knew–of course I knew–what I had to say, what had been asked. And I already knew her answer in advance. I knew how to interpret her silence. Sometimes it meant nothing, sometimes nothing good. I remember my raving, which was always the same. It was impudent, shameless. Yes, like anyone else, I could say, "How wonderful," and look at her artlessly or indulge in counting: beautiful hair, beautiful mouth... And if one of them interrupted me with "Beauty, bah!" and said that she didn't give a damn about it, and gave a lecture about what makes a person human–spirit and soul, or even worse, inner values–it was an offense, a crime against good taste. If I was in the mood, I could ask one of them to marry me. That was part of the game. I could carelessly say, "When are we getting married?" And sometimes, for fun, I had bought rings, cheap junk, and seen her happiness, her glowing eyes. Or when I began talking about children, I said, "A dozen," exaggerated, and sensed the sadness when one of them quietly took my hand. Or she called me a dreamer. I wrote letters, dripping with corniness, I tell you, and sent them off. I wrote, "Darling"–the beginning always remained the same. And at the end I begged them: "Come!" And they came. And yes, I surrendered or didn't surrender after all. And I heard their tittering and giggling and helpless silence when I said "Little one," when I said "Little girl," "Idiot," "Fool," or when I asked them to hold me:

"Hold me and never, never let me go again. Do you hear?"

THE REGISTER
PART II

1

"What do you think the percentage of all Austrians is, who can't imagine having Jews, or even worse, Gypsies as neighbors? What percentage would regard a Jewish or a Gypsy federal president as a mockery, as a slap in the face? And what percentage think it's true, true in principle, when people say that Jews are greedy, stingy, and that Gypsies are dirty and vulgar?" Kreszenz is holding the daily newspaper in one hand, a cigarette in the other. Now it's only a cigarette butt, and she is no longer smoking it. It's stuck between her fingers with an overly long, already crooked appendage of ash. And while she laughs derisively and says "Miscellaneous news," she looks at us.

We don't say anything—"It's probably fifty, seventy, ninety percent"—as we endure her gaze, try to endure it. How should I put it? She's really taking aim, and we, we're in her sights. It becomes unpleasantly, phantasmally still. In a single act of pouring, without stopping between our adjacent glasses, Kreszenz refills them and pours a drop, a symbolic sip into her own glass. What she says then—"I've got to stop drinking."—seems exactly as she says it, pedagogical, with an emphasis like that of a teacher who has been in school too long and can no longer shed her overly articulated speech patterns. She tries to add meaning to syllable after syllable, and combined with her meaningful glances, even a common, completely insignificant word becomes overburdened. More and more, her changing expressions degenerate into grimaces, and when she talks, her entire face is in motion. Sentence after sentence, it seems hidden in the creases and bulges, in the movements of the skin of her head. She is probably drunk, and her seriousness is the exaggerated seriousness of a drunken woman. "Why"—it seems to be a standard question, a set phrase that she inserts from time to time when she no longer knows what to say—"why don't you say anything?"

Next door—we let ourselves be distracted momentarily—first on the ground floor, a little later on the second and third floors as well, lights go on. They are rectangular windows in the darkness, without pretense. And in one of them, as if thrust onto a stage, a woman is visible, or rather, the silhouette of a woman. And when a man, the silhouette of a man, joins her, we become witnesses of a scuffle, witnesses of an embrace, or who knows what, or only of its prelude. The main part and the end remain hidden behind closed curtains, while in reverse order, first on the second and third floors, a little later on the ground floor, the lights go out again. We look at each other—"Should we be horrified?"—look past each other, and look at each other again. We look at Kreszenz, uncertain as to whether or not she saw it. From her vantage point, she probably didn't, if her apparent lack of concern is any indication. She drums, she slaps her fingers in a recurring rhythm on the table, alternately louder and softer, mechanically, and it only seems to accentuate her motionlessness, her indifference, the provocation or defiance of a child.

"Magda...." We've been waiting for that, but what follows comes unexpectedly: "What do you know about Magda's"—it's an ominous word—"attempted suicide?"

We remain silent. "What should we have said?" Nothing, of course. We rise at the same time and hurry across the room, toward the door, unavoidably followed by her gaze. In the corridor, we look at each other openly, conspiringly, as if we had who knows what to say to each other. Then one after another we go to the toilet, and it's the sound of the flushing, the thunder with which it begins, the slurping with which it ends, the murmuring of the water rising in the tank, that finally, finally makes us laugh. In the living room, when we enter again–together–Kreszenz is still sitting at the table. She turns her back to us without looking around, and it isn't until we're in front of her that we see the nervous twitch of her lips and–as if she is trying to wipe it away–the movement of her hand in front of her face. Her gaze betrays nothing. She has removed her glasses, and without them her eyes seem dull, two-dimensional, as if they derived all their glow only from the reflection of the light, its refractions in the glass. We sit down, and when we are seated and already think that we've escaped, she says it again: "What do you know...?" and a moment later, "Talk, Vinzenz." And it's hard to say why she begins leafing through the photo album again in the silence that has long since become courteous: "We see a street lined with palm trees, so long that its rows of trees seem to intersect far away in the background. Standing, or just about to stop–in any case the spokes of the wheels are visible–Moritz is sitting on a bicycle that is crosswise with the direction of the street. And we have to look again and again to see the smile that he has put on." And turning the pages: "Streets lined with palm trees," and further on, "Palms, palms, palms, alone or in groups, with virtual roofs of leaves. Or they are bare, disheveled, torn to pieces"..."Vinzenz enjoys the proverbial bathing in glory, or he simply lets it happen to him, carried on shoulders, surrounded by banners and red-white-red flags and pennants. And in his hands, raised high above his head, cut off at the edge of the picture, he's probably holding a trophy. And it isn't hard to imagine the confusion, the noise, a constant singing and shouting"..."At first glance he seems to be part of the inventory, Moritz from behind, in an office, bent over a desk, and there is something–there's no other way to say it–something reptilianly stiff about him. But it isn't the stiffness of other photographs, of some daguerreotypes. And in front of him an almost corny mountain panorama with snow-capped mountains is framed in the window"..."There are letters as tall as a man, made of styrofoam, H-O-L-L-Y-W, unavoidably expanded to a word, HOLLYWOOD, with Vinzenz standing in front of them. He's wearing an imperious expression, if you can still call it that, and it isn't hard to imagine a few bikini-clad beauties outside the picture–independent of whether or not everything is authentic or only posed." And further on: "Skyscrapers," further, "Ocean,"–and so on and so forth.

*

Anyway, it was an event when Moritz arrived in San Francisco with the obsession in his mind that he was there, there at last, and in the next moment, that he had done it. But he didn't think, or even want to think what he had done, because anything less than everything just wasn't enough for him. Suddenly there, he didn't know what his previously cultivated enthusiasm was actually aimed at. Was it country and people, when he knew nothing about them? Or was it actually himself and his self-infatuation, the fact that he too was in America? And if that was it, it was the coquettish thought of an Austrian who had been held down for years, and in former generations for decades and centuries, always connected with the same sentence: *I don't want to be one anymore*—a front-yard Vorarlberger, a rucksack Tyrolean, a Salzburg semolina dumpling, an Upper or Lower Austrian cider head, an SS Carinthian, a boring or stony Styrian, a bootlicking Viennese, a Burgenland-joke Burgenlander—*I don't want to be an Austrian anymore.* And besides that, kicking over the traces completely, there was a saying, picked up sometime, somewhere: *Only the best go west*—if nothing else, a successful rhyme. So far, so good. But wouldn't you have to be guileless, completely innocent, to rave again like you did the first time—about the land of unlimited opportunities, about the American dream that has been realized—or even to say solemnly, *once upon a time in another country*, and talk about the future that way, a future that—in that form—has been pushed inaccessibly far away?

It was astonishing that Moritz, at least at first, had to make something out of everything. He indulged in enumerations of ever so insignificant details, and in listing apparently equivalent topics one after another and side by side. And it sometimes seemed as if he had just learned to see at the moment of perception and couldn't get enough of seeing. In a sudden affectation, he became a photographically precise observer, especially an observer of himself and of himself as an observer. And when he got lost in his hall of mirrors, he was finally confronted with the question of how many steps would be necessary to be absolutely safe, completely self-controlled. In a childhood dream that he thought he had forgotten, one that suddenly kept recurring, he saw himself steering a car by remote control while simultaneously sitting in it. At first he was on a straight stretch that could be examined from his vantage point, but gradually it changed into a winding road with tighter and tighter, more and more frequent curves that were more and more often hidden. And while he had unsuspectingly fallen asleep in the back seat of the car, trusting his fate, he simultaneously stood excited on his control hill, steering wildly in the meantime, aware, afraid that if misfortune had not yet occurred then and then and then, it was happening now. And he himself seemed to blame. What was left? Speculations, idle and fussy, about the advantage of a) dying ignorant, or b) continuing to live while knowing that he was already dead.

In a university town, a good hour from San Francisco by bus, Moritz had his room in a house that lay on a street not far from campus. It was a street lined with palm trees, in a vertical grid of streets that were miles long and straight as an arrow. The houses were set back several meters from the edge of the street, and there were trees along the streets on strips of grass between the roadway and the sidewalk. English lawns and a variety of more or less exotic plants had been planted by the city fathers in their ambition, in their founders' ambition, in a mild climate that was balanced throughout the year. There were lemon and orange trees and garages with large limousines in front of them. And when the cars—suddenly real street cruisers—moved beneath the trees with their lights on in the evenings, after sundown when there was still light in the sky, they seemed to float.

It was a low, wooden house like a barrack, with large grounds and an overgrown garden. The other residents included a musician who was a piano teacher, a female music student, and Kathy, Stacy, or Tracy, another woman, a woman without details.

In the so-called best years of life, the musician was a man with manners, with an exaggerated politeness.

With his English accent he was the personification or rather the caricature, the cliché of a cavalier of the old school, a gentleman. And he even emphasized it when he greeted his piano pupils stiffly and asked them to go ahead of him into the studio, or when he withdrew with a tray of tea and sweets on Saturdays and Sundays. It was always at the same time in the afternoon, and a little later piano music could be heard throughout the house. But his Christmas concert in the city music school was a sensation: the way he appeared, in a black dress coat with tails that reached below his knees, and with a very dignified and tragic facial expression; the way he walked across the parquet; the way he bowed while standing next to the piano; the way he sat down and began to play at once in front of an audience of male and female piano pupils and their dolled-up mothers, just as if he were playing in one of the world's greatest concert halls; and the way he exited with a perfect bow amid the final applause. Once, when Moritz slipped into his bachelor's bedroom, he saw before him a soft bed with long legs, with dozens of bolsters and pillows. There was a pile of playfully arranged stuffed animals and all kinds of junk, velvet and lace, and a crystal chandelier that had supposedly been imported from Europe as the show piece. And everything was repeated, twisted, distorted in the mirrors of the mirrored wall.

In contrast—it seemed like a contrast—in contrast to the musician there was Kathy, or whatever her name was, a rail-thin, thirty-year-old teenager with a look, a smile that Moritz could only call innocent, at the next moment already uncertain whether it was innocence or craftiness, or just a game. Somehow, without knowing why, he couldn't rid himself of the impression that she was one of those ugly-duckling-beautiful-swan things who were pimple-faced, wore glasses, had braces on their teeth and spaghetti or chive hairdos, and blossomed from one day to the next, but even later remained unsure of themselves. And one day, when he suggested that they go for a walk, he was surprised at how she got rid of him, at how decisive, energetic, almost horror-stricken she was as she said, "No! No!" and then said "No!" again. And from then on she preferred to smile when he spoke to her, or to say "Oh!" when nothing else occurred to her, when she had not understood something. She said "Oh, Moritz!"–or rather, Maurice–"Oh, oh, Maurice!" And she was like all the women who withdraw into their constant friendliness when spoken to, or act as if it's a faux pas simply to speak to them.

In the music student Moritz saw a *thoroughbred woman,* a *vamp*–words that can only be used in italics–a *Hong Kong Chinese woman.* He shared the shower on the top floor with her and was already confused simply by the utensils that she had spread out everywhere. There were boxes, little bottles, and jars. Or it was her razor, her hinged razor, and unavoidably: images of her shaved arms and legs, her shaved armpits. He was all the more confused when he talked with her, or when she came into his room in her bathrobe and asked him to have a look in the shower, in the shower stall, and he looked and sprayed spiders and ants from the walls while she told him her love story, her tale of woe, her life story. "Is it O.K.?" she asked then. And he said, "O.K." And while she showered, he withdrew to his room, idle, apathetic, or suddenly filled with wild hope, with all kinds of sentences, sentence fragments in his head, shreds of monologues. And when she left the house later, all dressed up, and he stood at the window, it had already become the babbling of a child.

In a short time—just how did he put it?—he had made himself at home, at least as much as he was able to make himself at home. He spent entire days on campus, in lectures, seminars, and libraries. Or he sat outside for hours in front of the dining hall and watched the activity of students of both sexes in shorts, T-shirts, and gym shoes, who were suntanned and programmed to smile, smile, smile, as they walked from one building to another or sat somewhere in groups, or played some kind of ball game. And there were always frisbees in the air like UFOs, yellow, green, red, frisbees of every color. And when he crept home in the evening and tried to enter his room unseen, he couldn't get their image out of his mind, and he had to be careful not to compare himself with them. Their gaze—more than anything else it was their gaze, along with a standard situation from his childhood, his memory of Mother's "Look at me!" when he was suspected of having done something—and he had to look at her without blinking, without winking, without twitching, because blinking, winking, or twitching meant guilt—and slap, "Look at me!" And it seemed like they looked at him the same way, in impudent, unbroken innocence. When he sat in the sun with his feet up, or in the soft—in his words, painfully soft—light of a sunset, he sometimes felt like a tourist; or when his age had been overestimated again and again, not by years but by an entire decade. But that way he enjoyed picturing himself as a man with chocolate to give away, standing, lurking beneath the archway of a building with a sack full of candy, and—"Here chicky, chicky!"—luring in a whole swarm of children, girls and boys with enormous eyes and chubby faces. And to everyone's horror he seized them by their American funny-bones and jackets, and was suddenly a greasy Austrian, an Austro-Hungarian subject. And actually, when he looked around him, he seemed to have nothing to do with all that. Or nothing appeared to have anything at all to do with him. He seemed to have no responsibility at all, no opinion at all, or the opposing view was always there at the same time, a mass of confusion in his mind. What happened seemed to be unconnected to him, to happen in another reality, sometimes slowed down to a crawl—but usually in images that succeeded one another more and more rapidly, images that almost twitched, ripping his mind apart and breaking his heart. And in their framework everything seemed untouchable to him. In a different reality, from time to time he took the bus to San Francisco, by way of towns that were reduced to a few glances, to their names as he passed by them. He spoke their names again and again, just to hear the sound of them. Or he traveled along the Pacific on the coast: Pacifica, Half Moon Bay, and Santa Cruz. Or he rented a car. And when he was beside himself, exuberantly driving toward one of the large bridges, toward its approach, apparently straight into a cloud-draped sky, or back and forth through the already proverbial streets of the city with their breathtaking views—they couldn't be called anything else—down into the canyons between the buildings, across the bay, and out across the sea, always seeing them from different vantage points, he seemed to be at peace with the world, even if it was not his own.

And once, when he was vilified by a few young men, blacks, real picture-book blacks with their baseball caps, sweat shirts, sweat pants, and gym shoes, in a bus that was half or three-fourths empty—"Hey man, you gotta move!"—he stood up laughing, without feeling threatened or anything and said, "You're welcome." He would have like to say *Be cool,* as cold as ice, *Be cool,* and *Man, man, I swear*, while they confiscated his seat, talked about this and that in their singsong, in their blurred, hard-to-understand dialect.

Was it composure? Or what was it when he sat in the movie theater on the campus with a crowd of raving students on Sunday evenings, amid the whizzing of their paper airplane squadron, without saying *childish*, or with his index finger raised misogynously when they screamed, "Show us your tits! Show us your ass!" when women appeared in the picture even for only a moment?

Again and again, as a hitchhiker, he enjoyed sitting in the cab of a gigantic truck with popcorn, cola, *Coca Cola* in his hands. In his abstruse fantasies, he parodistically imagined that he was fleeing head over heels. And when he came home at night, he went for a walk in a supermarket, up one canyon of shelves and down the next, beside himself with excitement when he suspected that he was being watched on a monitor, step by step. And when he went outside, he remained in front of the building for a while, in the glow of its neon sign, watching the arriving and departing automobiles, far out across the parking lot with its fish-bone pattern of markings that became lost in the darkness.

And it was at that time that he began to pick oranges and lemons from the lower branches of the trees in the garden behind the house. He knocked them from the upper branches with a long stick, so that they sometimes, already overripe, burst apart on the ground. While in the neighboring garden a girl, a young woman, pounded her despair, her desire into a drum again and again, with rhythms that were always the same, da-da-dum, da-da-dum, da-da-dum-dum-dum.

In his letters home he raved and boasted. And whether he believed himself or not, at least there was no reason to doubt anything. Or if there was, what difference did it make–if there really was a reason–whether he *was* doing well or had talked himself into believing– or was determined from the beginning, was forced to believe–that he was doing well, out of naïveté or for some other reason? And we knew that he was inclined to be pessimistic, and that a correction was probably more necessary in the one direction than in the other. Finally he quit writing, and we could believe what we wanted, or leave it alone entirely, completely stop believing anything at all. And when his picture postcards came, with the view of a glacier breaking apart, Alaska; with the view of a beach with palm trees, Hawaii; with the skyline of New York City, and some terse sentences, it was enough just to hear, yes, he was doing well, always in the same words.

*

And Vinzenz and Magda? There were scenes like in a movie–without dialogue, hastily strung together, with mood music, or broken down into individual images, sometimes in black and white. And in the theater it always seemed like they wanted to use quickly deciphered codes to avoid telling anything, to avoid telling stories that couldn't be told or had been told too often.

In the Saturday evening convoy they had repeatedly paraded up and down the streets of town with other couples in other cars that had been washed especially for the occasion, among teenage girls and greenhorns in dress uniforms and all kinds of strange figures on the sidewalks. More than once they had sat on the terrace of a restaurant that was already closed. They had sat for who knows how long on chairs that were chained to the railing, head to head over the table that was similarly chained, with a gradually changing view of a sky that was illuminated by the moon and the lights of the city that lay below them. And on the way home they had always landed in the sandbox of the same children's playground. They had climbed up and slid down the slide again and again, laughing, screaming with laughter. Or they had sat together on a swing that lurched and swung out in the confusion of their concerted movements. They had—old-fashioned, to be sure—gone on outings on mountain and mountain-pass roads, and had sometimes become stranded in no man's land. They had gone on picnics, or had unceremoniously cruised through the villages in a convertible with the top down, playing themselves, wearing baseball caps and letting their scarves blow in the wind—and, of course, listening to loud music, music that was turned up as loud as possible. In the winter they had gone down-hill skiing or had often traveled for hours through trackless areas on cross-country skis. They had skied on frozen streams or even pushed their way further and further into canyons. Everything, everything was in *Cinemascope* so to speak, in its exaggerated illusions.

But Vinzenz never took Magda along to one of his races. And what's more, if she went anyway, he didn't hesitate to ask her to remain at a distance or as inconspicuous as possible. And in his strict differentiation between what was proper and what was not, there was nothing worse than so-called girl friends, wives, or women who wandered around the finish line for whatever purpose, in fur coats or fur jackets or distantly visible down-filled parkas of every color, overestimating their own importance. What you did when you wanted to do it right, when you wanted to do it completely, had to be done alone. That was his motto, and it was important to implement that isolation ruthlessly at the decisive moment. In our childhood, a movie—and that always meant a western—was a failure from the very beginning if there were women in it—except for Indian squaws—if they galloped at full speed into a godforsaken hole that was still called a town, with their Colts still smoking so to speak after train or stagecoach robberies and gunfights or real massacres, moving quick as a flash to the unavoidable flirtation with an innocent woman from the country or a woman in a saloon who was sometimes infamous and sometimes seemed to be no less innocent. And it was really bad if a man—how should I put it?—if, in spite of his legendary one-man rides against robbers, gangs of robbers, he united with a coffee-and-cake woman or a female matchmaker instead of riding off into a red, bluish-red sunset. Yes, it was still acceptable if he died in a hail of bullets. We wished that we could censor, cut out scenes of that kind—even though later we could watch because of them, strictly because of them.

Summer after summer they spent a few days in the village. And they were welcome guests in our uncle's hotel, at least as long as Vinzenz did his part, as long as he won one race after another. Time after time they cheered him, and depending on his mood he was painfully touched or completely unmoved, but never naïve enough to see anything else in it but ballyhoo: "Come on, Magda! We're going to show off! We're going to swagger. We'll show them who we are!" They could spend entire afternoons in the sauna, in the solarium, in the so-called workout room, sweating and groaning next to each other. Or they lay hand in hand in the swimming pool. It was a short pool, and if you dived into it head first, you glided under water from one edge to the other without a stroke. And sometimes they didn't leave the house for days and demanded everything that was to be had. Then they would leave again at the crack of dawn, and on days like that—when they pushed far into the forest or beyond the forest borders out into the mountains—on days like that, Vinzenz told his stories of Grandfather again and again. There were chapters from before, during, and after the war, each more elaborate than the one before it, with all kinds of fantasies—with anecdotes about the smuggler, the ski instructor, Hemingway, the hotel and cottage owner, fairy tales in picture-book style. And when he got completely beside himself, in batches of real delusions of grandeur with attacks of loneliness in which he didn't accept anything or anybody, it was too much for Magda: "When we're running, it always seems like we're running away from ourselves with our bustle, plans, and programs." And when it got to that point, he wasn't satisfied until he had penetrated her from all sides, in all kinds of positions, tirelessly, almost as if he were continually trying new and different entrances into a labyrinth, new and different ways to get inside, to reach its innermost core, attempt after attempt, despairing more and more and still trying everything more desperately. When he lay in bed next to her in the darkness with his eyes open wide, painfully wide, was it fear of the silence or—as he sometimes said—of the tangible progress of time in the complete cessation of motion? It seemed as if he were happy and really savoring his remorse and his already hackneyed and litanylike excuses. And nevertheless, it was an explanation—*impotence*—that was good enough to block his view into another abyss.

*

If anything at all was Austrian–if not the tomfoolery of tourist advertising–what was it? In the national, in the so-called national anthem there was nothing that couldn't also be in other national anthems: "Land of mountains on the stream, land of fields where churches gleam, land of hammers, with future bright," or something like that. Nor was what we learned in school anything characteristic: enumerations of mountain ranges and valleys, cities, rivers, and lakes. And there was a past, a great one that was also like other pasts, with magic words: *Habsburg, Habsburg-Lorraine,* or *access to the ocean,* and sometimes a confused dream of a glorious future. If it was not standards from history, from geography classes, it was far-fetched superlatives. And without the slightest embarrassment they spoke of an *alpha and omega*–A-E-I-O-U–of an *island of the blessed* as a platitude. And what does a cliché matter: that nobody has ever made his fortune in the country, or if he has, it has been against the country and against the people, against Austria and against the Austrians?

One day, in a rest room of the university library–as if he had never seen anything like it before–it was like a revelation when Moritz saw the graffiti that had been written with a felt-tip pen on the tiled wall above the urinals. Right at the beginning there was: A, B, CH, D and a few dots, and in the farthest, in the very farthest corner, over a poorly illuminated urinal that was continually plugged with chewing gum and cigarette butts, YU was written in blurred letters that had been renewed again and again. And suddenly it was clear to him how an index of the world would look, as an expression of Austrian national pride, Austrian national resentments of the worst kind. There would be a category A, exclusive, with exclusive countries, the U.S.A. and Germany

—even if you wished that Germany with its stupid, pompous asses, Prussians, and french-fry eaters would go to hell or who knows where. Category B would be hard to describe. Austria itself would be in it, with Sweden, Switzerland, Holland, and Canada, Italy and France without their southern regions, Great Britain without its proletarian districts and cities, broad portions of northern, western, and central Europe in general, Australia and New Zealand. And finally there would be C, a category of losers, with southern and eastern Europe, Latin America, Africa, and all of Asia, except possibly Japan, possibly. Sometimes evaluating themselves too high, sometimes too low, to a large extent the people of the country seemed to view a disturbed feeling of self-esteem as a significant part of their national consciousness. For that reason, an already proverbial bootlicking went hand in hand with the greatest brutality. Orally, apparently orally and mentally handicapped by difficult dialects, from the very beginning they were inclined to withdraw within the language community, in the worst case as foreigners, yes, foreigners. And they didn't forgive the Germans for being German, as they had always so arrogantly been—and the Swiss: the Swiss were Swiss were Swiss. And to hide their foreignness, they tried to lay it at everyone else's door, in an odd view of the world. And the results were visible everywhere.

    Back from the U.S.A., Moritz committed himself to a fastidious standard language, having decided not to swallow his pride again, or because it didn't work to pronounce a word like an American and in the next moment continue on in dialect, obscuring sound and meaning with impure, distorted vowels and swallowed or scratchy, throaty consonants. Or was it nothing but provocation? In any case, when he went shopping in one of his usual stores, as he left, he saw how one saleswoman turned to the other and mimicked his order word for word in an extremely affected tone. But when she noticed that he had seen it, a servile expression of the most zealous obsequiousness came over her face. Then a few hours later, on the same day, he was jostled by someone in the old part of town and even heard a curse instead of an apology. Torn from his pondering, he knew where he was. After that he once more found it important for him to apologize right away, to know in general, with the utmost matter-of-factness, of his guilt toward himself and toward everything else–the way he had unavoidably been guilty from childhood on. And the highest commandment was to look at his heritage, not to forget it negligently, thoughtlessly, not even for a moment. If he did that, he would be discredited for being ashamed of it, and people would look him over skeptically from top to bottom. It was always an event when one of the great ones of the country remembered his or her homeland, when he or she sent a message from somewhere in the world, an Austrian man or woman, someone like a clergyman or a dignitary, or like the president–even if it sounded like a funeral oration for those who were left behind, those who were left behind and dead at the same time–or when with sudden sentimentality one of them spoke of the most beautiful time of his or her life, of childhood in an Austrian hick town –or in fool's, fool's paradise.

In the period after his return, Moritz avoided talking too much, much less raving. Or if he raved, he made an effort to speak of the drawbacks in the same breath, in a balanced ratio–even if he felt like a do-gooder, a foolish do-gooder who was committed everywhere. Or if he let something sensational slip, especially something about himself, in the next moment he had to protest that he couldn't take credit for it, rather, that it was luck or who knows what. He always seemed guarded, and when he later talked without protecting himself, they let him talk, pointed to his quirks and the fact that he had been in the U.S.A. so-and-so-many years ago. "And since then,..." they said, "How should we put it? Crazy. Since then he hasn't been doing very well."

*

"World champion." It was already after the high point—or rather, it was the high point of his so-called career, when Vinzenz became the world champion, the world champion in the slalom. There were hundreds, thousands of pictures, and one, at least one had symbolic value. It was from a television interview, portions of which were broadcast again and again even days and weeks afterward. During the interview he said who knows what—it was uninteresting, unimportant, something. But just before it began, he had shaved, and little drops of blood came from tiny cuts that were on his chin, his cheeks, and distributed over his neck. And as more and more places appeared, spread out, and united with each other, suddenly—or did it only seem that way? —suddenly his entire face was raw.

At home a larger crowd than ever before had gathered for the broadcast of the event. Total strangers sat in the living room in the armchairs and on folding chairs that had hastily been brought in. Others stood tightly pressed together in the kitchen. Somewhere an old, halfway dilapidated, black and white television set had been turned on. And in a single vast confusion, everyone seemed to be talking at once, making ever different, more and more daring and even more and more idle predictions, conjectures about the results. And it wasn't quiet until Vinzenz's victory was certain, and then only for a moment. Then it started up all over again, louder, boisterous, with exaggerated congratulations and regular prayers of thanks in all directions. One person embraced the next or shook his hand, shook it and shook it and shook it. And there were tears, tears of emotion. Again and again anecdotes were repeated about who had been with him—Vinzenz—who had done what with him when and where. It was as though he had suddenly moved unreachably far away and they had to employ a net of who knows what experiences to ascertain that he was a human being. The telephone seemed to ring constantly, and Father ran to it. He took one telephone call after another and let them congratulate him, from time to time announcing who it was. And in between he went around and clinked glasses with everyone. They were drinking from bowls and dishes or straight from the bottles because there were not enough glasses. And suddenly, without any fanfare, he was exhausted and withdrew —and he was sick for days. But it wasn't until later, much later, that we spoke of his first heart attack. In the meantime, things went on without interruption, with more than enough wine. They toasted everyone and everything, Vinzenz and themselves over and over again. When they were drunk, they ascribed even more meaning to his triumph, as an irrefutable sign to the world. And it was midnight when they left and went from one bar to another, back and forth through the city, where there were spontaneously staged parties everywhere, and no closing time. And that meant all kinds of riots and lesser or greater atrocities. From the point of view of unwearying guardians of morality they were great–*Sodom and Gomorrah*. Afterward, people talked about them–either without any protest or in a tone of moral horror–in *never-before* or *never-within-living-memory* sentences.

When Vinzenz returned and it was necessary to prepare a reception, a so-called official reception for him, Father wasn't back on his feet yet. *City fathers*, with the mayor in the lead, took over the arrangements, and it turned out correspondingly opulent. Thus, early in the morning of the day of his arrival a procession began moving in the direction of the airport, a convoy of heavy luxury cars, polished to a high gloss especially for the occasion and decorated with little flags. Pennants of all colors fluttered from their antennas, and at the end of the already illustrious column came a rented Rolls Royce, a convertible with a chauffeur who wore a chauffeur's uniform and a peaked cap with all of the accessories. And there was champagne, cold, chilled, in copper buckets with snow and ice that had been scraped together on the edge of the street. And when they clinked the narrow, long-stemmed glasses together, there was a loud, almost shining, flashing clinking sound, and they drank in large gulps, playfully, in playful awareness of their decadence. In the reception hall at the airport, as if out of nowhere–as we arrived–a string orchestra moved into position and played a piece for practice. And we, side by side, unrolled our banner, as extras or simply as part of the stage set that Vinzenz entered a little later. Well, suddenly he was there, and things went topsy-turvy, with embraces and kisses and sayings that had been prepared and rehearsed especially for the occasion. And in the music that began immediately, everything was exaggerated, an illusion of an hallucination. In rank and file they stood there in their so-called Sunday suits, Sunday uniforms, and among them there was one—was there really one among them who gave orders?

Vinzenz sat in the front of the Rolls Royce on the way back, next to the indifferent, seemingly indifferent chauffeur, while at intermediate stop after intermediate stop different people sat down in the back seat and incessantly spoke to him—congratulations. And when even the customs officials at the border congratulated him, with their hands to their caps in salute, it looked like it was staged. As it did later, when we turned off the highway and went through the villages honking wild concerts, and idlers stood everywhere along the side of the road, children, school children with red and white or red-white-red pennants. And hallucination or not, if we listened, we could hear snatches of the national, the so-called national anthem as we arrived in the city.

In the car, which crept along slowly, more and more slowly, and finally moved at a walking pace with the top down, Vinzenz stood with all his insignia, with his medal glistening in the sunlight as it hung around his neck. In one hand he had a piglet that had been given to him hastily for good luck. With the other hand he grasped the edge of the windshield or waved, and it was an uncontrolled waving that swung out far to the left and the right. And whump, at the edge of town came the first bang. And whump, whump, whump, several gun salutes that almost visibly flickered over the valley, reverberating from one slope to another, drowned out the blare of horn music, the shouting of the people who stood closely pressed together on the side of the street, even the noise of the children with the wildly clanging tin lids that they called horse scarers, their trill whistles, and their drums. Church bells rang, following each other in quick succession. They started over again and again, and suddenly in the wind their tone seemed chopped up and frazzled. In tatters a linen sheet with words of welcome tore loose from the belfry of a church tower. While everywhere, when he came past, companies of riflemen moved into position, stood at attention, saluted, and from time to time one of the group stepped forward and presented his compliments on behalf of the others, outdoing, surpassing himself in military snappiness. It was already beginning—a party that they still talked about years later: "In an igloo and several ice cream parlors they gave out free beer, wine, mulled wine in paper cups, and quarter liters of liquor in the same paper cups. And in front of them there were lines, pushing and shoving, lines of people who were half or completely drunk."..."And now and then there were speeches from a snow-block podium that was decorated with flowers, plastic flowers. City fathers spoke, the mayor first of all, and a priest with his word of God."..."Did Vinzenz speak too?"..."Bands, brass bands marching on or off, one after another"..."Riflemen's clubs"..."Tipsy fraternizations"..."Fist fights, skirmishes"..."Always two by two, people in twos to the nth power dancing"..."Request program"..."Applause"..."Applause, applause"... "As people gradually withdrew—it had grown cold—there were buffets in several hotels around the city square, world-championship buffets, free, with all kinds of seemingly exotic delicacies and choice, really choice wine."..."And it was midnight when everyone—it seemed like the entire town—when everyone went outside at the behest of a self-appointed master of ceremonies. And suddenly rockets, firework rockets, whole swarms of them, climbed into the sky in the darkness, shot hissing from bottles that had been set up in rows, exploded, 'Oh! Oh!' and 'Ah!' And in their light the snow that had fallen the day before glistened in all colors, in a metallic, almost irreal brightness."

The next year, when Vinzenz went down unwept and unsung—at least that was the phrase they used—it came as a surprise, unexpectedly. His decline seemed to occur inexorably within a few weeks. And there were already signs of it when he reached the finish line a distant last in the *Criterion of the First Snow*, or when he lost every subsequent race before Christmas, even though he had respectable times. His renown was quickly gone. Then they began to apply a different standard and, depending on the circumstances, spoke more and more embarrassedly, more and more derisively, or didn't talk about it anymore at all. Suddenly *good* meant *good* or *bad*. Did he really encounter malicious glee everywhere? Or was it only his imagination, what he himself called his persecution complex? Nevertheless, he could remember more than enough cases—all kinds of stories that were told over and over again, always in the same words, about stars who had risen and then declined again after a while, stars and superstars, falling stars. And he knew how they were talked about, how delightfully, boredly, cruelly. It was peculiar that it distressed him, when it simply corresponded to his pathetic views about the rottenness of the world.

After Christmas it continued without change. Race after race his times were eternities behind, with horrifying consistency, although he always ran perfectly—as he swore to himself over and over, as all the coaches never wearied of swearing to him. And he was in the feared situation of running behind without knowing why. What was the problem? In principle, it was clear from the outset: the moment you begin to think, it's too late. And he had begun. And the less visible the reason was, the more he looked for it, and the more he got caught in a vicious circle. And in the end, his seeking alone seemed to be reason enough.

Late in the winter—it was his final move, and it can only be explained with a trite phrase: *the courage of despair*—he tried downhill skiing, out of naïveté—if it was naïveté. He actually seemed more, much more like a player who has gone out of control in a decisive game that is already as good as lost—and with it the stakes, the highest stakes of course—as he unhesitatingly, apparently without thinking, brushed off any misgivings: fear of drop-offs or even of jumps or peak velocities of far above 100 kilometers/hour. And just what did that mean: *slalom, giant slalom specialist*? Was it perhaps also stubbornness? Whatever the case, in his first attempt he took a disastrous fall, on so-called camel's humps. He was lifted off his feet and hurled in a high arc onto the rock-hard, prepared course, and from there, tumbling several times full length, into the bales of straw on the edge of the course. And he was still fortunate in misfortune—with breaks and torn ligaments, with bruises and abrasions over his entire body and a completely battered, scraped face. But at the same time, it was his final out. In the aftermath he lost his usual place on the team and was gradually expelled from all of the sections. And what else could he do? He announced his retirement. That was the customary phrase—you announced your retirement, your official retirement, and depending on the situation, you departed without a sound or at the peak of your success, with drums beating and trumpets sounding, as the world champion, champion in the art of impressive departure.

What remained was little, and Vinzenz seldom talked about it. He avoided questions, said nothing, or became entangled in contradictions from one sentence to the next. What seemed—as long as he was still at it—what seemed to upset him most was the fact that small things were suddenly held against him, things that at other times had been sanctioned. And it happened so abruptly that he couldn't comprehend it. At other times, when he had joked around before a race, it had always been welcome, or at least it had seemed that way, and suddenly he was considered to be a joker who could not be taken seriously. And where they had previously said that he was unassuming, agreeably so, suddenly they said that he was a bootlicker. Or where he had always smoked a cigarette at the starting line as an exaggerated gesture, at other times it had been provocative, and suddenly it was *mannerisms, a sign of his disorientation.* Often before races he lay awake for nights, and with the fear came the fear of fear. In his own estimation he was only a conglomeration of victories and defeats anymore— or of defeats alone because of his person or personality —when more and more newspapers attacked him, demanding that he not deprive someone else of a place. It was everywhere, even in the papers that had otherwise been so devoted to him. As much as possible, he accepted it indifferently, and in general—indifference as an attitude toward life—he let what happened happen. At least that found expression in his language, where there was hardly a sentence any longer with him as subject, hardly a sentence anymore with a predicate that wasn't passive. When he did something, in reality it seemed to have happened to him, in the reality of his language, and of course: *passive voice* —what a term. Only when it was a matter of diversion was he active. He undertook everything in order not to sink into the maelstrom of his ever constant doubts, and from time to time he succeeded in deceiving himself. Again and again he went out, even on the nights before races, and stood for hours in dance halls. Or if there was a casino or some other establishment in the vicinity, he was drawn to it. On the way home he was drunk, and while talking to himself or to a hastily acquired female companion, he indulged alternately in self-pity and all kinds of eccentricities and resentments.

There was already a rumor that at home he had begun to take his trophies from the shelves and the glass cases, that he polished them one after another and replaced them, polished, precisely ordered according to their importance. That was bad enough, but even worse was the fact that he suddenly used everything as an excuse to brag about his victories and so-called serial victories, his historic moments. And he always went into detail, with all kinds of dates—Kitzbühel, nineteen hundred such and such, St. Anton, nineteen hundred such and such—who took what place in which race, and when, with analyses as to why, and with time differences that he remembered for some reason—seconds, tenths, and hundredths of seconds.

*

In his memory it seemed to Moritz almost grotesque on the one hand, on the other hand pleasant, that Magda told him her truths so plainly and openly. When she accused him of being a half or three-quarters intellectual, she probably meant: *even less than none at all*. And just what did it mean to be one? Or when she lovingly called him a dreamer, without restricting the term to *feebleminded dreamer*. Moodily she reproached him—if it was a reproach—for talking only about himself, and perhaps about his brother and the father whom he revered, despised above all. And mother and sister weren't there or were not given enough attention. To say that he talked with her about things that he didn't talk about with others was, putting it mildly, a banality. It went far beyond stages of lesser or greater intimacy, and it wasn't easy to say more than that, or you quickly got into a spongy, nebulous area of pseudophilosophical dementia, where words got out of hand. Again and again, out of coquettishness or who knows why, suicide seemed to be a topic, always with the awareness that it was "in" to talk about it, and just as "in" to say *in* derisively. And when they created different scenarios again and again with the greatest enthusiasm, different short-circuit situations, procedures with a guaranteed death—combinations of a shot in the head, sleeping tablets, and a rope—they were nonsense, things that were far, far away. Or when they agreed that one would have to assure all kinds of people from the beginning that it wasn't because of them, basically every ever-so-distant acquaintance, or everyone in general—in a generous, almost Christianly stupid gesture—all people in heaven and on earth. They could get worked up, invent new and different reasons that were not reasons, more and more absurd, more and more far-fetched, then say somewhat precociously at last that there was no reason or that each was ridiculous. And it was even more ridiculous to commit suicide without a reason, in stoic calmness so to speak. And with how much abandonment, with what enjoyment of the entire paradox they uttered the word *paradox: paradox.*

In any case, Moritz was surprised–and not surprised, when Magda stood before him one day with her arteries cut open, weeping and laughing at the same time. Again and again in their upward swing her crying and laughter collapsed at their highest point in narcissistic, tipping acoustics. Blood seemed to seep hesitantly from her wrists, already crusted over in a blackish scab on the edges of the cuts, dried in spots, streaks, and spider-web threads on her bare underarms, her dress, and her forehead, and smeared into her gray, gray-white face. On a whim they had gone out into the country over the weekend to properly carry out a pregnancy test and celebrate the result with a few bottles, an entire case of champagne. And there had been a lot of commotion, at least for a while. But when Magda finally came out of the bathroom and mockingly said with trembling, twitching lips, "Pregnant," again and again, in all possible combinations, "stinking pregnant" or "ultrapregnant," it was as quiet as a mouse for a moment. And there was no doubt when she began to cry, torn back and forth. And as she wept and sat there weeping soundlessly in the silence of the hotel room, in front of the wall mirror, stiff, stiff as a board, she looked at herself with empty eyes. "What is it? What is it?" Was something wrong?

That evening they sat at the counter in a bar. She was dressed up, too heavily made-up, with her hair piled high, wearing a dress with spaghetti straps, and ballet shoes or shoes that resembled ballet shoes–*ballerinas* was her word. Moritz watched soberly as she drank one schnapps after another before the eyes of ladies and gentlemen who were perfectly positioned in their armchairs, gazing peevishly. And it went on and on, with different kinds of liquor. Time and time again she was saucy, coquet. And when she spoke, or when she alternately looked at the apprentice waiter and the waiter, "Piccolo" and "Poker Face," with yearning glances, it was already perfidious. They—Moritz and Magda—sat there without saying much, without looking at each other. And when they left it was after midnight, rather, when they tried to leave, when they took a few steps. And suddenly things happened in quick succession. Without saying anything, without a sound, Magda collapsed. And when she was carried out in front of the building and placed in a taxi, she gushed and gushed and gushed vomit over the back seat, and she came to rest with her head in the vomit. When they got out, she tore off her dress in the open air in front of the hotel, then unceremoniously entered it naked, with her panties in one hand, her bra in the other. Later, in the room, she lay crosswise across the bed with her arms and legs stretched far from her, grotesquely twisted, and her babbling—it was unintelligible stuff... And instantaneously a wet spot formed beneath her belly, quickly growing larger, forming a rivulet between her legs. Was it really urine, warm on Moritz's hand, the back of his hand, pleasant and warm?

When he was half asleep the next morning, Magda's absence was the first thing that he noticed. And when she came back sometime later in the morning, with her hands raised, weeping and laughing at the same time, in their upward swing her crying and laughter repeatedly collapsed at their highest point in narcissistic, tipping acoustics. And he could do nothing but slap her in horror in the first moment, only to embrace her in the next and say "Idiot, idiot woman," over and over again. Then he wrapped napkins around her wrists, quickly knotting them with loops that stood out wide in a sudden prank.

For some reason, that weekend he began to rummage around in Hemingway biographies for the first time. He looked at pictures, photographs of the master as a big-game hunter, deep-sea fisherman, ladies' man—the old litany—as a skier and a seriously or very seriously wounded man in the war. And there was one picture that didn't relinquish its hold on him, the half-length portrait of a defeated man—winner take nothing, loser, boozer—with an expression that said that he was instinctively withdrawing into a descriptive game, directed *somewhere* or *nowhere*. In his dull, empty expressionlessness, in that very condition, a beastly suffering seemed to find expression. And when Moritz read in the famous-infamous memoirs—key word: *Schruns passages* —what good times those days were, he all too easily lost himself in sentimentality, in broodings about the meaning and meaninglessness of life.

The next week Moritz went to a prostitute for the first time. It was the first time that he didn't back out at the last moment. It was in the railroad-station quarter, and it went quickly. Something in her face—guilt, innocence or who knows what—served as a stimulus. He spoke to her. She said, "Yes" and "Darling" or "Lover." And as he walked along beside her, half turned away, at a safe distance of a few steps, he cast a glance at her suddenly expressionless face from time to time, and everything took its course. Only gradually did he realize that she was drunk. Step after step it seemed as if she would keel over with her spike heels, and that in falling—in her black tights, in her black knee-length or higher than knee-length boots, in all her glow and glitter—she would shatter into a pile of sharp-edged fragments and splinters. And in the meantime she talked —it simply bubbled forth from her—about a toothache, about her pimp, in massive confusion about umpteen topics at the same time. Did she actually wear glasses? In a brightly lighted courtyard Moritz grew completely silent at the loud, ever louder clacking of her heels, as it reverberated from one wall to the other. He walked behind her beneath rows of narrow windows that reflected blackness, embrasures. And when they arrived at her apartment, he seemed to be out of breath. He was taken by surprise when she immediately got down to business: fuck, so and so much, blow job, so and so much, fuck and blow job–discount. And when she got undressed, at the first moment he didn't know where to look. Or when she ripped the wig–her golden, golden yellow hair–from her head with a single movement of her hand, and hung it like a trophy over a bedpost that had been lengthened for that purpose, stark naked, coy, a dishevelled bird, with her bald head, her blue, really blue eyes, and her crinkled mouth, bared once more in its harshly red, glistening strokes of lipstick. Or when she spread out a handkerchief on her velvet bedspread and moved into position in the middle of it, with her legs spread. Or when she turned around and knelt with the small of her back swaying, then lifted her bottom, and a tattoo became visible in the depression of her back, an elliptically distorted circle that was a ball, a planetary ball or the crystal ball of a fortuneteller. At that moment, the barking of a dog came from the neighboring room, and she got up, opened the door a crack, and with a completely different, softer voice said into the darkness, into the sudden silence behind it, "Do sit! Do be good! Do be quiet!" instead of *sit, be good, be quiet*. And she was lost in thought when she came back and knelt down again, her legs spread wide, with her arms stretched far forward, in a real picture-book position. In a combination of far too many movements, Moritz awkwardly bent over her and immediately, now, now, or now, lost his head. And all that was left was her theatrics, her "Yes," her "Yes, yes, yes," and "Oh!" and "Ah!" in a well and badly played moaning, in staccato sounds.

*

We knew everything else only approximately, and again–who knows why?–Vinzenz seldom talked about it. Or if he did, it seemed to degenerate often enough into a smug varying of some rumors. And when he pretended to talk about himself, in reality he talked about an out-and-out fantasy. He accepted what reached his ears –distorted or not–and when in doubt he passed it on even more distorted. And it was always a pleasure for him to work on his own image, on the destruction of his own image. And even when it was repetition, repetition of a repetition, everything that came from him seemed authentic. As stories with a first-person narrator as hero, they were true, independent of their *true* truth content.

In the winter after his retirement, he went to America and entered a series of races on his own initiative. That is, he ran a few slaloms, parallel slaloms, man against man–knock-out system–head to head with his opponent, his wheezing and the scratching of his edges, the edges of his skis on the mirror-smooth, rock-hard, prepared course, hearing the sounds of ankle, elbow, and upper-arm protectors striking against goal posts, and the fluttering and slapping of the banner cloths between the stakes. And how should we put it? One time he was the shadow of himself, another time the original. And unbelievable but true, he won, won, and won, usually in remote winter sport resorts, in front of a few dozen spectators, and he moved like a ghost through the newspapers as a *dark horse* or who knows what. For that reason, when he quickly gave it up again, it was all the more unexpected. *Hollywood.* If he talked about it at all, that was always the point when the ominous word came into play—*offer from Hollywood.* And it seemed to be enough by itself that we were speechless, or that we immediately began to imagine who knows what, in the brightest possible colors. And it was greatly exaggerated—if anything at all—an appearance, a single appearance a few minutes long. Vinzenz was supposed to play a ski instructor in a tiny role in a television series. And all he had to do was say with a broad smile, "I'm Austrian. Hi, I'm Austrian," and with tasteless tomfoolery pretend to be infatuated with bored, boring married women for a few hours. And he was always the same type, artificially kept fresh, with an expiration date that had been wiped out, counterfeited—corrections of his age—blond, blue-eyed, and suited for alliteration, not only for alliteration: stupid. He was supposed to give them a kick, and he gave them one. But for some reason the scene was cut out without any ado and it was never broadcast. In the meantime, his American dream seemed to have run its course as well, his dream of quick money. And he no longer saw himself able to attain it on his own merits. And if he still dreamed, it was of a good role, or rather, he forced himself to do it, doubting that such a thing existed—a good role. And what remained above all was his appearance. Apparently undaunted, still unbroken, he seemed ageless. As long as he could, he behaved generously. But there was also arrogance, even in the way he spoke, with an affected, seemingly arrogant accent. Or was everything only an act? Either way, as he went to casinos more and more often, it became less and less a matter of only his luck, only his money. It was a matter of life and death. It was not bad when he risked and lost everything–winning, winning and losing seemed to be the same, and all that mattered was the act, the thrill. What was bad was when the ante got lower and lower but more and more was at stake. And if that happened, if he lost–unimaginable. If he won, he won and won–and lost. There was no other possibility. He also wound up in some gambling den or other again and again, stood for hours at one-armed bandits, with styrofoam cups full of coins in front of him, became completely absorbed in the necessary maneuvers. And sometimes he fell into a trance, just with his ever constant, automatic movements, or when he saw himself multiplied in the rows of players, and there was nothing in their lifeless eyes, not even when their machines poured coins into their collection cups with a clatter that quickly died. But in his imagination he always saw the pupils that grew rounded, rolled or flashed as stars in the eyes of cartoon characters. And the comparison with marionettes that pulled their own strings in a puppet theater that was completely out of control was not far off. In his own stories, he always said that from one day to the next.... All right: from one day to the next he gave up gambling, and with his remaining money he traveled from coast to coast, back and forth through the country. It was a jumble of routes, a diagram made by a wildly moving seismograph needle with highest points in the extreme north, lowest points in the extreme south. And as far as possible, he avoided primary connecting roads and preferred to waste his time far enough back in the interior. We couldn't get anything more out of him, or it was sentences like: "In reality, or if you simply put it on a large enough scale, a course always turns out to be a zigzag line, a movement along stretches of road, and path after path becomes a detour."

When he came home, he was a different person—at least that's what they always said. He had lost weight and seemed emaciated, without muscles that had been developed through exercise, and his athletic body had become a pile of misery. Always brimming, overflowing and almost bursting at the seams with energy before, he now seemed ill, even when he was in normal condition. And if somebody wanted to know if he was doing well, he was evasive or put everything into question in an outburst: just what did *well* mean? In a short time he took up old habits that we thought he had forgotten, and he tried to get along in the ordered routine of the house with its precisely defined plan. He moved into his old room that had been left unchanged, and he was sometimes not seen for days. And when he appeared, he wasn't talkative. Often he sat somewhere, and suddenly, without his knowing it, hours had passed. And when he called it self-forgetful, that didn't seem to describe it well enough for him. Then, lost in thought, he became afraid when a moment later he didn't know what he had been thinking. And again and again he began talking to himself. And when he left the house early in the morning and didn't return until late at night or the next day, for some reason he behaved secretively. And with visible pleasure he refused to say where he had been. He hardly went to his old bars at all anymore, and when he went, he seemed to detest the fact that the people were always the same, with their same old shouting matches, their same old speechlessness, their same old malicious or hypocritical necrologues about him. And then he got drunk, or at least he drank enough and behaved as if he were drunk, for protection. And sometimes he kicked up a terrible row and raised the roof, or even threw up and—in the worst cases—remained lying in his vomit.

In all that time he was subjected to Father's attacks. Father didn't let himself be deprived of cutting him down. Every day he admonished him to do something, anything at all, and said that it was his own fault, suddenly his own fault, that he had not learned a trade. Or he went on and on with his fantasies that everything was open to Vinzenz anyway, with his popularity, his connections. But although he studied the help-wanted advertisements in the newspapers and even submitted applications from time to time—as half-heartedly as possible—he seemed to establish himself more and more in the only position for which he was suited, in his position of retirement—*letting other people work instead of working himself.* So that it was all the more astonishing when he came home with the news one day: a café—he had leased one in town, well, on the edge of town.

*

In the academy where he became an assistant after completing his studies, Moritz's illusions had been at a dead end from the beginning. When he watched the secretary in her office—that alone seemed to be enough—with her undaunted, incorrigible agelessness—or from one day to the next she became years older or years younger—he got the evil eye. Or even when she greeted him: "Good morning, Master," "Good morning, Doctor." And in a few years, if everything went well, she would address him as Lecturer, as Professor, with a precisely calculated smile, step by step, with her proverbial charm, always hoping that he would request of her,

"Yes, but yes, my dear, my dearest, my very dearly beloved, call me Moritz."

At some time or other he had quit seeing heroes in mathematicians per se, and besides, he had never viewed average types as anything but officials of a state apparatus who were more or less absorbed in their own self-satisfaction, in their own mediocrity: marionettes, straw men. In reality it was a few people who did all the work, a few here, a few there, distributed over the length and breadth of all continents. And you couldn't make a country with the others—or rather, you could make a country but you couldn't have science. And how ridiculous it was when those very people decreed what was *true* and *false*, or when they aspired to being godlike or who knows what in a creative act, in their turns of speech: let this be this and that be that. What remained was a contradiction between the glory of mathematics and the dullness of the mathematicians. Nevertheless, in the beginning he too had been addicted to their omnipotence of speech, their apparent omnipotence of speech and language. And everything seemed possible when he excitedly wrote something on a blank white page, in sweeping symbols at the top of it, or when he playfully said, "Let it be as it is, because it is as it is anyway." But he never forgave them for their normal, their stinkingly normal lives with their stinkingly normal desires, their stinkingly normal hopes and stinkingly normal fears, and he fell more and more under pressure to move, to break out. And it was clear that that did not—not simply—mean going to a prostitute from time to time or dreaming restively, in the belief that he was different, different from everyone else. And even his continually recurring desire to break out was nothing, only stinkingly normal. So he didn't have much to say in reply to them, except, "No, no, no." And he was hardly able to explain that he got headaches, stomach aches, and heartaches over sentences like: "I work like a horse"..."I'm going to the movies, the theater, or out to dinner with my wife"..."I'll spend the holiday at home with candle light and a bottle of wine and sex"... "And on weekends we go to the country–visit my parents or my in-laws–or we go swimming or skiing, depending on the time of year, or year in and year out to a matinee, to a soiree." And if there was nothing else to do on a Sunday or a Sunday afternoon, they withdrew and sat in their usual bars, in some coffee house or other, model citizens, men with wives and children. And when they had done it a few hundred or a thousand times, it was–well, what was it? In reality, in words that had already been used who knows how many times, it meant, there would be so much, so much to do if only one had a life, any life at all, and another, and again, again, and again another, and after each one, still one more, with a guaranteed right of exchange and return.

2

"In the early months, when Magda came back from the city, she lived in her parents' house, and there must have been who knows how many jobs that she started and lost again a few days later—secretary here, secretary there. Or rather, she quit, and when she talked about it, it was always appreciatively"..."It didn't seem as if she had intended, really intended, to do anything, and it remained unclear why she applied somewhere else again from time to time. Or there was something to the rumors that she was concerned about prospects for the future —they always said *prospects for the future* derisively— about a good match. But talk, there's a lot of talk."... "She was probably known all over town more quickly than she thought."..."She still looked good, but she had never believed that her looks were her only trump. And then suddenly she did, at least it seemed that way, and of course with that she lost all of her mystery."..."And it shouldn't be forgotten that she gradually reached the age...." Interrupting herself again and again, Kreszenz utters sentence after sentence while we look at her and nod from time to time. It's hard to say why she does it. Perhaps it is only her tactic to make us talk. The way she talks, it seems that she is on guard not to use the wrong tone, and when it happens to her once—a miscue, a cooing, a gurgling—she immediately recovers. And from then on she has herself all the more firmly in control. And she makes no distinctions. No matter what she says, everything is the same, a jumble of accusations that are always the same, wrapped in trivialities and banalities. Without continuity, sometimes without pausing, she brings up all kinds of things, her children—one after another we hear the names that we have never properly noted—all of the odds and ends of her everyday life, and to make matters worse, Father's book—"I have—believe it or not—I've actually read it." And while she looks at, or rather tries to look at us, her upper body jerks back and forth, rocking further out from time to time, as if involuntarily. And when it seems that she will tip over or strike the table with full force, she always pulls herself together—at least that's how she says it: "I must pull myself together."

We ourselves have already begun to hold back. We don't drink, that is, not really. We only sip at our glasses, and when Kreszenz refills them we let it happen reluctantly. We wince when her rocking reaches its high point. And sometimes we actually dart forward with our arms stretched out wide—and nothing—"What are you doing?" We are immediately rejected. If we say anything, it's as if we had come to an agreement without saying anything. We ask no questions, and our answers are answers to her momentary silence: "That's the way it is."..."What happens, happens."

At first hardly perceptible, growing louder and louder, a sound penetrates from outside. We turn around and look out the window. There is a brushing sound, a scraping across asphalt, a crunching in the snow, a scratching on ice. It is footsteps, multiplied it seems—"Army." And as the first soldiers become visible in the clip-clop of their marching strides—they are immediately visible as they come invisibly out of the woods—they walk in double file and turn with a bend, a precise right angle, in which those on the inside walk in place and those on the outside walk around them into the street. As they suddenly appear before us, we can't help but press our noses against the window pane to see more precisely how they step into the cone of light from the street lamps, one after another, and then disappear again, replaced by those marching behind them. They enter and exit—it's laden with symbolism if you will—with their field caps, their field jackets, field pants, and field shoes, with their belts with canteens on them, with their rucksacks and the handles of the shovels that protrude from them, with their assault rifles slung over their shoulders. And what is peculiar, or not peculiar in the limited light, is the fact that one face resembles the next, expressionless, when it rises out of the shadows and sinks into them again, blackened with burnt cork. And as they disappear down the street in cadence, column after column, we discover in the brightly lit windows of the neighboring houses rows of faces that are equally expressionless. And in their staring and marveling everything is theatrical, unreal, a spooky thing that is quickly forgotten again. "Do we have to look at that?"

Meanwhile—it's hard to say how much time has passed—meanwhile Kreszenz has begun to clear off the table. "You're not going to eat anything else anyway, are you?" And we watch how she hurries back and forth between the living room and the kitchen with her sleeves rolled up and wearing an apron that she has hurriedly tied around her waist. It probably has to be that way. She has to do something—make herself useful—at least maintain the appearance of doing something. And everything else seems that way—how should I put it?—ostentatious. We raise our glasses to her, and without wanting to we stare at the still corked bottle of liquor in front of us. Nothing else is left, only the candle that is burning down—and cigars. As a precaution we've swiped cigars from the little wooden box. Again we say nothing. We respond only to her gaze or look past her, if we can't do anything else, when she sits down and looks at us with her head resting in her hands and her face half covered. And suddenly: "You knew it from the beginning." She says it without adding anything, without her preparatory "Magda..." or who knows what. We know, that's the way she is, and what she means doesn't become clear until she continues. "You must have known that she was double dealing."

We don't react. We don't move away from each other, but pretend to concentrate completely on the noise of a car that is laboring up the street in front of the house, with its wheels spinning. Again we look out the window, and when the light from the car's headlights appears, it brushes shakily across the walls of the houses. It is aimed directly at us for a moment, momentarily motionless, soundless it seems. And it is as if we there in the middle–it must probably be viewed that way –have nothing to do with it all.

*

We had gone a long way, or rather, we had wanted to go a long way and had foundered, foundered even before anything happened. They could say that–sometimes agreeing, sometimes in resignation–as if it were a natural law, irrevocable, or as if it would require a different world with different people to revoke it. And if we said it more precisely, we said that we had sunk pretty low, or for fun, always only for fun–even when it wouldn't have taken much for it to collapse–that we had gone to the dogs. If they couldn't do anything else, they could excuse the greatest nonsense with their infatuation with language, tone, and sound. Or they could grandly say that they would sacrifice everything, reality, so-called reality, and themselves at any time for an effective word, an amusing sentence. And even more wonderful were words like *illusion, illusionariness*, or even *disillusionment*, a tongue twister—or when we said —who knows why—that we had ceased to dream, or that if we dreamed, we strictly separated our dreams and daydreams from reality and no longer hoped that they would be fulfilled, or hoped that they wouldn't be fulfilled, out of fear of their sudden triteness.

Had we always known it and for some reason, hastily constructed out of necessity, just not wanted to know? We had trusted Magda. That is, if asked whether or not we trusted her, nothing would have occurred to us immediately, or only that that was not in question. And we didn't try, not even with intimations, to cross-examine her. On the contrary, everything was settled with a few words: "Please, please don't say anything to Moritz," she said to Vinzenz. And to Moritz she said, "Please, please don't say anything to Vinzenz."

And they said, "Yes, Magda, yes," and felt that their secrecy was romantic, an expression of their childlike innocence.

Either way, we seldom encountered each other. And it was even more seldom—or never—that there was an encounter involving all three of us. As a result, not much changed, at least at first glance, when we found out about it, found out once and for all, and from then on avoided each other completely. And—it was easy—we also lost sight of Magda.

And suddenly—sentimentally—suddenly it occurred to them how little they knew about her. Or everything they thought they knew seemed to be too little. And they were not even immune to the thought that they would do everything differently if they could begin again from the beginning. Or if it was to be the same again, they would do it with a different consciousness. Or they could even say that a moment was present only for a moment, in reality, but in memory, in memory.... And it was important to be aware of the future usability of everything that a person perceived. What you forgot was not just forgotten, it was as if it had never been. It was dead.

We resisted and tried to hold on to what we could—even though we knew that we had part of our most pleasant memories in common, and not only memories. We gave her the same nicknames and pet names based on constantly different traits. In the beginning it was her hair. As children we had already invented the greatest gems. And at some time it was her nose—we called her Cyrano, Cyrano de Bergerac. Or it was her widely swinging gait, with arms and legs in motion as if it were a matter of running a motor and then walking with its help, with the help of the motor. And for lack of another comparison, we spoke of a jumping-jack or marionette gait, and it was natural to call her Pinocchio. And there was always her language, her dialect that was virtually interlarded more and more with foreign words that were always different. She used a complete hodgepodge of the most varied levels of expression, so that at first we wondered what was going on when she began with it. We wondered if she was trying to fool us into believing that she had something, exquisiteness, elegance, or who knows what. And in the worst moments we saw before us the dreadful sight of a country bumpkin clumsily trying to act like a lady, a lady of the world. But no, it wasn't put on, it was really her, or rather, her and her and her, always a different girl. Everything happened with the greatest matter-of-factness when she said *benign* or *malign, trivial* or *complex*. And her special words were *legitimate* and *feasible, legitimate* as an invitation to agree with her, and *feasible* when she already clearly understood a course of action.

Over and over, at shorter and shorter intervals between one visit and the next, Moritz went to prostitutes. He picked them up on the street and pounced on them in his parked car in a back yard, or in a parking lot—in the enormous, empty parking lot of a shopping center. Or he studied the pertinent advertisements in the newspapers—*thoroughbred woman, amazing bosom, Rubens type*—telephoned, and went there. And it went quick as a flash, in hastily prepared apartments with a hint, a trace of lower middle-class idyll, just as if the husband and children had gone to the movies or to the zoo—and perhaps they had—and would come back any minute. Or he went to tall apartment houses with gloomy hallways, with whole rows of unfriendly doors and unusual maiden names in the register. And for him—he said it again and again—for him it was a pleasure or who knows what, a privilege. He enjoyed playing cat and mouse and was unscrupulous enough to expand his game. Occasionally he had an affair with one of his female students. And usually he didn't pay any attention to the murmuring that went on all around him when it lasted for a few days. And usually it was with first or second-semester coeds, innocent things who looked up to him. And he always saw to it later, that he flunked them out on their ears; and if he talked about it—if he talked about it at all—he spoke of his sense of justice.

And Vinzenz? In his café Vinzenz played the pasha. That was only one term for it. Another was *cock of the roost*, and still another was *lothario*. And there was no doubt about who was the lord of the manor. Within a few days he could hire waitresses and fire them again. By the end of a year a considerable number had invariably been used up, and his reputation had grown worse and worse. And there was a rumor that he slept with them, or at least tried to sleep with them, using every means, every permissible and impermissible means. It was said that there were problems if they refused, or if they hadn't refused and suddenly began to make demands. Either way, sooner or later he always threw them out, or they left of their own accord.

At some point Moritz had ceased taking his work seriously. Who or what he was, who or what he had become didn't seem to matter. What mattered was that he resigned himself to it more and more. Always before, when he had said something derogatory about himself, it had only been to arouse a contradiction. It was clear from the beginning that he was not serious. But suddenly it seemed to be pure sarcasm, and what's more, it was expressed in the hope that with his acknowledgement of what he was people forgave him for everything. Instead of doing nothing, like all the others he did only what was necessary. And it was his good fortune that there was nobody except himself before whom he could lose face. And as always, he was able to envelop Father in some fantasy or other concerning what would become of him someday—*just wait a year*. And when he indulged in the most insane fantasies, he knew that he never had to be specific, and there was no supreme authority.

In his first year as an assistant, he took over a lecture, linear algebra, analytic geometry, or some such thing, and repeated it with minor deviations autumn after autumn. He always proceeded the same way, adhering to his lecture notes. And when he no longer needed to do that, his timidity disappeared, and nothing could happen to him anymore. Or at least he suddenly seemed to say that, and he said it without being frightened. Did he really enjoy it? In any case, within a short time he had become a favorite of the students, and in the institute itself his situation became better and better. His senior professor had retired, and people no longer regarded him as his water-bearer and flunky. What's more, everything was even straightened out with the secretary, and when she greeted him, he greeted her back without derision. To her satisfaction he said, "Good morning!" or "Good day!" And suddenly words—word monsters—like *working atmosphere* or *institute atmosphere* flowed easily from his lips. During all that time, he puttered around on some papers, marginalia, as he himself called them. And when he measured them by their abstractness, he still succumbed to their fascination, their exclusiveness, their charm of a world that did not exist. He liked the thought that they were written on the wind, or only read by who knows whom, by a few odd characters. And if he was in correspondence with them, it wasn't because he took even one of them seriously. It was because it gave the whole thing an even more abstract, an even more absurd appearance. Whatever the case, for some reason he seemed proud of his publications, and even if they didn't appear in the most renowned periodicals, they were nevertheless in respected, internationally respected journals. And when he had the galley proofs in his hands, he stroked the pages as if spellbound; and he couldn't stop stroking them, as if he could decipher symbol after symbol with his finger tips. And later, when the offprints came, he sent them everywhere in the world and kept a copy for himself, or one copy for everyday use and another, untouched, so-called *good* copy.

In the eyes of the others he was probably a contented human being when he came to the institute in the morning and disappeared again sometime in the afternoon. It happened so unobtrusively that for a time people said that he was a pussyfooter, a servile man. If somebody wanted to know how he was doing, he said, "Good, I've never been better, and you?" or sometimes very extravagantly, "Never better, never better!" And he gave every appearance of being serious about it. At some time or other—previously—he had responded, "Why do you ask?" or had said in general that he didn't tolerate such questions. But that belonged to the past, as did his scornful "Bah, a contented man." That was not what mattered after all. Another saying of his was also consigned to the past: He had always said that in reality it was about something else entirely. Then he had become silent or paused or stuttered when he tried to say what it was about.

In the mornings he let a period of time pass in inactivity, and sometimes he did nothing for an entire morning, or nothing but straighten up his desk and rearrange books on the shelves. And when that was done, he carried out the garbage, walked up and down, or simply sat at the window and looked out. By noon he could think that the afternoon was already as good as gone anyway, and when he thought about the coffee break in the middle of the afternoon, that alone seemed reason enough to let everything go from the beginning. As time passed, he could do nothing else. He had to call it his life and gradually straighten it out and make it bearable, or his sarcasm came into play again. And he vacillated back and forth between days when he believed he had time, enough time, and others when things were always out in front of him or running away like the rapidly spinning reel of a movie projector after a film breaks. And when he tried to imagine a sound to accompany it—first silence, a sleepy, soporific purring, and finally a bang—it was a sign of greatest alarm. He no longer heard what came then, or only a beating, the rhythmic beating of a celluloid strip against metal.

Above all he enjoyed the timelessness, as he put it—as he didn't hesitate to say—the timelessness that lasted for hours. And actually he could never get enough of his view of the airport. On some days he felt like he was really at an observation post, at a switchboard, and if he wanted to, he could believe that nothing could happen without him. When he sat at his desk, he saw before him, out beyond the runways, the low airport building with its control tower of reflecting glass and its visitors' terrace, as well as a few adjacent hangars. And if he bent far enough to one side, his gaze went deep into the approach corridor with its buildings that seemed as though they were cut off. On the other side it went out over the runways that seemed to come together in the distance as if they were running straight into the river when they broke off so close to it. Or sometimes, before it got dark, they seemed to meet at their vanishing point right there.

When a plane took off, he knew where it was going; when one landed, he knew where it came from. And depending on which it was, he either followed it with his eyes as it became smaller and smaller and finally disappeared, or he punctually took up a position and waited. Recognizable in the distance by their position lights, the arriving planes always seemed to stand still, and only when he had looked away and back, and away again, and back again, had they come further along. And when they passed by him at eye level, there was always still a second, a fraction of a second, in which they seemed to hang helplessly in the air, as if they had been painted there. And he saw their bellies with the landing gear already down or stared into the blurred circles of their propellers, and at the same moment the noise reached him in a trembling of the entire building. Otherwise it was noticeably quiet. But in the winter, on many weekends, the silence was really shredded by the hourly arriving and departing tourist bombers, the jet planes.

On nice days in the summer, he often watched for hours as the gliders were drawn up by a winch and released at its highest point. While the hook sank back to the ground on a parachute, the glider suddenly floated trembling in the air, seemingly undecided, and finally moved away majestically, yes, majestically–there was no other word to describe it. And when the gliders hovered in an updraft next to a cliff upstream, they seemed weightless.

More and more often Moritz sat in the coffee room in the morning. More and more often he let them talk him into it, and at some point he no longer had to be persuaded, or he even initiated it himself–even when he knew that it was regarded as a sign of his indolence. He had become a regular customer and passed the time with the others, with all kinds of games. There were games with matches and mental exercises, so-called mental exercises or puzzles. Or they played *battleship* on the blackboard. And it even got to the point that one of them drew a target, and they threw pieces of chalk at it as hard as they could and laughed. They couldn't quit laughing about the pile of dust and splinters that kept growing larger and larger on the floor, about the mountain of riddled wrecks—when it was harmless, mind you, when it was harmless. In other, less harmless instances, one of them opened a deck of cards, and they played a game of poker for money, or seventeen and four. And when they were really at it, one of them always stood lookout and warned them in time. Sometimes they were already drinking liquor in the morning, on some pretext or other, even if it was the pretext that there was no pretext. And it was only because they knew what was at stake that it didn't degenerate into a real binge.

That was the background—painted, if you will, painted in black, in black, in black and white. And it wasn't long until Moritz even had a bottle of liquor always handy in his office. At first he only took it out of a drawer in his desk when visitors came, but gradually he also took a swallow now and then, even when he was alone. Although he drank as a matter of course in front of others, making an effort to appear as dissolute as possible with who knows what sayings—he spoke banteringly of his bar or house bar—peculiarly enough, he always drank furtively in front of himself. And sometimes it seemed as if he were standing behind himself and watching all of his movements, all of his steps, in order to strike out at the right moment if he made a mistake.

They said that Vinzenz seemed to be the best customer by far in his own café. And even though they said that about all kinds of landlords—an inveterate cliché—there was something to it. Usually he simply stood around and idly watched. And even in the rush hours, when the waitresses couldn't keep up with their work, he acted as if nothing concerned him. Or if he did lend a hand somewhere, if he really had to, even if it was for only a moment, he reproached them with it in an enumeration of the things that he didn't need to do, things that it was not necessary for him to do, as he put it–for him as the boss. And that is what he wanted to be called. And when he went from table to table wearing an apron that was carefully tied around his waist with one corner always turned up, he didn't seem to notice it when he was in the way, or when he came at an inconvenient time. Out of the blue, he gave out rounds of drinks on the house. And sometimes he was regarded as sociable, sometimes as morose–*grumpy* was the word that they used–if he either didn't notice when someone came or went, or he stood overzealously at the door as a parody of himself.

He was always in his element with friends, with so-called *old friends*, and especially with skiers or in general with people from his time of glory. And sometimes closing time didn't come quickly enough, so he closed early on some pretext or other, in order to be alone with them. And then there was a drinking spree. And when he took the dented, faintly glistening trophy cups out of the cabinet–out of the mirrored cabinet in which they stood among liquor bottles–he filled them up and sent them around one after another. And while people clinked them together, in their tinny clang, in their absolute lack of tone, he was already in the middle of his ever constant sermon. At first people came on the basis of a personal tip, but finally it became fashionable to go to his place winter after winter when a race, a ski race, was being broadcast. People came, and at the beginning, when he stood on a beer box next to the television set and turned off the sound with a controlling gaze directed toward the television screen, it always grew absolutely quiet in the overflowing café. Finally he was known all over town for his commentaries. And when he looked at the clock at intervals of a few seconds, cleared his throat, or shoved the microphone from one hand to the other and always began the same way—"Good morning!"—in the black suit that he wore for the occasion, he seemed like a mediocre actor. And he actually seemed to parody a different television announcer each time—or was he serious? Again and again he poured a drink of liquor into himself and, depending on the situation, put on his happy or his sad expression. And sometimes when he was drunk, all of a sudden he digressed and told his own story, in a mixture of boasting—even though it was ever so timid and prim—and sentimentality.

On days like that—they were the café's days of glory—on days like that things were sometimes pretty lively, and in the general confusion the stink and staleness of the regular customers seemed neutralized. How should I put it? Everything was more colorful, brighter, and you could already feel it in the sound effects, in the background noise with its suddenly sharper, much higher tones. At other times it was an ordinary restaurant like dozens of others. Such places sprouted up out of the ground and quickly disappeared again. Or sometimes, for unexplainable reasons, one of them still existed after years, even if it was under a new name—the names were constantly changing. And Vinzenz's restaurant actually seemed indistinguishable from others. It stood at the intersection of two main streets, not in the center of the city, but not quite off the beaten track either. And what was striking was its lively, swinging neon sign, or even more, the revolving door that served as its entrance.

And when you entered, you seemed to enter an entirely different decade, it was so old and dusty. During the day it was especially tourists who came, tourists who had strayed into that part of town for some reason, or people out for a walk–chance customers. Or for hours there was nobody there. And things didn't really get started until evening when the regular customers gradually arrived. And they already knew who would come when and who would leave again when. Usually it was men in their so-called *best years*, or a little beyond them. They were ordinary figures, and at first it seemed impossible to see something in their outward appearance that did not correspond to traditional norms. But then you saw it in their shoes that were not quite polished clean, in their shirts and pants that were not pressed quite as smoothly, in their ties–they wore ties–that were not knotted quite so precisely, all in all exactly modelled as the image, as the embodiment of what? Evening after evening they sat lined up at the counter and stared at the waitresses. You could tell what they were thinking, or they were soused to the gills and no longer capable of thinking. And even if there were the most diverse types with the most diverse lines–silent men, windbags, dreamers–in the final analysis they all seemed the same: alone.

One summer–the story was told as if it were something extraordinary–for a few weeks, a prostitute stationed herself directly in front of the café. And after serving a customer or when she had stood around long enough, she always came in. And in the sudden silence, beneath the gaze of everyone she drank some seemingly extravagant cocktail and then disappeared again. Is that all?

But gradually the situation with the café went inexorably downhill more and more–even if it didn't seem alarming at first and was explainable in terms of seasonal fluctuations or who knows what. Or it was simply time. One thing came after another—Vinzenz indulged in the most audacious conspiracy theories—and when a new restaurant opened nearby with all the pomp and ceremony imaginable, one after another the regular customers quit coming. And if they came back again later, they came apparently crestfallen, with real feelings of guilt, once more, just one more time. And it was already the last act. Finally Vinzenz had to fire the last waitress, and even though he was alone from then on, he didn't give in, not yet. He tried to maintain the business—and did maintain it for a time, with opening times that constantly changed. Stubbornly he went there day after day. And when he remained open during the day for a week and saw that it was no use, during the next week he was open in the evenings, and vice versa, and vice vice versa, as he put it. And at the very end he was at a point where he seemed to open and close entirely at his own discretion.

We didn't know what to say when Father's book was suddenly there, and our flippant final word was: "Really." We took it from his hands, even though we had long ago quit listening to him when he talked about it, when he began again and again and sometimes couldn't be calmed down.
In the first moment they were startled when they saw it, with his name in large block letters, white on a black background, and the title that he had publicized for so long—"A title, a title, I tell you!" as he always said. They simply brushed their palms speechlessly over the smooth, glistening dust jacket.

It was beautifully done, bound half in linen, half in cardboard, with a frazzled, rough cut, and when we had opened it, the stroking began all over again, page after page. We didn't know yet that Father had already sent copies all around and given them to everyone, to friends and enemies, and that he had canvassed all kinds of book stores again and again, to see if it was displayed well.

Again we didn't know what to say when we had read it. We didn't know if we should be ashamed—or rather, we weren't ashamed, of course not, but the very fact that we thought about it seemed to be enough. We called it *Father's piece of trash* and were irritated that we didn't even know, couldn't know—because it was so jumbled—just what it was about. We only suspected that it was an artificial political scandal that was already a failure in its artificiality, interlarded with prejudices as it was. And packed in between in allusions there was a meager little love story, told naïvely. It was a totally half-baked little work. Its tone was confused, and there were purposeless and directionless sentimentalities and deviations in all directions. Sometimes it was querulous, sometimes coarse, or submissive, or arrogant, and between the extremes there was nothing, or only something even more extreme. It was accusatory, self-accusatory, much too personal, and full of exaggerated consciousness of guilt and consciousness of everything. And if it was intended to be truthful, it seemed mendacious because of its constant moralizing. And in its erotic passages, or rather, in the passages that were conceived to be erotic, it was a matter of squeezing around with a woman who was constantly denounced again and again. And by the same token, denunciation in general was the usual thing with regard to women. Characters that appeared were usually presented and dismissed one way or another in a few sentences, even before they took form, could take form. All that was left was a first-person narrator full of self-pity and conceit. And it was like a forced confession, and, even more, as if it were being told under torture, with the intent not to tell anything for as long as possible, and then, when there was no other alternative, to tell everything. In the entire hodgepodge the only ray of light seemed to be the fact that it wasn't more than a hundred pages long, in rather large print–in print for people with bad eyesight, as we derisively said. And fortunately Father had been clever enough to delete his dedication, something to do with Hemingway, Ernest Miller Hemingway–and so on and so forth.

We saw Father's whims. We saw his whims alone in the physical appearance of the text in his book, in the confusion of who knows how many paragraphs that often contained only one line or even only one word. They were interspersed with the most useless punctuation marks, with virtual accumulations of semicolons and colons. It was Father's story, Father's case history, and we had heard about his difficulties, his difficulties in writing. Supposedly everything began with the fact that from one day to the next he became unable to finish writing a sentence, and when he tried to force himself to do it, everything in him resisted. He had the sweats, real attacks of fear, and finally his slogan was: "Why bother, when you know what comes next anyway?" And just what did *correct* mean, *grammatically correct*? Sooner or later there were no longer any unsuspicious sentences anyway. There were suspicious ones and less suspicious ones. Just as there were no unsuspicious, only suspicious and less suspicious words. New and different words were constantly banned from his current linguistic usage, for almost insane reasons. Sometimes the way they looked in writing was already enough; or they were possible if typed, impossible if written by hand. *So-called* and *so to speak* became his most important aids. He almost seemed to strew them out, in constantly similar doubles–and a man, for example, was no longer a man, he was a man, a so-called man. Or what seemed beautiful did not simply seem beautiful, it seemed beautiful, beautiful so to speak. And in general it seemed as though they, *so-called* and *so to speak*, had a function between the words, not as words themselves, but rather as empty places, as punctuation. Most disgusting to him were endings in "e," especially at the ends of sentences, and he even said why: because sentences that ended in "e" or in some vowel were less complete, less closed. And at the same time the word *in* became an almost mandatory beginning for a sentence, *in* with a time reference when it was a matter of–and it could only be a matter of that–opening an entire cosmos. And in general the beginnings of his sentences always seemed like the beginnings of first sentences, the endings of his sentences like the endings of last sentences. In general the sound of the language seemed important, much to important to him–we knew where our infatuation with language and tone and sound came from. And he also expressed the idea that if he was going to say anything, he would rather say something stupid, and say it melodiously, with repetitions, repetitions of words and rhymes, than say something extremely clever or cocky and say it boringly, weakly.

We were painfully touched in general, but most painfully by Father's resentments. It was horrifying for us to have to witness how he created images of enemies for himself, stereotypes, and stereotypes of writers in particular. And even worse, we always knew who was hiding behind them. They were quickly decoded, or there was nothing to decode because it was obvious. His characters bore one-syllable names, names like lightning bolts, as he put it. They were homemade, a vowel and a few consonants placed together. There really did not seem to be many possibilities at all. Or there were graveyard or telephone-book discoveries. And if he adopted one, a single one of them, there was a good reason: Scribblerer, Scribbler, or Scribble, in an exaggerated word play with the verb *to scribble*, one that he carried to the extreme. And *scribble* meant to write badly, unreadably. Hidden behind that was his first cliché, an ambitious provincial hack. Depending on what was currently in vogue or rather regarded as avant-garde, he sometimes wrote one way, sometimes another, alternately hunger artist, dandy, and coffee house man of letters, with a real court in his usual restaurant. And in one place he called him a wheeler-dealer, in another a milksop, with his tailored shirts and jackets, with his wide-cut trousers, shoes with high heels, and all kinds of extravagances. Then he attacked others who thought they were progressive if they were only sexually vocal enough and used words like *knocked-up, diddle,* or *poke*—as if they could thereby who knows what, probably shock, who knows whom, other than themselves. He also attacked a few others who eternally lived in the past, or still others who were continually committed to some cause, always on the side of good. And all he said was: "Babble, socialist babble." Every filthy hole—o-sound—every filthy hole seemed to have its messiah, every filthy hole its unrecognized genius, its drunken romantic, every filthy hole its exile—even if it was only a seemingly exiled dialect poet who shamelessly peddled his mendacious exile existence and his similarly mendacious affiliation with the common people. And he could no longer be stopped in his mockery: "The voice of poetry."

Under the circumstances, it only seemed good—we said *deserving* and *right*—that the book failed. Since he had published it himself, it was limited to a small market from the beginning, but was not successful even there, and a large portion of the edition remained unsold. Reviews—there were no reviews, not really. In the district newspaper and in the *Blickpunkt* there were a few friendly lines, and in the daily newspaper a scathing critique. It did not lie in the displays in the book stores, was not displayed visibly at all, and quickly disappeared onto—and just as quickly off of—the shelves, becoming less and less real, and gradually nothing more, really no more than a fantasy, a phantom of our childhood—which it had always been.

3

"When did you last see Magda?" It's as if Kreszenz is once more trying to get us to talk, using questions that are as innocuous as possible, with the same beginning again, as if we were not already at the end. And again it seems like a television play.

We pretend to be conciliatory, and simultaneously we say: "At Father's funeral. It must have been at Father's funeral." We light cigarettes, with the exaggerated fuss of people who only smoke on so-called *occasions*, and puff silently for a while. Pensively, we follow the climbing smoke with our eyes, with the appropriate expression unavoidably on our faces, and we know that because of that fact alone everything that we say—if we say anything—seems, must seem important. We watch how Kreszenz uncorks the liquor bottle—she takes it unceremoniously between her legs—and how she pours the liquor into our glasses. And when she says something about a nightcap—*nightcap*, an unspeakable word—we get up and toast Magda for the umpteenth time. And of course we drink up and wipe our mouths with our hands—with the backs of our hands.

Meanwhile it is already after midnight, and even though we get ready to leave—we stand up and then sit down again—we don't go. We've discovered a deck of playing cards on the window sill, and when we pick it up from time to time and shuffle it, we try all kinds of tricks. We try again and again to pull it apart like an accordion. Or when we turn up the top card and look to see if it is an ace—still playfully, not with the seriousness of a real game—we know that it can't be long until we begin stuffing ourselves or boozing. In the silence, before Kreszenz's astounded eyes we build a house of cards, blow it down as soon as it is built, and try to find favorable or unfavorable constellations in the cards that have been blown down: "Magda's horoscope."

We shake our heads—"Is it going to go on forever?" —as shouts penetrate from outside, growing louder and louder. We turn around and look out the window. And again there is a group of people with torches, probably the same one, throwing snowballs right and left at the houses again and again. They walk close together in a bunch as if they had to mutually support each other, and when they are in front of our house, they stop in a line —men, only men—and urinate, unbelievable but true. A few even vomit or at least pretend to do so, and they sing, they actually sing something unintelligibly. It is an uncontrolled singsong. They interrupt themselves and immediately begin to syllabize Kreszenz's name: "Kreszenz, Kreszenz, Kreszenz!" so that we look around at her in amazement. But it is too late. She has already rushed out and is standing at the entrance to the house, talking insistently to them while gesticulating wildly. To judge from her gestures and from the shouts of "Boo!" she seems to want to get rid of them. But when a roar suddenly breaks out, a real howl of pleasure, we know that she has not succeeded, and they are already storming in, in a confusion of indistinguishable shadows. They jump over the garden fence, stumble, fall, get up again; and when they are in the hallway in front of the living room, there is one sentence: "We want to see Mazegger's,"—if we understand it correctly—"we want to see Mazegger's rivals." And we hear their provocative laughter. We barricade ourselves. We hide behind our glasses as they enter, pushing Kreszenz along in front of them. And it's quiet as we look at one after another, and she–Kreszenz–says: "Quickly, have a drink–then it's over. You get lost." Then she takes a glass, the glass from which she has been drinking, fills it, and puts it in the hand of the first, and presses him to drink all of it. And he drinks. And while he still looks completely dumbfounded, she is already handing it on to the next man. And when the last one is finished drinking, she remains waiting in front of them and lets it happen. While seeming to loath it, she lets them kiss her. She lets them give her a kiss, a little kiss, and act exaggeratedly as if they were all her ex-, her ex-who-knows-what, or rather–we look at each other with the words still ringing in our ears: "Cheers, Kreszenz, cheers! Tomorrow we will be rid of our darling"–Magda's ex-lovers. We don't listen at all to the other things that they say–memories, erratic, always one sentence, and in the next one they are somewhere else entirely–much less participate or tell anecdotes ourselves. And when they leave again, accompanied out by Kreszenz, we watch them disappear silently down the street, sobered, it seems. Only a few minutes have passed since they entered. We again light up the cigars that have gone out. It appears to be so complicated. We refill or glasses, clink them together, and drink. "We could have gone with them."

 We remain sitting calmly when Kreszenz comes back and says, "It's time." We watch how she wipes off the table with a cloth, how she picks up the armchair cushions and brushes them off, how she bends down again and again and picks up lint from the floor. And in general it seems important to her to drive us away. Suddenly–we don't react–suddenly it's actually like it is in a restaurant immediately before closing time, with

Kreszenz as the sullen waitress. And we, we're the notorious drinkers at the bar, for whom it never remains open long enough. "Who is Mazegger?" We look at Kreszenz. "Who is Magda's husband?" And no, it doesn't become quiet, no quieter than it already is anyway.

We don't wait for her answer. We take the cards and lay them out in four rows next to each other: hearts, diamonds, clubs, and spades, and it is actually a complete deck: sixes, with the six of diamonds wild, sevens, eights, nines, tens, jacks, queens, kings, and aces. Then nothing stands in our way any longer. We can begin. And as Kreszenz says, "Good night," and leaves, we wave her away, simply mumble something—"We'll be leaving right away too,"—while we lay our money on the table, all that we have, coins and bills. Then we declare suit and trump, and play, play, play. And of course—a matter of honor—we don't leave, we don't stop until one of us is broke. "We play, of course, for everything."

*

When Father died, more than anything else it was a relief, at least that's what we said. Again and again we were able to say it grandly, but in the next moment we distrusted the statement.

There was no reaction that they felt was their own, that hadn't been learned by watching others or simply through their constant self-observation.

We knew what we were doing, we knew what we should do and we knew what not to do.

Their view of themselves was intact.

Instead of crying we thought about what it would be like to cry and observe ourselves doing it and simply on the basis of the observation think that it was not authentic. And we would probably have seemed to ourselves like ham actors in a traveling play, or perhaps something less corny, and for that very reason even cornier if we had laughed, had not been able to continue for laughter, had not been able to laugh anymore or anything. In reality it didn't matter what we did. We could do what we wanted, or do nothing. Cliché remained cliché. Did we want to experience Father's death as creatively as possible?

Sometimes they felt that the trickiness of their thoughts was the only appropriate reaction–to say they could react this way or that way, if only they wanted to, but they didn't want to. Or there had to be ways to react that didn't exist.

In their abstruse thoughts they saw a weakness in dying. It was the only possible, the only real weakness that one accepted, could accept for himself during his entire life. And it came as a person was so bent upon maintaining composure. And that proved to be so true in Father's case. It was a confession of his final defeat, a confession that everything was a mistake. The night before the burial, they had opened the coffin once more in the funeral chapel. Standing side by side, with the lid in their hands, they had stared in the candle light at Father's corpse, with its wrinkled mouth that had shriveled up without his false teeth, with its eyes that were not quite closed, and with the hair that was combed in such a way–falling over his ears, with bangs and a part that was too far toward the middle–that it gave him a peculiarly idiotic appearance.

We had leaned the lid against the wall, and with a jerk we had thrown back the silk cloth in which Father's corpse was bedded. Without hesitating–or no, we had hesitated. Finally trembling, we had unbuttoned the jacket of his suit and the shirt beneath it, button after button, and had stroked his naked breast and his naked belly with groping hands. We had felt along his back and around his neck. We had gone deep into his waistband. We had opened his fly, searched his genitals and his lap, and had followed his thighs with our fingers —with the tips of our fingers—without finding anything. We had examined his body centimeter by centimeter and had found nothing, nothing at all.

The funeral was pleasantly normal. We simply assumed the roles of extras and gave Mother and Kreszenz the parts as the mourners, the bereaved and surviving members of the family. We stood a few steps behind them and unfeelingly let the procession of funeral visitors file past us, knowing well that we must seem like the incarnation of evil or like evil itself, with our flamboyant mirrored sunglasses. And we were not affected in the coolness that we had adopted until we saw Magda. In her short black skirt, in her black and white striped blouse, in her high-heeled shoes among all the depressed people—the people who were displaying their depression —she seemed like a vision from a different, really different world, all the more so when we talked to her, even though it was only a few empty words, words that said nothing and everything and nothing.

At first there was not much to it. It was a game, banter, as we began to look for a guilty party or guilty parties. But more and more it went beyond that, with newer and newer accusations, ever more severe, more sharply conceived punishments. Finally it was always fantasies that ended in murder and mayhem. From one time to the next their images became harsher, more inhuman, painted in a harsher, crueller language. We were well coordinated and we alternated with each other smoothly in the worst tirades, and it even went so far that we no longer knew what came from whom, or why.

Their first target was always the family doctor. They reproached him for having sent Father to the hospital too late and for having treated him improperly, mistreated him—there were not enough words—in general for years. They called him a worthless quack and said that they would have liked to bash his head in with a hammer and chisel. Next—they were already in gear—next came the chief physician, who had called them young men in the hospital, young men on their way. And when they wanted to, they could see in him a former SS officer, and they said that they would have liked to stand him against the wall—and ratatatat. Or the female ward physician, who was still talking about Father's appendix or something or other when his heart was hardly making a peep any longer. They wished everything on her—whatever, whatever there was. They wished everything on her head, the most unspeakable diseases, and said that she should feel every word that she uttered, as if it had barbs, with every letter burning as a brand on her body, and that she should die a miserable, wretched death. Or the nurse who kept bringing him normal food when he had already been lying in a semi-coma for days. They called her everything that a human being has ever been called and wished that she would choke to death on her own food. And finally—as the high point—they always got around to talking about the hospital priest, a frail man, who in his frailness seemed made for the role, a man in a cassock, disguised in a cassock. And they celebrated it properly: on the cross, on the cross with him, and they would have liked to watch, or they would have preferred, much preferred to drive in one nail after another themselves, with powerful strokes of the hammer, when they heard him murmur about the Lord God, or about heaven, or when they only saw him with his hands folded in prayer, with his ecstatic, insane–in the truest sense of the word–expression.

When we later remembered the day, the day of Father's death, we knew that we constrained our memory with erroneous images. And we always began with the fact that it–phantasmally–never really got light. It snowed for hours, in enormous flakes that seemed counterfeit, immediately two-dimensional, as soon as they had landed. Snow lay in the city–we couldn't get away from that–as it had not lain in human memory, and cars moved ahead only at a snail's pace anymore, or got stuck completely on the slightest rises, or were snowed in in their parking places. And they were often no longer visible, buried in formless heaps of snow. Beginning at dawn, snow plows ran all day, and there was a pack of them. There were who knows how many that combed through the streets one after the other. They were uncanny, with their yellow lights that brushed across the house façades, with the scraping of their blades, the clanking of their chains. And at first it always seemed as though they were completely soundless when they came toward us from a distance. And it was only at the last moment, when they were already even with us–or at least it seemed that way–that the noise reach us as well. And we saw how the snow flew up from the blades, spraying against garden fences, walls, and houses, with a sound that could not be imitated. Then it fell down. And within a few hours piles of snow towered meters high along the edges of the roads everywhere, and it continued to snow unceasingly.

We had never talked much about Father. We had answered questions about him only carelessly or as evasively as possible. And at an age when we could still hardly talk, we had already felt uncomfortable when we were asked to whom we belonged and were supposed to say who knows what to designate him. In town it was his name, and even if it seldom meant anything to them, as the name of a man who had moved there, there was nothing else. But in the village there was Grandfather's name, his first name, and sometimes that of his father. And only that made father somebody, and with him we became somebody too. And descending from one generation to the next, the relationship always remained one of ownership: "To whom do you belong?" was the question that asked who we were, and if we tried to change that, we tried to change ourselves, our entire existence. We didn't kick at it as long as Father was alive, and when he was dead, we were asked about him less and less often anyway, out of so-called *consideration*, or because he was gradually forgotten. And if we were asked at all, it was by strangers, whom we told nothing or something or other. And we even sometimes claimed that he was still alive, out of an unconfessed wish, out of sudden mischievousness, who knows, or because a dead man in the family seemed just as bad as a drunkard or a criminal or a sex offender.

From then on we no longer had to fool anyone. Not that we let ourselves be restricted, but what was wrong, was also wrong, among other things, because Father's gaze was upon it. It seemed to be his way of looking at things that tore our reality apart and left it in pieces that did not fit, pieces that could no longer be put together.

So that our lives sometimes seemed like one of his pipe dreams, one of his fantasies—as if we were subject to the confusion of his constantly changing prophecies. One moment they said that something, something great would become of us, and the next moment, nothing. Perhaps we had defied him too little as children and had to make up for it now—now, when he was dead—with the result that we let ourselves go. Put a different way: finally released, we tried free fall—if we were not already falling in free fall. Anyway, in our inheritance we saw less a safety net than the chance to accelerate everything. And when we said that we would only do what we wanted anymore, at first that meant: nothing. We remembered Father's saying: *Money makes a person happy, money makes a person h...* And we remembered our religion or philosophy teacher: One day he began to burn a piece of currency in front of the assembled class, to prove that it was nothing, a piece of paper—smoke and ashes. But it had not occurred to him that a twenty proved nothing at all to us but his inclination toward miserliness.

Nevertheless, Vinzenz finally reached the point where he closed his café. From one day to the next he no longer went there, and he hung a sign on the door that said: *Temporarily Closed.* And as he wrote it, he hesitated for a moment, because the phrase *gone fishin'* occurred to him. He had read it somewhere in America in the display window of a store, and *gone fishin'* seemed appropriate to him. He wandered aimlessly through town for days, on forays that became more and more extensive and brought him from the center of town further and further into the outlying districts. And it was especially in areas of town that he didn't know, that he felt like he had free time or that he was on vacation. And only there did he really become aware that he was doing nothing. Or when he tried to do everything that he considered to be part of *enjoying himself*—getting up late, eating out, or sitting with a six pack of beer and snacks in front of the television set—it occurred to him more and more that that was not what he, or rather, what people meant by it. And in his usage the concept didn't exist at all, or only as mockery. Weekend after weekend he went to the soccer field. And sometimes he lost himself in the crowd and had to see a television summary of what he had seen, in order to know that it was real. Otherwise, he stayed home and began to move the furniture around when worst came to worst; or he dug around indiscriminately in his papers, or did something else, anything at all, only to reverse it in the next moment. And then in the evening he didn't see how the time had passed. Or he polished his trophy cups, actually took them from the shelves and glass cases one after another and replaced them polished, precisely ordered according to their importance. That was bad enough, but even worse was the fact that he began to make the rounds of tourist attractions, so-called tourist attractions and museums, and once he even rode back and forth through the city in a horse-drawn coach with the top down.

Finally there were excursions in his car, first in the immediate vicinity, into some valley or other, and then, after a brief stay, or without stopping, out again. One day he went to a village, the next day to the neighboring village—and so on and so forth, on half-day tours. And only when he saw why he was doing it, for the driving, only for the driving, for the old peace that he found in it again, did he expand his drives more and more. And more and more often he drove across the border and spent a night or didn't return until morning, exhausted. And from one time to the next he actually went a little further, and in time it was half of Europe and more. And he was able to sit at the steering wheel for hours without getting tired, or rather, he became more and more able to deal with his weariness. If at first it was six or eight hours without interruption, only with the necessary fuel stops, later it became twelve, sometimes fourteen, sixteen, eighteen. And he pushed his record further and further. Finally it was twenty-four hours. In his imagination, the end, the only end always seemed to be the ocean–there was only one–and if he spoke grandly about the edges of the continent, he spoke about them and about the fact that there were not four but three hundred and sixty directions, and that for him it was no longer possible to be anywhere but on a trip, on a literal trip, not a mystical one.

In the meantime, Moritz took a semester off, and he couldn't clean out his office and his desk at the institute fast enough, even with the idea–or the certainty–that he wouldn't return. He was no dropout–dropouts were wimps–but what he knew, he knew. Thus his favorite saying–when he didn't understand something, or when for some reason he refused to understand it–was: He had done a job, his job; whatever the case, he had done it, and now he wasn't doing it anymore, and that was all. And in general he could only bring forth tautologies about it. And after an interlude–a few weeks in the army–he was unperturbed. He sat day after day from morning until evening in some café or other and tried to imagine how things would go from there. It was not that he was nervous, it was more that he was curious. But he knew that it was important to tackle his inactivity properly, or, as he said, that tackling it didn't come automatically. And actually, when he began, his inactivity was strictly divided up, with prescribed times to which he adhered. He went to the university library in the morning and spent the entire forenoon reading, at first indiscriminately, whatever came into his hands: scientific or pseudoscientific stuff, and finally more and more literature, novels that he seemed to choose by their thickness. Later he went for a walk. There was a shorter route for bad, a longer one for good weather. And in the afternoon he returned to continue reading. In the evening he was always in a state in which he felt invulnerable, completely withdrawn from everything on his inevitable forays. And when he was in his usual restaurants, he succeeded without effort in radiating an ice-cold arrogance. And that was it—paltry enough—that was his triumph.

We gradually adapted, and doubt concerning our choice was not permitted. The way we lived kept us alive. And anyway, there was no going back anymore.

In rumors that constantly recurred, it was said that they were often seen drunk. When he came back from his trips and was in town for a few days, Vinzenz called himself half mockingly, half seriously, or just to use the phrase, a *quarter drunk*. And Moritz was constantly on the move or babbling quietly to himself. And when Magda's invitation came—handmade paper, parchment-colored, with a barely perceptible fragrance—they were more than content with themselves and their circumstances. They were not afraid. And actually they were at the peak of their fatalism, at the peak of their audacity, or at their peak in general.

EPILOGUE

I don't know who thought out the seating arrangement, or for what purpose. Or it's too transparent, the way we sit here, one next to the other, or rather, a man next to a woman, a woman next to a man, always a man, a woman, a man, a woman, with place cards and bouquets of flowers, and, it appears, with the married people separated from the unmarried, younger people with younger, older with older, or possibly–even if it is obscure–according to some other grouping entirely. In the middle of the hall beneath a crystal chandelier several tables have been placed together in a grouping with the bride and groom sitting at the head of it, Magda and–in the meantime already–her husband. Around them are tables arranged in a checker-board pattern, with pink, old pink table cloths and elegant place settings, with cloth napkins and silver eating utensils, with virtual towers of plates and several glasses and candles arranged in groups, usually in groups of three. Reflected back and forth in the wall mirrors all around, bent and broken, the scenery seems unreal enough that we can confidently believe that it's real. A few tables away I see Vinzenz looking at me. I see all kinds of people with whom I am more or less acquainted. I see Magda. I see Kreszenz. I see the priest–Schoißwohl, Schimpfößl, or whatever his name is. I see the priest–Schoißwohl, Schimpfößl, or whatever his name is. I see Kreszenz. I see Magda. I see all kinds of people with whom I am more or less acquainted. A few tables away I see Moritz looking at me. I try to read something corresponding to the day and its festivity into all of the faces, but for some reason it's difficult for me. I see nothing but everyday faces. One in all, all in one. I can convince myself that I see, have seen something in them, anything, but I spare myself an enumeration of all kinds of emotions and say only that it is a beautiful wedding dinner—just the way you say: *a beautiful corpse.*

Meanwhile—it's the middle of the afternoon—meanwhile the hors d'oeuvres are being served, some exotic trifle, or rather *petítesse*, with accents in its name and who knows what kind of taste. And suddenly it becomes quiet. First in the middle and at the entrance of the hall, but finally at table after table, the conversation, the chatter, yields to the clatter of the eating utensils and the clinking of the glasses. And actually, for a while it is quiet enough that you can hear the noise from the highway in the distance.

I look at the eaters. Sometimes their movements seem synchronized and sometimes they go up and down, as if transferred by a crankshaft from one to the next. And when I imagine them stopped, with their arms in the most diverse positions at the same moment, seemingly constrained, I have to think of the handing on of water buckets to put out a fire. And as a mental image, but not only as a mental association, the waitresses hurry back and forth between the tables at a trot. In their orthopedic shoes, in their knee-length, black skirts and white, starched lace serving aprons they seem like caricatures of themselves. And if you address them, you usually don't know quite how, or embarrassedly you say, "Miss," or you say nothing to begin with.

With a single glance I see the most diverse eating habits. I see people who peck at their food. I see gobblers, people who gorge themselves, morsel swallowers.

I see mouths that joyfully melt away in all directions and others that keep who knows what to themselves with lips pressed together. And what I see is broken into tiny splinters, but still coherent, a mosaic of nothing but partial faces, with sometimes this, sometimes that added to them.

In my imagination I see a woman. It's a fat woman who is climbing into a bathtub or is already sitting in it and scrubbing her back with a long-handled brush, and it's possible that she is singing. Or it's a man who is standing at a blackboard writing I don't know what—hieroglyphics. I see the cheeks of his butt clenched together. I see the outlines of his underpants against his trousers, and I suspect that they are too big for him, with expanded leg openings into which his penis slides when he walks, sometimes on the left side, sometimes on the right.

At some moments the faces of the eaters seem to be nothing but chewing muscles that have grown far too large. They are provisionally covered, with lumps and swellings that explode beneath the skin, and with eyes, ears, and noses that eat along with them almost violently. While they are lifeless again, they are masks. And if one of them eats with pleasure, for another eating seems to have guilty overtones, as an act of some dull necessity. When you see what all is human... But a sentence like that, a sentence with a beginning like that can't end well at all. It can only end in an aphorism or in a distinct blunder.

Now the musicians provisionally take their positions in one corner of the hall. They tune their instruments and say, "One, two! One, two! One, two, three!" into their microphones as seriously as if it were a matter of who knows what, and it becomes quiet again. They seem to enjoy the quiet and they fiddle around longer than necessary, and finally, before they quit, they play, yes, they play a fanfare.

I see that something is happening at the table of the bride and groom. There is a pushing back and forth, playfully and hesitantly. With apparent hesitation, Magda's husband stands up and makes a speech, or rather, he says two or three sentences. It is probably nothing worth mentioning, and I hardly listen. There is a proper measure of sentimentality and emotion about himself in his voice, and it appears that at any moment it could break and fail completely or deteriorate into an unintelligible croaking. And as if to prove it, when he pauses or stops speaking entirely, his mouth performs the wildest escapades, seems to go wild, to melt, sometimes in one direction, sometimes in another. It trembles, twitches, and stops short from time to time in an imperceptibly flickering condition. It reminds me of a writer who, while writing, forms the characters with his lips before or after he writes them.

I remember a fellow pupil in elementary school, against whom I had to compete in an arithmetic contest at the blackboard, he on one half of it, I on the other. We set to work with erasers held in front of us and with scratchy, squeaky pieces of chalk. And as improbable as it may sound, when I saw the corner of his mouth twitch, at first hardly perceptibly, but then more and more, I was momentarily ready to lose. I still remember how the victor, the faster pupil, had to turn around, stand at attention, and shout his result to the class. And yes, I still remember also, that I didn't do it.

As soon as Magda's husband has stopped speaking, they all stand and propose toasts, and for a moment it appears as if they—every man, every woman—have each prepared a speech. I hear the clinking of glasses against each other. At first it is isolated, but finally there are the most haphazard sounds, sound sequences, superimposed on each other. And I imagine that everyone clinks glasses with everyone else, even if it is not that way. I imagine all the permutations, and how many of them there are, and I can't help myself, I immediately see the corresponding formula. I see it: $n \cdot (n+1)/2$. Then things become confused again: "Cheers!" And everyone drinks or at least they act as if they are drinking, and—I don't know what—they give their blessing or secretly utter a curse. In their unaccustomed clothing it is difficult to see through them. They are imitations of an original that they themselves have never seen, copies of their own fantasies. And when they try to radiate a kind of indifferent nobility in their behavior, it seems grotesque, and no matter what they do, in one way or another it is always too much or too little. Or if things go well for a while, they unexpectedly give themselves away, in some trivial thing, or in general. Their movements seem awkward, disjointed, as if they had been planned for too long and had happened contrary to all the plans. And in the end it is always a stalemate. Their joints seem to tremble and come to rest at an unexpected, unnatural angle. Their entire body seems to be purely mechanical. And if they become conscious of one part, it appears that they immediately wish it gone, and especially their hands, regardless of whether they keep them hidden or in constant motion. They are compulsive smokers when they inhale the smoke of their cigarettes with the greediness of consumptives. And it seems as if they all, men and women alike, have their lips painted red. And they seem to have mouthpieces—even if they don't have any—so elegant and urbane does the very act of smoking seem. And when they let the smoke virtually pass through themselves, with their eyes closed in enjoyment, it is like a thought process. In the smoke rings that they blow out, there are thoughts, or rather, there are fantasies that rise high into the air before they blow apart. Is it cunningness? Sharp-sightedness? In their faces there is a sudden glow, and the moment of greatest enjoyment actually seems to move along with a kind of illumination.

I look across the tables toward the entrance to the hall and see that the soup is being served, a dumpling soup, and there is the same synchronized walking of the waitresses, with enormous trays that they carry at the level of their heads. It goes quick as a flash, as they say, when they put down their trays and empty the soup bowls into the soup plates. And when they say "Enjoy your meal," somehow it seems flippant, and you don't know if they mean it, or if it is mockery. When one of them bends over you, you can see part of her bra in the neckline of her blouse, and pinned over her breast there is a name tag with her first name. It clearly identifies her as married or single, *Miss* or *Mrs.* And if you can believe the tags, the young ones are married and the older ones are not.

I remember that as children we saw more femininity in waitresses than in any other women—with the possible exception of nuns, because of their black and white habits, as peculiar as that may sound. And it's hard even to say what *femininity* is supposed to be. In any case, it was something that attracted us, something mysterious that has an uncanny attraction for some reason. In their bustling around the waitresses seemed to best represent all of what was obscurely forbidden, everything that you didn't even talk about. Or if you did talk about it, you did it in such a way that afterward it was even more obscure. They seemed to have something that other women didn't have, at least in our circle of acquaintances. It was up to them to join in the conversation, or sometimes they even set the tone when they talked like men and used words which would usually have caused everyone to blush or at least to act as if they had done so. It was their gripping, sometimes coarse language that seemed to abolish a double gulf between us and them. Because in that, on the one hand, they didn't behave as untouchable adults. On the other hand they were also not the fragile, completely frightened creatures that we didn't want to have anything to do with anyway.

I know, there are more ways to eat a dumpling soup than you might think, depending on whether you divide the entire dumpling up first, or eat it piece by piece, and whether you eat it before or after the liquid of the soup, or with it, as seems to be customary. Or you can put the whole thing in your mouth and swallow it, if it's small enough.

I look at Magda's husband and see how he awkwardly loosens his tie. Red and white spots seem to alternate in his face, as if he were ashamed and frightened simultaneously. And when he fans himself, it is as if the air casts shadows; or there must be something in his changing facial expressions. Does he squint? At least he seems to squint. When he looks nervously around, he seems disoriented. And what is amazing is the fact that he always avoids Magda, just as she always seems to avoid him with glances that are no less nervous. Is that just my impression? Even earlier–when I saw him for the first time–before the ceremony, he was extremely agitated. I watched him from a distance, and something in his manner, in his movements–there was something hectic that affected me, and I saw that I was somehow like him. That's the only way I can put it, even if it sounds so vague. He seemed to touch something in my memory, without my knowing or wanting to know what; and he was real and unreal at the same time. When I was introduced to him, I liked the way he talked, in a well-balanced mixture of standard German and a dialect that I hardly knew where to place. That was reason enough not to connect him from the beginning with the same old claustrophobias. I also liked the words, the very special usage: speaking of a *calamity* when in reality it was nothing or a mishap that was not worth mentioning, or saying in all kinds of situations: "It degenerates." And only when it really degenerated was I cured of my raving, when he wanted to know how I was doing. He asked several times, one after another, "How are you doing?" and didn't listen when I began to talk, or at least he interrupted me again each time. I can still feel his handshake even now, damp with perspiration, warm, almost hot; and a moment later, when I wipe off my hand, it's ice-cold. And I know that I must be careful not to dismiss him, not to write him off from the start.

In the meantime the light in the hall has changed several times. It has grown dark and then light, dark again, light again, and each time the sun seems to have moved imperceptibly a little further onward. Even if you don't perceive it, not really, you imagine that you perceive it. And it is always different faces that radiate in its glow. It is the same faces, but they always seem to be different in the changed light. And particles of dust actually dance in the rays of sunlight, and if you look carefully, the air seems to tremble in many places, as if time were going to stand still, or go on more slowly.

And a little later, in the shadows, it again seems faster. And the conversations at the tables seem to be exactly the same way, sometimes softer, sometimes louder. The movements, depending on whether they are more or less abrupt, seem sedate, the expressions sad, happy–and unquestionably distinguishable from one another. In the alternation between light and shadow everything seems like a play of what is and what only seems to be, but it remains unclear what is what, and now, as the candles at the table are gradually lit, it seems like a preliminary decision.

In the babble of voices one and the same sentence stands out again and again: "Mr.," or rather, "some Mr. Schratt, a teacher, killed his wife," yes, his wife, "and himself." I see him before me. I can't help it. I see him, Mr. Schratt, in front of me as he comes out of the school building on the day of the disaster, right after his last class, or a little later, in order to avoid the swarms of pupils who rush outside in wild confusion at the bell. I see him walking alone across the yard in front of the school, sometimes with his head bowed, at other times with it raised. I see him go to his car, stop in front of it, in front of a compact or medium-sized car, new, not used–or is it a dilapidated rattletrap? I see him from the front, from behind, and again from the front, and really, he's like a daydreamer, a sleepwalker. And he must have driven off just that way, like a daydreamer, like a sleepwalker, sputtering, with a stalling engine, or suddenly, with squealing tires. A moment later I see him drive past the middle-class houses in the center of town, past the swimming pool, the *Post Hotel*, the *Stern Hotel*, and the dairy with its gateways and ramps, past the state school dormitory, the boarding school, a building with a crudely decorated façade, high, barred windows, and a high wall around the garden, past the post office with its enormous parking lot. I see him drive for a while across open, undeveloped land, past a wooden fence with reflectors—it has a tattered cadaver lying hidden at the end of it, no longer recognizable, a reddish-black heap. I see him drive past an automobile dealership with several automobiles standing outside for sale, with a mountain of old, tattered wrecks that are pressed together, with towering piles, cylinders of dull, black tires of different sizes in the background. He drives past the soccer field with its high, seemingly tarnished wire-net fences, past the low building of the central market, past the meat market, past the row of farm houses that stand side by side with parallel gables, past filling stations, and finally past the last buildings. He is already outside the city limits. I see him arrive in one of the neighboring towns, and once he walks toward his house across a lawn sprinkled with crocuses. Another time he walks hesitantly, stride after stride. I see him enter it. And for some reason everything is completely silent.

I look across the tables toward the entrance to the hall and see that the main course is being served. We have our choice of fish or meat, artistically arranged, with enough decor and frippery. And we hear "Oh!" and "Ah!" in every tone, sometimes amazed, sometimes hungry. Or is it only an act, and in the final analysis feigned horror? It grows quiet again. Conversation ceases, first in the middle of the hall and at the entrance to the hall, but finally at table after table. The babbling yields to the clatter of eating utensils and the clinking of glasses, and for a while it is actually quiet enough that you can hear the distant noise from the highway. I watch the eaters, and at the sight of their chewing motions it occurs to me again that as children we couldn't even imagine that other people—women, or our heroes—also had to go to the toilet, and neither could we find such descriptions in books. We could stand around a tree or around a fire with friends and urinate together, see who could do it longer or further, and whoever stepped out of the circle too soon lost face.

I still remember, once at home, when Father and Mother were away, one after another we stood on a windowsill and urinated in a high arc out of the wide-open window. And for days and weeks it seemed to us like a heroic deed. And it must have been exactly the same when we collected our urine, poured it together, and drank it. It was a real ritual, or at least the seriousness with which we did it seemed to go far beyond a children's game.

During all that time we had no shyness about exposing ourselves in front of each other. And later, when we became shy about it, we didn't know what was more embarrassing for us—that we had never been shy before, or that we suddenly were.

Disgusted, I see how devotedly everyone sits there and eats. And it doesn't matter whether they act as if they haven't had anything for days, or if they behave inconspicuously, or, on the contrary, mime the connoisseur. And I see the way they drink the wine along with it, like water, or as if it were a delicacy that is being wasted. And while one envelops his glass with his entire hand, or even with both hands, like a bowl, another takes it by the stem. I see their swallowing movements, the way their larynxes bob up and down. And depending on whether they have their eyes closed or open, their faces seem more or less distorted. That way their mouths all seem to play pieces, and when you see the shapes they have, no comparison is satisfactory. I see in them internal organs turned inside out, and what is noteworthy is that it seems as if they had a life of their own, independent of the body that belongs to them, or as if they were the only thing on it that is alive at all. As if that were not enough, a few of those who are eating are already drunk, and they become loud or withdraw more and more. And suddenly the seating arrangement becomes clear to me, or at least it seems as if willingness to drink—or whatever you want to call it—has been one criterion. And while the faces at some tables blur more and more, begin to resemble each other more and more, or in general look like one face, dunked and not properly dried, smeared, or look like no face, the faces at other tables still seem completely intact.

I say, "Cheers!" and drink a sip, and from every side I hear: "Cheers!" "Cheers!" "Cheers!"

All at once I can hear the noise of a car from outside, a car that is being maneuvered out of a parking place. It seems as if it keeps getting stuck in the snow again and again or jerks forward and backward with spinning wheels, with the engine roaring, with r.p.m.'s far into the red area. In between, when the gears are shifted, there are virtual breathers, and who knows if we imagine it or if the noise from shifting gears actually penetrates to us? Just as it can also be our imagination when we perceive a trembling of the windowpanes when the noise reaches its peak, just before it falls off. Or hardly perceptible, the sound of bumpers striking each other. I see that more and more people in the hall have stopped talking. They listen with faces that are almost distorted with pain. And when the car comes free, the proverbial sigh of relief goes through the crowd, and we listen to how the gears are quickly shifted from one to the next as it drives away, and to how the sound, growing softer and softer, dies away. Then it's quiet, as if everyone were waiting for one final noise, for who knows what, perhaps for the bang of an explosion. And there is enough time, useless, unused time.

A few tables away, I see Vinzenz looking at me. I see how he takes off his jacket and rolls the sleeves of his shirt up past his elbows. And when they are rolled up, he rolls them down and then back up again. I see all kinds of people with whom I am more or less acquainted. I see Magda. I see Kreszenz, and it doesn't occur to me to see something, anything special in her. I see the priest–Schoißwohl, Schimpfößl or whatever his name is. I see how he lights a cigarette and inhales the smoke greedily. And when he puffs the smoke out in rings, it is spiritual. I see the priest–Schoißwohl, Schimpfößl or whatever his name is. I see how he lights a cigarette and inhales the smoke greedily. And when he puffs the smoke out in rings, it is spiritual. I see Kreszenz, and it doesn't occur to me to see something, anything special in her. I see Magda. A few tables away, I see Moritz looking at me. I see how he takes off his jacket and rolls the sleeves of his shirt up past his elbows. And when they are rolled up, he rolls them down and then back up again. And I know that he's imitating me. And I still try to read into all of the faces something that corresponds to the day and its festiveness, but for some reason it is difficult for me to do it. They are nothing but everyday faces, one in all, all in one.

I see Mr. Schratt sitting at the dinner table with a newspaper, with no shoes on his feet, or with his feet resting on a chair across from him, with a sheet of paper under his shoes. Sometimes his face is unmoved; at other times what he reads in the newspaper seems to be reflected in his features. I see him put down the newspaper when Mrs. Schratt enters and serves the food. I see him look at her wordlessly. Or he says who knows what to her, or looks past her, or even worse, he nonchalantly continues to read. I see–if I want to–how he kisses her; and it is an awkward kiss, out of nothing but absent-mindedness. I see him make the sign of the cross, say grace, and say, "Enjoy your meal." He says, "Enjoy your meal," or he says, "So," with an "o" that is so short that it isn't an individual letter. In its customariness it must have been an established fact: how they sat across from each other, Mr. and Mrs. Schratt, taciturn or drowning in the usual torrent of words, depending on the situation, the way they always did, with exactly the same movements, exactly the same lack of movement, with exactly the same back and forth, in a virtual stalemate, in a game with stricter and stricter rules and stricter and stricter penalties for a violation of the rules. Or is it the case that all moves have already been marked out, so that an additional move brings nothing, only misfortune?

Is Magda happy? I turn to her, and again, and just like a couple of times before, it seems as if she is avoiding me when she immediately turns away and tries to converse with her husband. But it can just as easily be a coincidence. Just as it's possible that I looked at her too long, as she ate her fish gingerly, awkwardly, too carefully, chewing piece after piece to nothing, in her own inimitable way of spitting out the bones or brushing them from her lips with stretched-out fingers, without feeling embarrassed. Her lipstick is still smeared, and her mouth, with its indefinitely extended corners, seems exaggeratedly lascivious, a contrast to her bashfulness when she looks around and lowers her gaze when she notices that she is being watched. Her face seems too heavily made-up, with red, reddishly highlighted cheeks that somewhat give her the look of a juicy peasant girl who is bursting with vigor. And it has the same effect that she had as a child when she almost glowed with excitement, with shame, or with anger. Her hair is put up. It's an exact arrangement–coordination between chaos and order, more or less successful–an allegory, symmetrical, asymmetrical, with corkscrew, spiral, or curlicue curls that have been manipulated, turned so that they fall accidentally or as if accidentally against her cheeks. And it can't be corny enough at all to talk of their colors. There are so many tones of red, so many different ones in the play of light and shadow–*romance in rouge* is the phrase, and I no longer remember where I got it from. Did it come from the label of a cheap wine in a night club, from the cover of a dime novel? I watch the way she drinks, surprised that it is still her typical pose, with horizontal upper and lower arm. And when she swallows, she makes her swallowing noises, reason enough for her to excuse herself all around. And there is still something sensually deliberate about it when her lips enclose the edge of the glass. And when they let go of it, it happens with a peculiar indolence. In general her movements seem heavy, delayed, and carefully thought out. There is a glow in her eyes, intensified by the alcohol and the candlelight. And it's clear that it can be attributed to all kinds of causes, perhaps, perhaps even to her happiness.

    I remember–as if it were already who knows how long ago–with what enthusiasm they put the rings on each other's fingers, Magda and her husband: "Yes, yes, I do, yes." And it seemed as if they wanted to do it in front of the altar, before the eyes of everyone–the way they stood hand in hand, turned toward each other, in the rain, in the drizzle. And something in their faces made it seem that they were trying to see that moment as the most beautiful moment of their life, of their lives—or at least as something that they would always remember, whatever it was. And it was an event, on the one hand a mass, on the other hand not a mass—to satisfy their belief in God, or rather that of their relatives and friends, while at the same time not having to be ashamed of them. It was a farce. In the yard where the ceremony took place—a place that was partially paved, partially covered with boards, bordered on three sides by buildings, old, well-preserved farm houses, open on one side—folk plays, or so-called *Tyrolean evenings* were performed in the summer before an audience that was addicted to applause. And this was a folk play too. It began with the priest who had degenerated into a moderator, and who, as far as possible, stayed away from the liturgy and gave directions, stage directions, with hand gestures that he had practiced beforehand. At his command, the unseen string orchestra began—it had been placed on a balcony decorated with garlands—and at his command it ceased playing. At his command children stepped forward one after another and recited intercessory prayers, bungled, stuttered together on their own, or as if on their own—that was the effect it was supposed to have. And the substance of their prayers was the very same "Long live the bride and groom! Long live the bride and groom! Long live the bride and groom!" that resounded again and again in the subsequent shouting, in all kinds of variations.

It was children in general who carried out a large portion of the program. We were supposed to find them cute, nice, with their sayings. And when they joined together and intoned together: "When the dog...uhhh...

with the bitch, when the tom...when the tomcat...uhhh, uuhhh... with the pussy cat...," we knew for what purpose children, children's blessings were being used.

The accompanying mothers stood in the background. They moved a pace or two forward and were the first to clap, looking around, surveying those around them, alternately proud and ashamed. And in the same way, proud and ashamed, they clapped during the reading, a reading from a book of fairy tales instead of from the Bible. It was presented by a woman with a French accent, with words and sentences that were breathed out over and beyond themselves. They were so soft, so quiet, so gentle that you couldn't call them anything but *soft*. And when all of us stood there with velvet gazes, dumbfounded, halfway senile, it was as if they were vainly going to indulge once more, and yet again in reveries, in purposeless and aimless extravagances.

What the priest said then was not a sermon. It was an indistinct, blurred retelling of the fairy tale, with a moral. And it seemed as if only the good or the well-intended existed. In fact, it was that abstract, precisely that abstract.

A female photographer gyrated around among the assembled people, acting harried and important, as if to draw attention to herself and the clicking of her camera. The latter was inaudible, and if it had been audible I don't know if it would have reminded me of the ticking away of time, at least because of the rhyme. How she laughed before she disappeared behind the enormous lens, just as if it were directed at her and somebody, whoever it might be, just as if she were saying, "Now, smile now, now." And how beautiful–how very conscious she was of her beauty; and the different positions that she assumed–sometimes crouching down, sometimes standing up straight—made her poses seem like those of statues.

When the ceremony was over, Magda and her husband went arm and arm up and down among the people with a basket full of bread and distributed it. That is, they broke pieces from large loaves before they distributed them—that was the point. And if the scene didn't disgust us because of its forced symbolism, it was because of the rain that came streaming down. We all sought refuge under the balconies and stood drenched, pressed closely together.

It has grown dark in the hall, and if I look outside, I see heavy storm clouds. What comes in from outside, a reflection, mingles with the candlelight, and an undecided, greasy twilight comes into being. In it, the faces of the eaters seem pale, pale as a corpse, or as if without color. Or the colors are unusual, dark olive, dark violet, and one is inclined—paradoxically or not—to speak of a kind of lightlessness, a kind of lifelessness. In the faces and in the sometimes momentary flickering of the candlelight, there seems to be an irreconcilable rigidness, and one resembles the other, resembles a prototype that has never been seen. And every smile, every laugh is an act of grimacing, and if you don't look carefully at it, it seems fragmented, chopped up. Only later, in the electric light, is the hall evenly lighted, in a brightness that penetrates every crack. It is reflected back and forth, bent and broken, from the wall mirrors all around. And the impression that we have the scenery of a film in front of us, a stuttering cartoon with an insufficient image frequency, immediately disappears.

I imagine how an argument between Mr. and Mrs. Schratt began. In one instance it is a triviality, so ridiculous that one is forced to laugh, even if the laughter quickly fades again. You just can't describe it, or if you can, then without understanding, with the understanding of a tabloid reporter. Nothing is too trivial, and if you say *for no reason*, that it began without a reason, it means exactly that. In another version it is orchestrated theater, always with the same beginning and end: that she carps at him until he says "That's enough!" and begins to scream at her. Or he carps at her, and in total contrast she becomes quieter and quieter and finally becomes silent, or vice-versa, less trite, with the roles reversed. I see him with a bright red face, while her face is pale. And his entire body seems to tremble with emotion, while hers seems motionless. And if he sometimes forgets what he is talking about because he is so beside himself, she always seems to know exactly what is going on. And one word leads to another; one of them is riled up more and more by the other, or they have quit talking to each other. I imagine that at some point, perhaps from the very beginning, old stories, little stories are brought up, misunderstandings that they believed they had endured, petty jealousies, justified or unfounded, fantasies. And who knows, if he called her a whore, she will hardly have hesitated to call him a pig or a weakling.

I remember what a female pupil, a former pupil of Mr. Schratt told me a few hours ago: "In school, more than anything else, Mr. Schratt was notorious for his gray suit that never changed. It was a relic from another decade, with trousers that were cut too narrow at the top and too wide at the bottom. The jacket was fitted at the waist, one of those pieces of clothing where you get goose bumps from looking at it or feel sorry for the wearer. There were rumors that it was an heirloom, his uncle's wedding suit, and that he wore it out of gratitude. Or they said that he was bound for life by an oath, or that there was no reason, that he was a personification of tastelessness, nonchalance, and miserliness. And when he appeared in a sweater, a sheep's wool sweater, or only in a shirt and pants a few times a year, we immediately began to speculate. The companion piece to that seemed to be his car, a black, rusty monstrosity with red leather seats, a car next to which the other cars in the parking lot in front of the school seemed like machines with two-cycle engines. It was a diesel–often enough with a dark cloud of smoke trailing behind it when he drove up, when he drove close to the school building in a curve that was as elegant as possible, stopped, and got out on stiff legs. Even in the worst condition, it seemed, it was a status symbol that elevated him far above his status, the status that he himself despised. It elevated him above all the teachers, the people who made their living by teaching–state parasites. And if he didn't grow tired of enumerating advantages with respect to some crate or tub, it was clear that he meant himself and viewed his colleagues as poor wretches.

"We," she continued after a pause, "we didn't know how serious he was about his sayings, whether he was concerned about laughter when he made a mistake or when he let himself be carried away to new and different pirouettes, to new and different capers. We didn't rack our brains about it, because we pardoned everyone for everything. 'Talk and let talk,' we said, as generously as possible, as grandiose as possible. And we preferred not to take something seriously rather than to counter it with a *no*. Politics disgusted us. We didn't understand it, didn't want to understand it, and pushed it off unexamined into the realm of a sordid, dirty world that didn't concern us. And it wasn't out of cowardice, at least not just that, when we didn't contradict him. It was because there was hardly any contradiction, because we were familiar with the very same tone at home. In his storm-and-stress periods the slightest provocations were enough to drive him wild. He only had to have seen a politician who didn't suit him on television the night before; he just had to have encountered the right fellows—worst of all was the chancellor, or the finance minister, the *Pighead*, as he called him, the *State Pig*, or his bag man—and everything broke loose, in tirades of curses, in a single torrent of words. *Long-haired fool, fixer, pot brother,* and *dirty pig* were synonymous. He called the girls *Gitschen* [dialect for *young girls*] or *Fräuleins*. *Weiber* [women] and *Tschuschen* [derogatory term for foreigners] had the same meaning as everywhere else in the country. But now and then minute distinctions were made, between *fathead* and *bumpkin*, between *Dardanelles stinkers, camel jockeys,* and *spaghetti eaters*. And there was hardly any difference from one time to the next. At the end he constantly prophesied that nobody needed to come after him. He would stand there, and bang! As if he were constantly being threatened with death or bodily harm. Or he even brought up his favorite topic, skyjackings in all their details. 'Not me! No! No!' he could say amid our laughter. He wouldn't let them get away with it. He would make short work of them, and ra-ta-tat-tat, he'd place them against the wall, the riffraff."

In the hall, first near the entrance and in the middle of the hall, desserts are already being served, sweet things in all kinds of forms and colors: cake, pie, and tarts with whipped cream, and small pastries in large glass bowls. Pots full of coffee and tea are being placed on the tables, and again and again you can hear "Coffee!

Coffee!" sometimes stressed on one syllable, sometimes on the other, or "Tea!" sometimes with, sometimes without "th." And whoever wants to can continue to drink wine as before, heavy wine, red, so red that it even looks black, with points of light and reflections in the glasses. It is carried in in narrow-necked one or two-liter carafes, and at first it seems to get stuck when it is being poured. Then it seems to explode when it comes out, with the bubbles that enter the belly of the carafe. And a very peculiar gurgling arises when waitresses have just carefully poured it from bottles with napkin ruffles and cravats. At some tables they are already beginning to drink hard liquor, that is, a home-made liquor. A so-called home-made liquor is being served in brandy snifters with stems, for the most part in rounds. Entire trays are full of it, and if they were calling it *a drop of brandy* only moments ago, it is now being called *liquor.* Cigars, long thin ones, thick short ones appear, stogies, Havanas or not. Their smoke, getting thicker and thicker, hangs motionless in the air. And the process of lighting up seems to be the most important thing when you see with what engrossment they are puffed into action again, when they go out after hardly being lit. Or the status is so important that sometimes even nonsmokers don't decline. Meanwhile there is a peculiar confusion of sounds. And when a champagne cork pops somewhere and the champagne seems to fizz to silence in the glasses, the popping is imitated everywhere with index fingers that snap out of the hollows behind people's cheeks. And it doesn't become quiet until Magda's father stands up and makes a speech. I see how he stands there, his hands resting on the table, how he eyes the bride and groom or looks around the hall, apparently lost in thought, and how he unavoidably describes the course of a marriage and gives advice, mostly platitudes. The musicians move into position again, and while he is still speaking, they begin to play–Thank God! And in my vicinity there's a know-it-all dialogue, and I don't know why, but for some reason I am unable to keep from listening.

"Waiting in a crowd on the edge of a railway platform, you are startled by your own thought of pushing someone, somebody or other onto the tracks, or of jumping yourself, and you step back a pace just in time. Or in tunnels, you imagine steering your car into the approaching traffic and then sputter off at a walking pace, honking with fright. Or in the pedestrian zone of a big city, in the confusion of a Saturday morning, you can hardly keep yourself from causing a blood bath, a massacre: controlling authority between delusion and insane act."

"And a fraction of a second is enough, a blunder, a misfire, and you're already running amok. Yes, you seem not to trust yourself when you're completely crazy, and you're alone in a room with a set of kitchen knives that is laid out in plain sight, and you don't know which way to turn, or you see the woman at your side as a destroying angel. Or in a car, when you just barely get past the only tree far and wide on a straight stretch of road that goes on for miles. Is it a vortex?"

"People live in the high-security cells of their apartment houses, their concrete blocks, stacked on top of each other by the dozens, and they imagine well-staged blood baths. And the thrill of it is that it could be them. They could be murderers or victims, and when it gets to be too much, just before a shot, or a stab, or a blow, they let the image fall apart again in their philistine world."

I turn around and see that it is two older gentlemen at the next table who converse so pretentiously. The one always continues without contradiction exactly at the point where the other one stops. And because they are in such total agreement, it seems as if only one of them is really talking. In similar, similarly gray suits with red-white-red striped ties, they sit across from each other, and in their doubling they seem not to belong to the wedding party. They are like supervisors, watchers, like twins who have remained behind and escaped from their own watchers. They are both fat, with heads that move back and forth almost cunningly on motionless bodies. And in light of their fullness, their limbs—which are too short—have the appearance of lacking a function, of playing. They seem like toys. And it must also be a game, the way they blow the smoke of their cigars into each other's eyes, with one of them always doing it while the other is talking, as if in reinforcement. It's fun to look at their little faces, their pink little pig faces, or at the way they take the cigars in their little paws between their index and middle fingers and are careful not to let the ashes break off. They brush them off, knock them off on the ashtray and pensively stare into space. And from behind, the austere pattern of their haircuts is visible. And beneath the hair, with rolls of skin glistening with perspiration at the nape of the neck, I can see their scalps, between little ears that lay close to their heads. And their entire appearance somehow reminds me of dogs, so-called *killer dogs*.

Meanwhile, the band has reached its stride with the greatest difficulty; and if they were playing waltzes just a moment ago, now, as promised, as the bandleader says —he probably calls himself a bandleader—they are playing evergreens, super-hits. They are hit songs, tearjerkers, from who knows how many decades, rendered sometimes more, sometimes less in the pop style. And gradually the dance floor fills up with couples who turn round and round, and around each other, mostly older couples, children dancing in a ring. And more than anything else it brings to mind a beach or health-resort dance on a Sunday afternoon. I look at the musicians absently. In their costumes, illuminated sometimes in red, sometimes in green, sometimes in yellow, they seem smaller, less conspicuous than they did before in civilian clothes, with their walrus moustaches, their permanent waves. Three of them have those—curly, artificially curled, as if they were kinky—while the fourth is a black man who wears his hair smooth, pulled down flat. Children stop in front of him with pointing fingers again and again, and now it starts, "Look, Mama, look! A Negro, a real Negro!"

A few tables away I see Vinzenz watching me. I see how he leans back and lets his gaze wander over the dancers, trustingly, tenderly—or how should I put it? I see all kinds of people with whom I am more or less acquainted, a solid hodgepodge of white, black, and all kinds of colors. I see Kreszenz, with a ponytail, as if for the first time, dancing with the priest—Schoißwohl, Schimpfößl, or whatever his name is. And I see how he puts his arm around her waist, smoothly, lithely. I see Kreszenz, with a ponytail, as if for the first time, dancing with the priest—Schoißwohl, Schimpfößl, or whatever his name is. And I see how he puts his arm around her waist, shyly, awkwardly. I see all kinds of people with whom I am more or less acquainted, a solid hodgepodge of white, black, and all kinds of colors. A few tables away I see Moritz looking at me. I see how he leans back and lets his gaze wander over the dancers, trustingly, tenderly—or how should I put it?

Will there really be no bride's dance? I remember how much Magda disliked dancing, how she said "No," at first hesitantly, but sharper and sharper if you came back, until she finally offended you. She talked about it uncertainly, disparagingly, and seemed to have something against it from the very beginning, when she called it *hopping* and talked about *dance-school dancers*, a term that conjured up images of effeminate men, men who were called feminine, images of prim provincial ballerinas. Anyway, if she could, she evaded, and she avoided dubious situations or slipped away to the rest room and didn't return for a long time, if at all. In the few instances where someone succeed in dragging her onto the dance floor, she stood there motionless, obstinate, and talked about her abstraction, about her insignificance. Or she swung, shook her arms and legs, threw them wildly, like a wild woman, in all directions, and usually withdrew right after the first dance. She said, "You will excuse me!"—it was always the formal *you*, because she didn't dance with anyone that she addressed with the informal form—and left her astonished partner where he stood, in order to get out of his reach as quickly as possible, still shaking with uneasiness. I don't know if this has anything to do with it, but once, many years ago—I have to begin in such a fairy-tale fashion—we, Magda and I, danced up and down in her parents' living room, experimentally so to speak, across the inlaid floor and the carpet. As we danced, sometimes I must have led her, sometimes she must have led me. And what is important: we did it without music. We ourselves hummed melodies and sang the lyrics. And no, I no longer remember which hits they were, only one: "There are millions of stars...." And then, as we continued to sing, on and on, and to dance, imitating a drum as if to keep time, there was "There is a lot of money and property in the world, but there is only one you for me." And everything that had begun as fun, as a prank, had suddenly collapsed and become serious, so serious that we didn't dare say it. And what was left for us to do? We laughed, laughed, and laughed.

I don't know which of the gentlemen says it: "Actually it's enough that you have the possibility to kill yourself at any moment," spoken verbatim. And as I turn toward them again, they act as if it were neither of them. There is that much about them that denounces and points fingers. And as if to hide everything, they take their napkins, which still stand there undisturbed, and wipe their foreheads with them. There is something roguish in their eyes, as if they were only saying anything they said in fun and meant nothing or something else. And actually, as they continue to speak, all of their megalomania is as if it had been wiped away, and they indulge in some trivialities. They are gossips for whom one bit of scandal is as good as another. In their vicinity sits a woman–one must probably give her the title of *Lady*–who has already listened to them for a while. Suddenly she crosses herself, placing one mark of the cross on her forehead, one on her mouth; and her breast, or rather her bosom begins to surge, as she makes the sign across it. And really, the most peculiar words occur to me, for example: *countenance*, when I look at her and know that I don't dare say it. She wears her hat–more a little cap–askew, as if to give herself a frolicsome appearance. But it's so ridiculous that it probably isn't on purpose. And if her headgear isn't appropriate, her arm-length gloves–which she doesn't remove, hasn't removed, not even to eat–are much less so. I see her jewelry. There are rings on all her fingers, and bracelets, whole bundles of them, on both hands. She wears them over the gloves, and when she moves, an exaggerated glitter goes out from them in the light, and there is a jangling that can't be heard. She is wearing earrings, shoulder-length, and a diadem in her hair. Her entire face goes into motion when she begins to speak and stifles it at the last moment. And a description, now this way, now that, is completely out of the question. And then she unceremoniously adds make-up and makes the most improbable faces in front of her pocket mirror, and beneath her layers of make-up she must be tanned, a few shades too dark. In her hypertrophy she seems like one of those women who begin to age alongside older men, as playmates, as wives who for years pretended to be older than they were in reality. And suddenly, when their age catches up with them, they fight against it with money and gold, with all of the baubles at their disposal. And that only makes it worse. And if they have seemed like wall flowers at first, later, in their thirties, or even later, they seem like women of the world, like women with money, or even like *femmes fatales*, like nymphomaniacs—and if they kick over all the traces, like whores.

I turn away and let my gaze wander over the dancers again, trustingly, tenderly—or how should I put it? I look at Magda, and suddenly there are the old sentimentalities that are always the same. I thought that I was finally immune to them. There are memories of shared summer days at the city swimming pool, of our aimlessly urgent wandering around, of trips that the two of us, the three of us made on motor scooters, on Saturday afternoons, on forest and meadow paths far out into the surrounding countryside. There are memories of the enchanted, wildly over-grown monastery garden where we crept in to steal fruit, and memories of the empty wing of the monastery, a building that was several stories high, where we had gained entry and sometimes sat in a narrow cell at night and breathed in the dusty air, the dismal secret of a monk's loneliness, of a terrifyingly senseless world. There are memories, too, of our first kiss, of Magda's soft, large mouth, her warm, wet tongue, and of how both of us said, "I like you," in the same way, and shoved our hands under her dress, seeking support against the bells of the monastery clock.

"In principle it goes quickly. At one moment you're alive, still alive, and at the next moment you're already dead. And in between there's a point of unsteadiness, between the life curve, so to speak, its up and down, and the zero curve of death. Or you imagine a steady transition, breathing your last breath, proverbial as it is. And it becomes less and less, less and less, with an established convergence."

At some point it was probably enough, that is, too much. Too much was probably said; too much probably happened, and everything was probably talked to death. And maybe without knowing what he was doing, what he was on the verge of doing, Mr. Schratt probably dug a kitchen knife out of a drawer, one with a long, slender blade and a mother-of-pearl handle, one whose weight felt good in his hand. And maybe he stabbed immediately, or he walked up and down with the knife in his hand, fully conscious of his theatrics, not aware, not yet, that he would play out the piece. And while he gesticulated in front of her, she–Mrs. Schratt–probably goaded him, "Do it, go ahead and do it, you coward." Or who knows? Maybe she retreated in fright. I imagine that her first reaction was amazement, when she felt the blade, or didn't feel it; when she only knew that where she felt nothing, there it was, in her chest, in her belly. And she probably didn't say anything, try to say anything, until she began to explore herself with trembling hands. In the meantime, her blood came into her mouth, visible in the corners of her mouth. And in her eyes, in her wide-open eyes horror probably spread–in her glistening pupils. I see her in front of me, how she feels along the knife, centimeter after centimeter, and finally clasps it. And when she lets go of it, her hands are smeared with blood; when her gaze falls upon them, it is pleading. And when she sees blood in front of her on the floor, drops, one next to the other, one merging with the next, it simultaneously seems to depart visibly, abruptly from her face. And it drips, drips, and continues to drip, shattering, splattering into crazy, many-pointed little stars. In one version I see how she collapses, slumps together right there. Another time she begins to move slowly, step by step, without lifting her feet; or it's a weak-kneed, high-heeled stalking with hips rocking up and down, uncontrolled. And this way, that way, or the other way she probably crossed the room and walked from one room to the other, in wild zigzag lines. I see her–and it's the final scene–as she stands in the bathroom, bent over the wash basin, and begins to wash herself. I see how she looks in the mirror with her bloody, blood-smeared face and doesn't seem to see anything but dream images, nightmare images, hallucinations. And finally, when she lies there bent, involved, she looks down at herself and sees everything, and her amazement is there again–and then nothing more. While on the floor, growing gradually larger in all kinds of different forms, Rorschach tests, a puddle of blood forms, as if vomited out, with traces, perfectly straight traces of blood in the cracks between the tiles.

A few tables away I see Vinzenz looking at me. Or no, he isn't looking at me; he's sitting there with his eyes closed, probably drunk. And somehow it's as if he believes that he's invisible if he simply doesn't look over here–the way children believe that–and a realm of absolute soundlessness seems to surround him. I see all kinds of people with whom I am more or less acquainted. I see Magda. I see Kreszenz poking around in her mouth with a toothpick. She holds her hands in front of her with one hand in the other She is bashful, impudent, and she sucks in air with a hiss between her teeth. I see the priest–Schoißwohl, Schimpfößl, or whatever his name is. He lights a cigarette and inhales the smoke greedily, and when he puffs the smoke out in rings, it seems overpowering. I see the priest–Schoißwohl, Schimpfößl, or whatever his name is. He lights a cigarette and inhales the smoke greedily, and when he puffs the smoke out in rings, it seems overpowering. I see Kreszenz poking around in her mouth with a toothpick. She holds her hands in front of her with one hand in the other. She is bashful, impudent, and she sucks in air with a hiss between her teeth. I see Magda. I see all kinds of people with whom I am more or less acquainted. A few tables away I see Moritz looking at me. Or no, he isn't looking at me; he's sitting there with his eyes closed, probably drunk. And somehow it's as if he believes that he's invisible if he doesn't look over here–the way children believe that–and a realm of absolute soundlessness seems to surround him.

I see Mr. Schratt in front of me once more. He follows the dying woman's zigzag line step by step, pausing when she pauses, and he's careful to maintain enough distance, as if her dying, dying in general, were something contagious. He alternately looks away and watches with interest like a man whom it doesn't concern, benign in the sense of *everything that is, is right and proper.*

And he probably didn't say anything, and one, two, three, maybe he counted his own heartbeats, or hers, or the seconds. Time crawled; it was slow-motion time, and silent, as if it were without a single sound for the first time. He probably also washed himself in the bathroom. And who knows, maybe he really did rush out of the house, slamming the door, as if he were out of his mind. And from there on there are only two possible ways to fantasize how the story ends, depending on whether he was sentimentally conciliatory, or unforgivingly hard, with enough corresponding memories, whichever way it was.

I don't know if he knew what he was doing, or if he wanted to know, as he climbed into the car, into his sacred, beloved automobile, probably already groggy, being counted out like a boxer before the k.o. Did he weigh things back and forth during the journey?: *Should I? Shouldn't I?* Or did he simply drive on without thinking about it? Whatever the case, you can see it the way you want to, and why not? As the final scene, I see an image before the unavoidably ultimate end. It's the car, as it hangs high above the ravine—in the air above the nearby ravine—with its wheels still turning.

Meanwhile the music has grown louder and louder, and one piece seems like the next, indistinguishable from the others, played in a rhythm that remains the same. Or it is drowned, at least its uniqueness, in the stamping of the dancers. Gradually the older couples have withdrawn, unappreciative, envious, or having come to terms with things, with their fate; and it is the younger ones who are dancing. They are not couples for the most part, or not recognizable as such, and in among them, unavoidably, there are still children. In the active movement of the people back and forth, the rigid seating arrangement at the tables has dissolved long ago, and whole crowds of spectators stand at the edge of the dance floor, in double or triple rows, and gaze, stare in at the dancers or direct empty gazes who knows where. Others walk around in the hall; they virtually promenade in their holiday finery–that is probably the best way to put it–from one table to the next, nodding and greeting other people. Still others, acting secretively, separate into couples, into groups, into little groups; and whoever remains in his seat exposes himself as a pitiful little mouse, asking for sympathy.

Between the pieces of music, again and again the voice of the bandleader comes from all the loudspeakers. Not that he says anything, no, just occasionally, *"Caramba!" "Carajo!"* and "Let's go!"

Near the entrance a table is being cleared right now, to the accompaniment of applause. Now it stands there, stands there like an altar, with entire batteries of wine and liquor bottles, and you can serve yourself. Suddenly the light goes out. It is unclear whether it is planned, as part of the staging, or if it is only a chance happening. And immediately a perplexed, many-voiced murmuring begins. There are loud whistles; people shout "Boo!" A tumult arises that changes gradually to approval–"A good gimmick!"–which means, whatever has happened, people adjust to it. And when the candles burn down, one after another, they are not replaced. Who knows why? In order to end everything or simply to get things going even more. People lie in each other's arms, men in women's arms, women in men's arms. And when it becomes quite dark–it is a sated, abundantly equipped darkness—I can already see it snowing outside. It snows heavy flakes that are artificially orange in the light of the street lamps. "We're still alive! Hurrah! We're alive! Hurrah! Hurrah! We're still alive!"

The author's work on this text was subsidized by the German Literary Fund.

AFTERWORD

In the famous letter that he wrote in 1919, Franz Kafka attempted to achieve a reconciliation with his father by illuminating his perceptions of their respective natures and the causes of their estrangement. His letter became a detailed compendium of the family relationships, characteristic experiences, personality traits of family members, parental behaviors, and other factors that contributed to his development, both as an individual and as a writer. At the same time, it also defined the existential problems that provided the focus for his literary creations.

Kafka's letter presents the author's private, personal version of the classical conflict between father and son, a conflict that has informed countless works of literature over the centuries. From his perspective, key elements in the continuing tension that existed between him and his father included the tyrannically patriarchal dominance of an inaccessible man who refused–or was unable–to communicate meaningfully and constructively with his son; the son's continuing failure to meet parental expectations; a feeling of personal worthlessness that the father instilled within his son through constant criticism and refusal to accept the son for what he was; and, above all, the son's inability to assume a viable role in the world of practical human endeavor. And in Kafka's case it is clear that the psychological pressures generated by that adversarial relationship gave rise to many of the peculiar visions of human existence that are contained in his narrative works.

Like Kafka's letter to his father, Norbert Gstrein's

novel *The Register* can be interpreted as a treatise on the conflict between father and son—in this case son*s*—and as a compendium of the factors that contribute to the development of the son figures as individuals. More important, however, is the fact that on a general level there are visible parallels between the basic problem statement of Kafka's narratives and the central ideas of Gstrein's novel. At the same time, on a different level, there are also distinct similarities between specific details in some of Kafka's works and important aspects of Gstrein's story. In that light, a brief analysis that compares pertinent components of Kafka's writings with corresponding features in *The Register* may yield useful insight into Gstrein's literary purposes.

The works by Kafka that focus on the conflict between father and son specifically reflect the tensions that existed between the author and his own parent. As a result, they are thematically and structurally related to each other in several ways. Of their common features, the following are significant for the present discussion: (1) Tension between father and son, caused by the son's failure to measure up to the father's expectations. Typically, the father declines in power for a period of time, allowing the son to assert himself, but then the father regains power and destroys the son. (2) Female figure(s) serve as a source of tension in the family configuration. (3) Alienation and/or betrayal of a friend figure by the son, with the friend figure occupying the role of a *son after the father's heart.*

In *The Register*, each of the general features listed above is clearly visible. It is important to note, however, that Kafka's basic pattern is not simply duplicated here. Rather, the elements of his conflict situation and its resolution are reduced and modified to yield a picture of life that is no less tragic, but somewhat more positive and optimistic.

The clearest relationship between Kafka's presentations of the father-son conflict and *The Register* lies in the parallels between the earlier author's father-son-friend character configuration and Gstrein's portrayal of the tensions between the two sons, Moritz and Vinzenz, and their father. During their childhood, both Moritz and Vinzenz resemble Kafka's son characters—and Kafka himself, as he depicts himself in the letter to his father—to the extent that their father regards them as potential failures who will never amount to anything. Gradually, however, a distinction arises between them: Moritz remains a failure in his father's eyes, while Vinzenz moves into the "friend" role by becoming a *son after his father's heart* through the skiing victories that eventually lead him to the world championship in the slalom. In this connection it is important to note that in some of Kafka's variations of the triad, the friend figure is depicted as an alter ego of the son, or as the son's better self. Through stylistic manipulation of the narrative, Gstrein frequently creates "mirror-image" descriptions of Moritz and Vinzenz by presenting facts about one of the brothers and then repeating the statements in reverse order when describing the other, thus creating the impression that they are different representations or aspects of one and the same character.

Like the corresponding Kafka characters, the father of Moritz and Vinzenz gradually declines in power, permitting his sons to assert their independence. With that, however, the similarity to Kafka's pattern seems to end. Unlike Kafka's father figures, Gstrein's character neither regains his power nor destroys his sons. Rather, he himself dies. Nevertheless, a closer examination of the narrative reveals that Gstrein uses the father of Moritz and Vinzenz to create what amounts to an ironic transformation of Kafka's real-life situation. A major factor in the tension between Kafka and his father was the older man's perception that his son's literary activities had no practical value. By portraying the father in his novel as a weakening man who writes a worthless book and eventually dies, Gstrein actually reverses Kafka's pattern for that particular generation of sons.

It is interesting to note, however, that in a different sense the death of Gstrein's father figure is actually in harmony with Kafka's standard problem statement. The power-figure model in *The Register,* the man who corresponds more precisely to Kafka's practical, business-oriented father, is really the paternal grandfather whom the father constantly holds up as a model for the lives of the two brothers. Viewed from that perspective, the role of the grandfather's son is consistent with Kafka's variations on the theme of the unviable weakling who perishes without measuring up to his father's example.

The relationships between Gstrein's female characters and those created by Kafka are also significant. In Kafka's novels and stories, the son figures typically fail in their attempts to create positive relationships with members of the opposite sex. Moreover, the young women with whom they associate inevitably contribute to the respective tensions between father and son and between son and friend. In *The Register,* Gstrein's Magda parallels Kafka's female figures in some respects, while Kreszenz represents an ironic reversal of the typical Kafka woman.

The most consistent characteristic of Kafka's females is their dual nature. On one level they are attractive to the male characters and are viewed as potential or actual allies in the existential struggle of life, but on another level they are a source of guilt that is associated with impure thoughts and behavior, and their sexuality belongs to the seamy, base dimension of personal experience. In her relationships with Moritz and Vinzenz, Magda clearly reflects both sides of Kafka's duality. The two brothers are attracted to her sexually, but she is also an object of their ridicule, and their experiences together frequently belong to a guilt-tainted realm that must be kept hidden from open scrutiny. Even more pointedly, she is a primary focus of the events corresponding to the standard Kafka situation in which the son betrays and alienates his friend—which is doubled and reciprocated in what transpires during Magda's involvement with Moritz and Vinzenz.

In her role as their sister, Kreszenz is also a potential ally of the two brothers, as well as a source of tension within the framework of the narrative. But unlike Magda or the typical Kafka female character, her impact on the male figures is unifying rather than divisive. By pressing Moritz and Vinzenz to explain and come to grips with their own failures, she brings them together and causes them to put up a united front in their resistance to her efforts.

In addition to relationships between central character configurations and problem statements, there are other interesting similarities between Gstrein's novel and specific works by Kafka. They range from parallels in background and atmosphere to connections between secondary characters and details of situations.

It is almost as if Gstrein has taken images that elude firm definition in Kafka's fantasy constructs and transformed them into concrete aspects of the real world. At the same time, he seems to weaken more threatening elements of the earlier author's nightmare visions and deprive them of their destructive power within the framework of modern reality. In that sense, for example, the initial oppressive moods in *The Register* and Kafka's *The Castle* are similar, but the nebulously isolated, nocturnal, snow-covered world of the latter novel is replaced by a physically similar, but specifically defined, dark, frozen landscape in the mountains of real-world Austria. Similarly, Kafka's mysterious protagonist, who professes to be a surveyor but is never permitted to pursue his vocation, is supplanted by the mathematician Moritz who actually performs the duties of a surveyor during the glacier-measuring expeditions with his mentor.

The most vivid instance of Gstrein's reduction of a pernicious Kafka image to something less threatening occurs in connection with the introduction of two minor characters near the end of the story. *The Register* resembles Kafka's novel *The Trial*, in that it presents evidence in an indictment leveled against the male protagonists and suggests that the two brothers may be worthy of death. In Kafka's narrative, Josef K. is eventually slain by two seedy executioners who come for him one night. The trial of Moritz and Vinzenz, on the other hand, ends in a different way. The executioners are replaced by two piglike men who sit near Moritz during Magda's wedding dinner. They talk about death and seem to suggest that their listener really should die. But when confronted with the young man's gaze, they emerge as powerless to enforce the sentence that they have figuratively pronounced, and they are forced to change their topic of conversation.

While a comparison of *The Register* with important

works by Kafka exposes definite relationships between the creations of the two authors, it also reveals that their literary goals were different. In fact, *The Register* might well be interpreted as a critical response to Kafka, one that rejects the fantasy worlds of the earlier writer's tortured nightmares in favor of a sometimes brutal, even tragic, but less malignant reality, while replacing Kafka's pessimistic fatalism with the feeling of relief and cautious optimism that is expressed in the novel's final lines: "We're still alive! Hurrah! We're alive! Hurrah! Hurrah! We're still alive!"

Lowell A. Bangerter